FOR LOVE OF A LAIRD

Irvines of Drum
Book One

Mia Pride

DRAGONBLADE
PUBLISHING, INC.

ARE YOU SIGNED UP FOR DRAGONBLADE'S BLOG?

You'll get the latest news and information on exclusive giveaways, exclusive excerpts, coming releases, sales, free books, cover reveals and more.

Check out our complete list of authors, too!

No spam, no junk. That's a promise!

Sign Up Here

www.dragonbladepublishing.com

Dearest Reader;

Thank you for your support of a small press. At Dragonblade Publishing, we strive to bring you the highest quality Historical Romance from the some of the best authors in the business. Without your support, there is no 'us', so we sincerely hope you adore these stories and find some new favorite authors along the way.

Happy Reading!

CEO, Dragonblade Publishing

Additional Dragonblade books by Author Mia Pride

Irvines of Drum Series
For Love of a Laird (Book 1)
Like a Laird to a Flame (Book 2)
Maid for the Knight (Book 3)

*** Please visit Dragonblade's website for a full list of books and authors. Sign up for Dragonblade's blog for sneak peeks, interviews, and more: ***

www.dragonbladepublishing.com

Dedication

To my sweetie, who spared no expense and gave so much time helping me research for this book and series. Your support and efforts mean the world to me.

The Irvines of Drum series is very personal to me as the hero and heroine are my grandparents 14x removed, which I had not been aware of until I was researching my genealogy after having already plotted this story. Some things are just meant to be.

A special thank you to the lovely people of Drum Castle in Aberdeen, Scotland who took the time to answer my questions and send me research materials so that I may properly recreate Robert and Elizabeth's world in 1411.

Ballad of Gude Sir Alexander Irvine

"Gude Sir Alexander Irvine,
The much renownit Laird of Drum,
Nane in his days was better sene,
Whan they war semblit all and some.
To praise him we sould nocht be dumb
For valour, wit, and worthiness.
To end his days he there did come,
Whose ransom is remedyless."

CHAPTER ONE

Dunnottar Castle – Clan Keith lands
1411

T HE FIRE FROM the hearth leapt at the chance to devour the parchment, wax seal, and all. The moment her eyes saw the crest of the Laird of Drum Castle, home of their rival clan, her skin had begun to crawl. No doubt the missive had been delivered bearing the unwelcome news she had dreaded for years: that the time had come to marry a man more than three times her age.

As the second sister to the Marischal of Scotland, Elizabeth Keith had been betrothed to the old Laird of the Irvine Clan for years now, a means to an end and nothing more. Their clans had been at war for decades, but tensions had escalated beyond the theft of cattle and border disputes. It had been a bloody few years before her betrothal, aye. But no peace treaty was secure until she was wedded and bedded by the enemy, or so her elder brother William liked to remind her.

As the fire popped and hissed, Elizabeth licked her dry lips and stared into the dancing flames, burning the missive that had indeed borne bad news, only not the sort she had expected. Her betrothed, Thomas Irvine, had died in his sleep, peacefully, thank the Lord. Elizabeth made the sign of the cross and kissed the rosary around her neck, the one made of pearls that her mother had gifted her before she passed. Papa had always called it a sin to make a rosary out of something as fine as pearls. Morally corrupt, he had called it, but it was Elizabeth's finest treasure and clenching her wee fist around the cool white beads, she said a prayer for Thomas' soul, and for her own, for surely feeling relief over his death was a foul sin.

Standing up from her seat, Elizabeth smoothed her sweaty palms over the wool fabric of her bright blue dress and walked over to the narrow window on the other side of her chamber. The angry waves of the North Sea pounded upon the cliff below her window and on a clear day such as this one, Elizabeth could look straight ahead and see the horizon, wishing she could turn into a dove and fly away from the whims of men. But the wheel of fortune was always turning and her mother had warned her that no lady was safe from its wrath. One may rise in fortune, then fall at the stake. And her fortune had been declared today.

Her betrothed was not yet cold in his grave, nor even buried she suspected, yet she had already been promised to another, his eldest son. She had met the lad but once several years ago on the day of her betrothal to his father and he seemed kindly, if not boastful. He had been a man of twenty years, and she a lass of ten and four years. His brother Robert had been in attendance as well, though he had seemed more pensive and less in need of attention, the way a second brother should, she supposed. Still, she remembered his soft brown hair and deep blue eyes even now. He had spared her but a look before staring straight ahead and leaving the Drum Chapel without a word. Alexander, her newly betrothed, however, had seemed outspoken and prone to foolery, even at a time of ceremony. Aye, she remembered his dark blond hair and light blue eyes, as well.

Sighing and gripping her rosary once more, Elizabeth closed her eyes and concentrated on the sounds of the waves below. It was no great fortune to be a pawn in the game of war to be sure, yet she supposed if she must be married to the enemy for the sake of peace, it may as well be with a man closer to her age. She was a woman of ten and eight now and it was time she was married. Whether she wanted to be or not was not her choice to make. Alexander Irvine was as good a match as any, she supposed, and if it put an end to the senseless loss of innocent lives, she could see her duty as a greater cause.

A light rap on her chamber door had her spinning on her slippered feet, wondering if it was her maid come to ready her for the nooning meal or if it was William come to check in on her, as he tended to do more often as of late. "Enter," she called and straightened her spine. She did tend to slouch, and her mother had always slapped her wrists for it, but only because it did make her look frumpy and less appealing, she knew.

"Ah. My wee sister," William said with a smile, his reddish-blond hair glowing in the few rays of sun that seemed to beam in through her small window. He sniffed the air and smiled. "I am afraid burning the missive willnae change yer fate, Lizzie."

"Oh, I ken that well enough," she sighed and sat down once more, feeling her stomach clench in knots. "Still, 'tis verra satisfying," she grinned widely. "A lady has but little control of her life. Burning the missive commanding my fate simply felt necessary."

"It shall save thousands of lives. Ye are doing right by Clan Keith." William walked in slowly, scratching his short beard before sitting beside her and taking her hand in his. "I confess that while I am saddened to hear of the loss of Thomas Irvine, I am grateful that our peace can still be maintained and my sister may marry a man her own age. I do want for yer happiness."

"I ken that, as well, Will. I have always kenned I would marry where I was expected to. 'Tis my lot in life. I have never been filled with the whimsies of love. Arthur and Guinevere. Tristan and Iseult. They all end in despair, do they not?"

Sighing, William nodded and looked her in the eye. He had the same honey-colored eyes with a hint of moss green that she had inherited from their father, a handsome man most revered. "I do wish ye werenae already so disenchanted by life, Lizzie. Mayhap ye and Alexander will have a love like theirs, only not ending in treason or death."

Snorting loudly and slapping a hand to her mouth, Elizabeth grimaced. That sound had gotten her in more trouble than her slouch over the years. "Och, I doubt we will ever be embroiled in treason… or love. But I shall be a good wife so long as he is a good husband. That is my best offer," she said with a side grin.

Chuckling, William stood up and put out his hand, helping her to her feet. "That's all I can ask of ye. I do hope ye attempt to care for him but ken that if he is brutish or treats ye poorly, I shall run him through and peace will be dissolved. However, despite my dislike for their family name, I dislike war even more, and I have heard nothing but satisfactory things about the man's character."

"Nor I. When last I saw him, he was being rather disrespectful in the chapel yard just before my betrothal to his father, but he seemed to keep himself in line once inside the sacred building."

"He is merrymaking, so I hear. That cannae be all bad, Lizzie. He will be a fine husband. Now, shall I accompany ye to the nooning? Our hunt was most successful and we have boar roasting."

Looping her arm into his, Elizabeth nodded and walked through her chamber doorway with her brother, the kindest and gentlest man she had ever known, at least when dealing with his sisters. On the field of battle and when dealing in politics, he was said to be comparable to a lion, but to Elizabeth, he was the greatest champion she could ever have asked for and she felt certain that if she should ever need use of his sword arm, he would ask a total of one question. Giggling, she cuddled closer to him and smiled.

"Ye seem rather happy," William observed, descending the stairs beside her. "Already warming to the Irvine knight, Sir Alexander?"

"Och, nay. Just remembering the one question ye said ye would ask should I ever need yer sword arm."

Scoffing, William nodded, remembering the conversation and they both repeated the question in unison before stepping into the great hall. "Where is the bastard?"

DREAD GRIPPING HER gut, Elizabeth folded her last chemise and shoved it into the wooden chest at the end of her curtained bed. The old hinges groaned when she shut it with a resounding thud, the sound of her life at Dunnottar Castle coming to an end.

"Mistress Elizabeth, I told ye I would pack yer belongings for ye. Ye neednae labor so." Matilda made a reproving sound and ran over to the chest, throwing open the lid to inspect its contents thoroughly. "All seems accounted for. Do ye have yer mirror and yer comb? Ye mustnae arrive disheveled."

"Tilda. I can manage to pack my own belongings, ye ken." Elizabeth smiled at her dearest friend. Though Matilda was her lady's maid, they had grown up in the castle together and sometimes Elizabeth even snuck Matilda into lessons with her tutor, hiding her behind ancient tapestries so the lass could have an education, as well. T'was most unfair that the poor lot had no education and Elizabeth had wanted better for her companion. It was a fine idea until one day when the dust from a tapestry made Matilda sneeze and she was almost whipped by the tutor. Having no desire to see her friend punished for her doing, Elizabeth had confessed and accepted the lashing instead, and the sting on her arse still stayed with her years later. But, it had been worth protecting sweet Tilda.

"I ken well ye can manage, Mistress, but 'tis my only job to serve ye. When ye do it for me, I believe I am failing." With a sigh, Matilda plopped on top of the chest and looked warily at Elizabeth. Her tight red ringlets escaped the confines of the white linen tied in her hair, and her freckled nose crinkled the way it did when she had something to say but was not sure of her place.

"Dinnae call me mistress when we are alone. I hate it verily. Ye are my best companion. I willnae make ye work for me or address me as yer mistress in private. Do stop. And I ken ye have something ye wish to say. Out with it, then."

"How can ye tell?"

"Ye always wrinkle yer nose as if someone broke wind and ye are too polite to run in the other direction." Elizabeth put her hands on her hips and smiled widely at her friend.

"Do I? Och, how unappealing. Verra well. I was only wondering if ye are slightly relieved not to have to marry such an old man. I hear Alexander and his brothers are verra attractive men."

Clutching her rosary, Elizabeth sighed and sat beside her companion. "By my faith, 'tis but a sin to feel the way I do. But I am, indeed, relieved. He was a kind man. He betrothed me for peace but I ken why he never married me. I was young and though he had a right to my body, he never laid eyes on me more than necessary. He let me be yet kept to the terms of the peace treaty. There has been nay trouble between our clans since then. I am saddened he is gone, but aye, I am grateful not to have to bed him or bear his children. Do ye think they would be born already middle-aged?"

Matilda burst out laughing and covered her mouth quickly, before anyone heard her behaving inappropriately with her mistress. "I havenae any idea how such things work. My education was received behind dusty tapestries. I was fortunate to hear more than three words in all those years. But my mam was much younger than my pa and I was born a wee lassie. I dinnae believe ye will birth a gray-haired babe, nay." She giggled into her hands and cleared her throat. "But now that isnae a concern, Lizzie. Ye shall wed and bed Sir Alexander, the fiercest knight. He fought in France ye ken!"

"I ken. So did every noble lad in the kingdom. 'Tis not so grand. I have met him and Robert, but I have never seen Reginald and wonder why he wasnae at my betrothal."

"Mayhap we shall never ken." Matilda shrugged and stood up. "We must ready ye for bed, Mist… Lizzy. We leave for Drum on the morrow. 'Tis not a long journey, I am told, except we will have a retinue of people and must take all yer belongings. Though ye shallnae be needing yer fine bed, now that ye will lie with Sir Knight." Her brows waggled and Elizabeth rolled her eyes.

"Ye are much more excited about my private life than I am, sweet Tilda. I shall do my duty as a wife must, but truly, he is just a man, nay different than his father, simply younger."

"As ye say."

Matilda removed Elizabeth's dress and under tunic just before slipping a fresh one over her head. Turning down the sheets for Elizabeth, Matilda stood aside as she climbed in, relishing the softness of her sheets against her skin. Sleep was a wonderous thing, yet she knew she would achieve little of it tonight.

"Now, ye try to sleep and if ye cannae, think of Sir Alexander and how long and hard his—"

"Tilly! Ye are a wanton lass, indeed! Haud yer wheesht!" Elizabeth blushed and put her hands on her cheeks.

"I was going to say sword," Matilda shrugged and closed the damask curtains around Elizabeth's bed, just before Elizabeth buried her face into her pillow to stifle her laughter.

CHAPTER TWO

W ATCHING AS HIS brother clenched his fists under the table, Robert Irvine knew Alexander was doing his best to prevent lashing out at his men. It was not their fault he had to bury his father, take on the responsibilities of a laird, deal with his new bride, and now hear about impending war all in one cursed day. Pity for his elder brother clutched at Robert's gut as he stood behind Alexander in the laird's solar.

"Anything else?" Alexander asked slowly, squeezing the bridge of his nose. Since the death of Father, Alex had been plagued with blinding headaches and Robert hoped another was not coming on. How glad he was not to be the eldest son, yet he would do all he could to support his new laird and their kin.

"The Donald is expected to arrive with an army of over ten thousand men by mid-summer, Laird. He is accompanied by several Highland clans whom are all in aid with the English king. And, well... he has threatened to burn Aberdeenshire to the ground on several occasions."

"Och, I ken this, Richard," Alexander replied testily. There was no way to avoid war. If an army was marching toward them with intentions to burn down their lands, Alexander had to tell their commander, the Earl of Mar. They had just arrived back from France not so long ago, but the world seemed to be ever in a state of chaos. A man, a warrior, a laird, and a knight. Alex was all those things. Soon, he would be a husband and mayhap a father. But one thing was certain, he had a mighty load of shite to deal with and Robert did not envy him. Gone were his carefree days of frivolity. Aye, he had trained his entire life to be a laird, to fight, to protect his own. But it seemed to all be happening at once.

"Thank ye, Richard," Robert said calmly, dismissing the messenger. "Please head to the great hall. Cook will have a meal awaiting ye." Richard nodded and the other men in the room knew better than to speak. Robert knew Alexander was more than grateful for his help since their father passed a sennight past. It had been a most taxing time and their pa had been much loved and respected by all, especially his three sons.

"Alex, I am sorry to have to put this on ye now of all times," Reginald, his youngest brother, chimed in from the corner of the room, facing a window that looked down on the courtyard. "But it appears yer young bride has arrived with a retinue of Keiths. I do hope ye plan to see this through, because we are surrounded by the enemy. They willnae stand silent if we break our oath."

"I have nay intention of backing out, though I have sacrificed much." The pained sound of his brother's voice made Robert frown, patting Alex's shoulder in comfort just before walking over to the window. Alex had a long-standing lover named Mary whom he had intended to wed one day. It was no wonder the lass had refused to speak with him since the day he signed the betrothal contract to Elizabeth Keith. She was heartbroken, as was Alex, but they both knew there was naught to be done.

Looking down into the courtyard, he saw a wee lass atop a horse surrounded by several Keith guards, all with their plaids draped over their shoulders and swords missing from their leather belts. Their men had done well, removing weapons from the enemy before they entered. Should something go awry, no Irvine blood would be spilled.

Wearing a black under tunic with long flowing sleeves and a matching black surcoat, the lass even wore a black kertch in her hair. At least she had the decency to pretend to mourn her deceased betrothed before being married to his son the following sennight, Robert thought wryly. In truth, he knew nothing about the lass, except for what he had seen of her four years past when she was only ten and four. She had appeared nervous being on her enemy's land, unsure if it was a trap. He could not blame her then. However, this time, she appeared to hold her spine straight, shoulders back, and head held high. He smiled slightly, wondering why he felt a wee bit of pride for a lass he knew naught about, except that soon she would be his sister... which did seem more natural than her being his mother by marriage, considering she was five years his junior.

"She sure has grown!" Reginald said with a chuckle, and Robert scowled at his younger brother.

Alex still held his head in his hands at his desk, not showing any signs of interest or curiosity about his new bride, yet still being a gentleman enough to defend her honor. "I do hope ye arenae commenting on the size of my bride's arse, for I would be forced to run ye through, wee brother," he said with no amount of determination in his voice.

From Robert's bird's-eye view, he knew exactly which of the lass' features Reginald was referring to, for it appeared her modest attempt to conceal her ample breasts was futile. Yet, she was their sister, or would be soon, and Reginald had better remember that. Robert shot Reginald a warning glance and his impetuous brother only shrugged.

"Charles, have a missive sent to the Earl of Mar immediately. Warn him of The Donald's impending invasion. He likely kens already. Tell him he has the full support of the Irvine Clan. All he needs to do is sound the alarm." Charles, one of Alex's best warriors and companions nodded his head and went to do his laird's bidding. "I suppose I must see to the comfort of my bride and prepare to bury Father." There was no mistaking the repressed pain in his voice. He did not wish to marry Elizabeth, that was clear enough, and Mary had done as she should and walked away so Alex may fulfill his promise. Yet the loss of both his lover and father all within a sennight was clearly affecting Alex.

"What can I do to aid ye, Alex?" Robert walked over and slapped his brother on the shoulder. "Anything at all?"

"Anything?"

"Mostly…" Robert scowled at his brother.

"Marry the lass for me, so I may wed with Mary. Does it matter which Irvine brother she weds and beds, so long as it keeps the peace between the clans?"

Robert felt himself blanch. Alex was generally the merry sort, but this was no light matter and Robert was not certain if his brother was serious or not. "Surely ye jest."

"Aye, I do. My name is already on the contract and her brother would see it as a slight against her honor and run us both through. I am unfortunately stuck with her."

"Mayhap she isnae so bad."

"Let us go find out, aye?" Alex shouldered Robert and forced a pained smile before exiting his solar. Following behind closely, Robert took a deep breath and prepared himself for perhaps the longest sennight of his life.

THE INNER BAILEY was filled with Irvine men and women wearing their light blue and green plaids as arisaids or over their shoulders. Elizabeth gripped the reins of her palfrey to prevent her hands from shaking. The afternoon sun beat down on her, and the thick black wool she was swathed in caused her to sweat and itch like a boar covered in ants. Not at all the best way to be formally introduced to her future husband, but one did not generally still become betrothed while in mourning. The old laird had not even been laid to rest yet, and it felt a wee bit disrespectful to have his funeral followed by her wedding to his son. But she understood the dire circumstances and need for peace on both sides.

The sooner the entire mess was over, she could settle in as Lady of Drum Castle and begin her new life. It had felt as if she were in purgatory for the past four years, wondering when she would be called upon to do her duty. The time had come. Clutching on to her pearl rosary as she often did, she said a quick prayer for strength as she saw two familiar faces approaching, followed by another man she had never seen, yet he had similar features as the others. Was he the third son?

The brother she recognized as her newly betrothed approached first and bent gracefully at the waist, bowing his head. "My Lady Elizabeth Keith, welcome to Drum Castle. My name is Alexander Irvine, third Laird of Drum. These are my brothers, Robert and Reginald." The two men bent their heads and smiled warmly toward her, and she felt herself relax slightly. They seemed fine enough men and not at all like the monsters she had concocted in her head during her entire journey.

"Greetings, Laird. We are sorry for the loss of yer father. He was a kind man to me. Ye remember my brother, William Keith, Laid of Dunnottar Castle and Marischal of Scotland?"

"Indeed, I do." Alex tilted his head respectfully to her brother. "We welcome the Keith Clan to our lands and look forward to a lifetime of peace and the blending of clans." Putting his hands out, Alexander gently lifted her from the palfrey, his eyes going slightly wide when he placed her on her feet. She knew what had caught his attention but there was nothing she could do about the unusual size of her bosom. It was a burden to be sure and one men seemed unable not to gawk at. To his credit, he simply cleared his throat, sent a strange look to the brother he referred to as Reginald, who just smiled and shrugged before Robert elbowed him. She looked at the three brothers strange-ly, deciding she would rather not know what they were communicating without words.

"Reginald, I am pleased to meet ye. Ye werenae in attendance at my previous betrothal, I believe."

"Aye. I had the pox. The poultry kind – not the small kind." Matil-da laughed from her horse behind Elizabeth's, but all she could do was nod her head and force a smile.

"I cannae tell if ye are jesting or not, but I am glad ye are hale. Robert, 'tis good to see ye once again. I suppose we shall all be seeing each other quite a bit from now on." Her nerves were on edge, and she fought the urge to squirm or slouch, gripping her rosary once more.

"'Tis lovely to see ye again, as well. I wish it was under different circumstances."

"Aye, as do I," she said as she nodded, wanting more than anything for this public greeting to be done with so she could be out of the sweltering sun and find her new bedchamber.

As if reading her mind, Alexander stepped forward and took her hand in his. "Ye are most welcome. I have some private matters I wish to speak to yer brother about. Robert will show ye to yer new quarters."

Stepping forward, Robert smiled and put out his arm. She accept-ed, looping her arm through his and smiled when she saw Reginald help Tilda down from her horse so they could follow. "My thanks," she replied, observing the crowd and seeing a red-haired woman with tears in her eyes. When their eyes locked, the woman simply turned away and disappeared from the crowd. Elizabeth may be wee in size and sheltered, but she was no fool.

Alexander had another woman. He was reluctant to get too close to Elizabeth and had already pawned her off on his brother. The woman was quite bonnie, and Elizabeth felt sorry for the lass. Entering through the main entrance, Robert showed her the great hall with the trestle tables all set up as servants put out fresh linens, preparing for what must be a grand feast to welcome all the Keiths and celebrate the life of the lost laird.

Servants stopped for only a moment to stare at their new lady, and Elizabeth gave them all warm smiles, hoping they would welcome a Keith willingly into their clan. Too much blood had been spilled and she was certain a few people would give her trouble for deeds she had no fault in, but she must prepare for it, just the same.

A large hearth occupied the west wall, large enough to roast an ox if needed with its stone arch and granite sides. The north wall had a large head table dominating its length with a wooden screen just behind it, no doubt hiding the kitchens and buttery.

Tapestries with the Irvine crest decorated with holly leaves and their motto were on either side of the great hall, as well as tapestries depicting great war victories and chieftains long passed. Fresh rushes crunched beneath her riding boots and Elizabeth decided that at least the hall was well kept and clean. Her job as lady and chatelaine of Drum would be easy enough, though she wondered who had been running the keep with their mother gone and no wives yet in residence. "Who is in charge of running the castle? 'Tis quite well kept," Elizabeth offered, breaking the silence between her and Robert.

"Mary has been since our mother passed. Her mother was our mother's maid and, growing up alongside us, she had learned the ins and outs of running the castle. Our steward is my Uncle William. He has kept the books and managed the tenants for decades now and does quite well, though he is in his mid-fifties and has recently asked me to prepare to take over his duties, as he only had three daughters, whom have been married off to other clans by now."

"Oh, I am sorry to hear that. 'Tis a hard time, watching those we love age. It has just been me and my brother running Dunnottar Castle for quite some time. Rest assured, I am competent at running a household. However, I respect that Drum is already well run and would soon like to meet the staff and establish myself as chatelaine."

Robert stopped abruptly and she almost bumped into him before he grabbed her arm to steady her. Had she said something untoward? Clearing his throat, Robert looked at her with uncertainty in his eyes. "Of course. May I escort ye upstairs into the tower? Yer rooms have been readied and I hope ye approve of them. We can continue the tour on the morrow. I am certain ye are tired and would prefer a wee rest before my father's funeral and then the great feast."

"Aye, my thanks." A sudden awkwardness lingered thickly in the air and she wondered what was so irregular about her wanting to meet with Mary and William to discuss her duties. It was like he was trying to get her out of the way, saving the tour for another time. But, there was no sense pushing the matter and Elizabeth was quite tired and would appreciate a bath before changing into her black demask mourning surcoat.

Falling silent once more, Elizabeth walked up the winding steps leading up to the tower, hearing Reginald and Matilda following closely behind, laughing about some shared conversation that Elizabeth suddenly wished she was a part of. She felt entirely out of place in this castle, the enemy who unwillingly tore apart true love – if such a thing existed. Alexander wanted nothing to do with her, that was as clear as the loch on a summer's day. Robert was kind, but awkward, having no idea what to do with her and clearly hesitant to have her talk to some of the staff.

Arriving on the third floor of the tower, Robert threw open a thick wooden door and Elizabeth was relieved to see the hearth fire lit and the room warm with a bath awaiting her. Sighing, she stepped in and looked around the room. A four-poster bed with heavy curtains occupied the far-left corner of the room. A large oak cabinet was to its left with a desk on the other end. Just in front of the hearth were two plush red velvet seats. "This is truly lovely. My thanks, Robert. I really do require a bath before the ceremony."

Nodding, he stepped up to the hearth and warmed his hands. "My thanks for wearing black. Nobody expected ye to be in mourning."

Feeling slighted, Elizabeth furrowed her brow and stepped beside him. "Thomas was my betrothed for four years. Aye, he was three times my age and it was an alliance for peace, nay love was involved. But, we exchanged letters and he was kind to me. I cared about him. William and I truly do mourn his passing."

Looking rather surprised by her honesty, Robert nodded once more and looked her in the eyes for the very first time. Her heart skipped a beat and she felt her stomach clench. He was a handsome man, there was no doubt of that. But so was Alexander, even if he was in love with another woman. And Robert would be her brother, so any attraction she should feel must remain on the surface. Besides, she knew nothing of the man. He could be as foul as the devil for all she knew.

"Reginald has seen yer maid to her quarters. She is just next door to ye, and a door behind that tapestry connects yer room to Alexander's."

Panic washed over her. Somehow, she had not even considered that within a sennight she would be expected to bed down with the man. She had hoped to get to know him better before they were wed. But if he continued to avoid her, that would be next to impossible. Although, she was aware that the man had lost his father, took on the lairdship, and had to take a new wife all at once. If she was overwhelmed, he must be barely hanging on. Perhaps she could be of help to him in his time of need and prove that, even if they never loved one another, she would be a dutiful wife. And she was rather good at chess and, between her and Tilda, she could drink whisky like a warrior. Aye. Elizabeth knew how to make merry just as much as anyone, and she had expected Alex to do the same, but mayhap she had been mistaken.

"Thank ye, Robert. That will do."

"Mary will be up shortly to help ye bathe."

"Oh... n-nay. Tilda can help me with such things."

"It is customary for the lady of the house to bathe guests. I am certain ye follow the same code of conduct at Dunnottar. It would be a grand insult to turn her away. Once ye are lady, Tilda may bathe ye."

Pursing her lips, Elizabeth nodded. She knew he was correct and offending anyone was not a good idea. It was the lady's duty to make guests feel honored and see to their needs, after all. "Verra well, ye are right."

Just then, a woman walked in carrying a handful of wash linens and a bar of soap. "My lady," she said quietly, looking down at the floor as she curtsied. Robert walked out of the room and shut the door behind him just as Elizabeth recognized the woman who had been crying in the courtyard earlier.

Stunned and gripped by a sudden palpitation in her chest, Elizabeth stood speechless before the woman. Mary was the beautiful red-haired woman and, if Elizabeth's instincts were as refined as they usually were, she was in love with Alexander. The question remained... was her future husband in love with this woman and, if so, how was Elizabeth going to live knowing she was the cause of their suffering?

Words escaped her, which was a rare event, indeed. But if she was to make Drum her home, it was best not to make instant enemies. "Mary, is it?" she asked with a smile so forced, she feared she may look rather touched in the head. "Please, do call me Elizabeth."

"As ye wish." Mary bent over to place the linens on a table just as several young lads came through carrying a massive wooden bathtub, placing it on the floor of her new chamber before departing immediately.

Licking her lips, Elizabeth twisted her hands in the folds of her dress, standing awkwardly as another line of servants, this time a group of young lassies, came through with steaming buckets of water, praying at least one of them would stay in the room to break the awful tension that seemed to swell and surround her with every new breath.

When the last lass smiled and walked out of the room with an expedient curtsy before slamming the door behind her, Elizabeth sighed and looked at Mary. It seemed, however, Mary was determined to avoid eye contact, staring at the steam rising from the bath water.

"Turn around, my lady." Elizabeth looked at Mary, who finally pulled her gaze away from the water long enough to glance at Elizabeth. "Ye need to disrobe before entering the bath."

"What? Oh! Aye," Elizabeth tittered nervously and turned around, feeling Mary begin to tug on the laces of her bodice. She was making a cursed fool of herself. Mary must believe her utterly lacking any senses. "'Tis been a long day, ye ken."

"Aye, I ken," Mary replied, stepping away when the dress grew slack enough for Elizabeth to step out of it herself, most gladly. This was an unforeseen situation and between having to marry a man she did not know and being bathed by the woman she supposed love him, Elizabeth was ready for a dram of whisky, or four.

She needed answers and to break this tension. They were grown women. There was no need for such floundering. "How long have ye lived at Drum, Mary?"

"My entire life," she responded, turning her back to test the water.

"Do ye ken Alexander well?" Was that question too bold? When Mary stood up straight and stiffened, her shoulders becoming rigid, Mary grimaced.

"Aye. I do."

"I see," Elizabeth murmured, removing her under tunic and quickly stepping in the bath while Mary was still avoiding eye contact. The water sloshed over the rim and burned her arse, making Elizabeth hiss from the pain.

"Is it too hot, my lady? I can fetch some cool water." Mary nearly bolted for the door like a mouse escaping a cat, but Elizabeth shook her head. "Nay, 'tis perfect," she forced, despite her scalding flesh. "And my name is Elizabeth, or even Lizzie, if ye prefer."

Nodding, Mary got down on her knees, lathering the soap against a linen cloth, her hand shaking as she placed it on Elizabeth's arm.

"Can ye tell me a wee bit about the castle?" Elizabeth persisted, feeling like a fool with every word, yet determined to get through this rather peculiar ordeal.

Mary stopped scrubbing and looked at the door with a frown. "I... I just realized that I forget something..."

Elizabeth looked at the bed and saw a fresh linen ready to be used once she needed to be dried off. Nothing was missing as far as she could determine. "What have ye forgotten?" she asked, but Mary was already on her feet, tears welling up in her eyes just before she looked away once more. Oh, bollocks. This was not going well and more than anything, it solidified her believe that this bonnie woman meant a great deal to her future husband.

"Just... uh..." Mary wrung her wet hands into her faded blue dress before trying to wipe away more tears without notice. "The lavender oil... to... scent yer water." Mary rushed toward the door and Elizabeth cringed, feeling an ache in her heart for this woman.

"Truly, 'tis not nec—" Mary was out the door, slamming it behind her, and Elizabeth stood in the tub so fast, she nearly slipped. Curse it all! She was getting out of this bath and dressing herself before this torture had to continue for either of them, and curse that dolt, Robert Irvine, for not simply allowing Tilda to do the task!

CHAPTER THREE

"Is it customary at Drum Castle to have the laird's mistress bathe his bride?" Robert choked on his wine and grabbed his linen napkin to wipe away the red juice dripping down his chin. Elizabeth pursed her lips to stifle a giggle.

Harps and flutes played in the background as minstrels sang before the hearth, but suddenly they were not the most amusing thing in the room. "Pardon?" he asked and looked her in the eyes for the first time all evening. She had shared a trencher with Alexander and conversation had felt easy enough, but she had not missed his wandering gaze continually landing on Mary sitting at another trestle table looking miserable. Elizabeth didn't miss it either, and her heart ached for the two, though she knew not what could be done.

A man wearing the Irvine plaid had approached Alexander not long ago and he kindly excused himself and disappeared up the stairs of the tower, no doubt to his solar. Left alone at the head table still wearing her black demask dress from Thomas' funeral earlier, she decided to try to make conversation with Robert, but apparently lacked the skill of subtlety.

"When I arrived with my kin, the courtyard was rife with wary faces, but one face was devastated, tears streaming down her face.

When I looked at her, she looked away and ran off. I was aware of the situation at that moment. But when she came to bathe me this evening, well… that was an unpleasant experience for us both, I must say. And now I see Alexander was staring at her during the meal."

Scratching his short beard, Robert struggled to come up with a response, but Elizabeth decided to spare the man. "'Tis all right. I understand this was an unexpected arrangement. I have nay illusions of love and expect this to be a marriage of convenience for our clans." She truly was not hurt or jealous. It was just as well if her husband had another lass to occupy him so she could see to her duties around the keep.

Clearing his throat, Robert tugged on the neck of his tunic and surcoat. "Are ye enjoying Drum thus far, my lady?" Elizabeth smiled and looked down at the remains of her pheasant meal just before a young lass came to take it away. Clearly Robert did not wish to discuss the situation, and she supposed that was well enough.

"Indeed, I am," she said with a proper nod and her hands folded daintily in her lap, deciding that she should attempt to remain ladylike, though it was always a struggle. Grace and decorum did not come easy to her. "Yer father's ceremony was beautiful, as is yer chapel."

"My thanks. He is greatly missed. He was a good man, ye ken."

"Aye, I ken," she agreed with a nod. Robert was easy to talk to and polite, even if she got the sense he felt trapped into conversing with her since Alex had departed the table. Twiddling her thumbs under the table, Elizabeth looked away from Robert and scanned the great hall for Matilda. She just needed to see one friendly face, even though the room was filled with her kin as well as her future kin. At some point, her brother had disappeared, and Elizabeth wondered where he may have gone off to.

Feeling out of place and suddenly lonely for home, Elizabeth clutched her rosary and continued to glance around her surroundings, wondering how she should proceed. Without Alex, was it rude to stand up and walk away from the head table? If she spoke too frequently with Robert, the clan would accuse her of poor character, accuse her of interest in the wrong brother, even though the one she was betrothed to gave her the least amount of attention he could without being overtly insulting to their arrangement. She would not care, except for the fact that she now felt abandoned and embarrassed in from of all her kin, new and old.

"Lady Elizabeth," she heard Alexander say from beside her and both relief and dread filled her at once. Looking up into his light blue gaze, she was startled to see such a serious expression on his face. "I apologize for having been pulled away."

"Ye are Laird of Drum. I suspect an important issue shall take yer attention now and again." She smiled and tried to look calm, but she was tired from the day's travels, followed by a funeral, followed by this feast. Sleep and time alone to manage her whirling thoughts were all she wanted at the moment. "Mayhap I may be excused to my bedchamber and be readied for bed? I am quite tired. The feast was wonderful and I thank ye for accommodating my kin."

Nodding stiffly, Alexander scanned the room before looking at her once more. "We are allies now and I am glad of it. Yer kin is always welcome, Elizabeth. Matilda has already gone up the stairs to ready yer chamber and light a fire. I do hope ye enjoy yer night in yer new chamber and rest well, my lady. In fact, I have need of Robert in my solar just now."

Glancing over to Robert, she felt the air shift between them, like something dreadful was on the rise. Scotland had been a tumultuous place since their young King James had been kidnapped by the English some years ago and his power-hungry uncle became regent, often siding with the English and Highland clans for more power and land. Too many times she had seen similar looks upon her brother's face and it generally meant trouble was brewing.

"I do hope all is well?" she asked and stood from her seat, looking between the brothers.

"It shall be, aye. Care for me to see ye to yer chambers?" Alexander asked and gently took her hand. It was the first bit of affection he had shown her since her arrival and though she knew he meant it only in an amicable way, it helped to make her feel less intrusive and more accepted. Alexander understood that none of this was her doing, just as it was not his. Mayhap she was not alone, after all.

"Nay, I can see ye have pressing matters. I thank ye once again. I shall see myself to my room."

"Verra well, have a good night, Elizabeth," Alexander said and spun on his heels, heading for the stairs with steps three times her stride. She stared as he sped off urgently, knowing something was amiss. There was never rest from trouble it seemed.

"I must go, as well. Enjoy yer night." Robert bowed and stormed off after his brother.

Standing by herself, Elizabeth began to slowly walk toward the stairs before an idea struck her. She was alone for the first time all day. She did not need to return to her chambers right away. Mayhap she should give herself a tour of the kitchens and the rest of the keep before retiring. Besides, her legs could use some movement and her arse was quite sore after sitting in a saddle all day and sitting on hard benches all night.

Deciding she would take just a wee stroll, knowing Matilda would be up waiting for her, Elizabeth slipped past the screen separating the great hall from the kitchen area, glad to be away from the music that had begun to give her a headache. Fresh rushes crushed beneath her leather slippers just before entering the bustling kitchen as woman scrubbed pots and plates. One woman in particular shouted commands at the other ladies while she swept the floors. Not wanting to be a burden and deciding she would take a moment to meet more of the staff on the morrow during a less busy time, Elizabeth turned and stepped back around the screen, when she collided with another body.

Grunting, Elizabeth almost fell to the floor before managing to grip on to the wall to steady herself.

"Och, I am so sorry," Elizabeth squealed, looking up and then faltering once more. Of the several dozen people occupying this hall, why did she have to run into this person? "Mary, correct?"

The red-haired woman nodded and huffed out a deep breath, closing her eyes and pursing her lips. "My apologies, my lady." Bobbing her head, she attempted to move around Elizabeth, but she stepped in Mary's way, blocking the path.

"Wait."

Stopping in her tracks, Mary stopped but stared straight ahead, stiff as a board. "What is it, my lady?"

"My name is Elizabeth and I am not the Lady of Drum just yet." That made Mary flinch and, more than ever, Elizabeth was certain of her instincts. "Ye dinnae care much for me, do ye?" Her voice stayed low and calm, hoping to discuss the situation with the woman.

"I dinnae ken ye, so how can I like or dislike ye?" Mary began to walk off again, but Elizabeth gently placed a hand on her shoulder.

"Please. Just let me go," Mary begged so quietly that Elizabeth almost missed it.

"This marriage is for peace. Not for love," Elizabeth whispered back.

Turning to face Elizabeth, Mary attempted to wipe the tears running down her cheeks and Elizabeth frowned. The woman was heartbroken, and it made her feel sick to her belly to cause someone such pain.

"Why ye marry isnae my concern, my lady."

"Aye, I think it is though, is it not?" Elizabeth crooked a knowing brow and gave a reassuring smile. "I may be a Keith, but I assure ye I'm not addled in the brain. I can see ye are in love with Alexander." Mary gasped and clutched her breast, turning white with horror and shaking her head.

"That... that is untrue. I... I—"

"And, he is in love with ye, as well." Elizabeth added. "It is as obvious as the black death upon one's face."

Sighing and hunching her shoulders, Mary nodded. "I understand why ye must marry. I cannae interfere with peace. T'was not so long ago my grandfather was killed in a battle between our clans. I shall live in misery every day of my life if it means yer marriage ends the bloodshed."

"I feel the same way. We women are just pawns, are we not? We do as we must to survive and to help our people. Ye and I arenae so different. I am simply the one in a position to end this war, and I am terribly sorry it is at the cost of yer happiness. I want ye to ken that." Elizabeth gripped Mary's hand and, for the first time, Mary looked her in the eyes and smiled slightly, before swallowing hard.

"Ye are a bonnie lass. I had hoped ye had warts on yer nose, if I may be honest."

Elizabeth laughed heartily at that and tilted her head back. "Mary, ye are as bonnie as I, if not more so. He is in love with ye, not me. Dinnae forget that. He pays me the necessary attention to not offend my brother or my kin, but he stares at ye the entire time, afraid to upset ye."

"Alexander is a good man. He will treat ye well."

"Aye, I ken that. I do hope ye and I can be friends. Truly."

Mary seemed to hesitate for a moment before blowing out a lungful of air and slouching. "Aye, I would like that, as well. I thank ye for speaking to me. Since the day he told me he had to fulfill the marriage contract for his father, I have been in agony. We were going to wed."

"I am so terribly sorry, Mary. I will do all I can to alleviate yer pain, but I dinnae ken how. I have a sennight until the wedding." Elizabeth frowned and squeezed Mary's hand once more before releasing it.

"My thanks. There is one more thing, my lady. I shouldnae say but..."

"Elizabeth. My name is Elizabeth, and if we are to be friends, ye can say aught."

"Och, fine. Elizabeth," Mary said slowly. "I am with child. I havenae told Alex yet. 'Twill only make him more upset, mayhap cause him to call off the wedding. And I cannae risk ending peace."

"Ye carry his bairn?" Elizabeth gasped and felt herself go dizzy. This situation only became more complicated by the minute.

Mary clutched her middle and nodded her head, more tears rolling down her chin. "Aye. I believe I am at the end of the third month. I was going to tell him, and then..." she hiccupped and Elizabeth rubbed her back soothingly.

"I... I dinnae ken what to say, but we will remedy this. I shall think of something. Good night, Mary. Dinnae fret." Elizabeth walked away from her new companion toward the tower stairs. She had to flee the room. Nothing but dread plagued her. She did not wish to make enemies and this situation was becoming more unbearable by the moment. Out of sorts, Elizabeth climbed the stairs to the third floor, found her chamber, and opened the door.

Hopefully, the morrow would be less exhausting than today had been, and she would get an opportunity to see more of the castle grounds, meet the staff, and speak to her brother about the situation. There had to be an answer. Finding Tilda sleeping in a chair near the hearth, Elizabeth grinned and went to wake up her companion and explain all that had happened during dinner and with Mary, leaving out the bairn. Tilda was known to gossip and the last thing Elizabeth wanted was any shame to befall Mary.

"Always meddling, ain't ye?" Tilda said with a chuckle while she helped remove Elizabeth's dress and under tunic, replacing it with a warm chemise that had been close to the fire awaiting her.

"Ye ken I cannae abide the lass being unhappy on my account. I would prefer a friend, rather than a foe." She yawned and climbed into her bed, which had been delivered from Dunnottar and reassembled for her in this new chamber. It felt enough like home with her chest, bed, and Tilda by her side. Stretching and burrowing deep into the clean blankets, she closed her eyes and began drifting off to sleep, but not before she heard Matilda mutter a stern warning to her.

"Dinnae go off and fall in love with the wrong brother now, Beth. I saw the way Robert looks at ye. He fancies ye."

"Ridiculous," Elizabeth mumbled, half-asleep. "He was occupying me because Alexander was too busy to do so himself."

"Ye keep telling yerself that, Mistress."

"I shall. And, I'm not yer mistress." She yawned once more and drifted off to sleep, just as a solution to all her troubles began to brew in her half-conscious mind. If she were to be used as a pawn, she may as well make the smartest move to everyone's advantage and, suddenly, that move made itself known. Smiling, she found herself actually looking forward to the morrow.

CHAPTER FOUR

"I N LESS THAN a sennight's time, there will either be war, massa-cre, or mayhap both. Donald, Lord of the Isles, is fast approaching." Robert leaned against the solar door and listened as Alexander, William, Reginald, and several others heard the messenger's announcement.

"I ken The Donald is planning an attack, wanting to seize the lands north of us that rightly belong to the Earl of Mar, but I had nay idea he was already on his way," Alexander groused and rubbed his forehead with his hand. "I only just had a missive sent to the earl today."

"He kens already," Charles, their best informant and fastest messenger, replied. "He is the one who sent this new information to us. The Donald wants to seize the lands of the Earldom of Ross, believing he has a stronger claim than the regent. He is a bloody fool, but he has several Highland clans ready to fight beside him for power."

"Our cousin willnae stand for this. Being the Earl of Mar, he will have nay choice but to gather an army, and fast. If The Donald is threatening to burn Aberdeenshire, we have nay choice either," Reginald responded, standing beside Alexander with his arms crossed.

"Aye," Alex scowled and looked around the room. "We must prepare for battle and march north to meet the earl. How many days away is The Donald?"

"Mayhap three at the most. He just defeated the Mackays and took Dingwall Castle, one hundred miles west of here and is marching toward us. Most men are on foot, so they cannae travel quickly, but word is the battle was already three days ago. We have enough time to gather our men and supplies and march north."

"Bastards never let us have peace. They will fight against the Stewarts and kill innocent Scots simply for land and power that was never theirs!" Alexander cursed and stood from his desk.

"Ye have the arms of the Keiths with ye, Alex, but ye must marry Elizabeth before we depart for battle, or else the contract for peace isnae fulfilled."

Robert looked at Elizabeth's elder brother and saw a strong family resemblance. The shared honeyed hair and eyes. It was also clear the man valued her greatly and wanted peace as much as they did.

"The wedding will have to be rushed," Alexander agreed. "On the morrow. I have nay choice. But I will have nay time to court her ye ken, William. It will be a ceremony, a bedding, and then I am off to prepare for war. 'Tis the only way."

William nodded and frowned. "It is most unfortunate, but it is the only way. She willnae be pleased."

"I ken. I am not pleased, either, but if we are to fulfill our peace treaty and prepare for war, she will have to understand." Alexander huffed and ran a hand through his hair. "I apologize. I dinnae mean to be insensitive to her needs, but I dinnae have time to consider them with so many lives at stake."

"I understand, as will she. Elizabeth is a reasonable lass. She hasnae complained once of her fate."

Robert looked at the men in the room, contemplating the strange woman. She seemed resigned to her fate, aye, even complacent, and not at all put off by being passed from father to son. She seemed to have a strong will and a stronger faith, if the pearl rosary she kept snuggly tucked into her bosom was any indication. He knew being rushed to the altar was going to cause her angst, and he wasn't entirely certain why that bothered him as much as it did. She seemed strong-willed and capable, yet she was soon to be married and left alone in a castle with nobody except her maid and her husband's mistress.

Shaking his head, Robert snapped back to the moment. War was coming. Lives would be lost, mayhap his, which would be preferable to the loss of his kin. He needed to focus. Life was unpredictable and dangerous in Scotland and everyone had to make tough decisions and face their own fates, even Elizabeth Keith.

Alexander strode past the men and walked toward he door. "If ye will excuse me. It has been a long day. I will retire now. But on the morrow, we meet in the lists and practice, discuss the situation with our men, and prepare for our journey. We must leave some men behind to protect Drum and the village in case The Donald decides to make good on his threat to burn us down."

Silently, everyone nodded and watched as their laird walked away. Robert had never seen his jovial brother looking so defeated or drained, but knew better than to pity him. He was a knight, a member of the Earl of Mar's elite army. He had fought in many battles and would survive this one as well.

Once Alex was out of earshot, Reginald grunted and leaned against the desk. "I have never seen Alex this way. Usually he would be chomping at the bit for a battle."

"'Tis not battle that he dreads," Robert grumbled and scratched his beard before looking at her brother warily. "Nay offense against yer sister, William, but my brother is still grieving our father, taking on the lairdship, preparing for a battle and—"

"And giving up a woman he loves to marry my sister. I ken."

"Ye do?"

"Aye, and so does she. 'Tis been bothering her since the moment we arrived, not because she is envious, but because she believes true love is rare and she doesnae wish to destroy theirs." William rolled his eyes. "If only she wasnae so innocent to think that he wouldnae keep a mistress."

Robert looked at William and crinkled his forehead. "Ye say it as if ye dinnae mind."

"I dinnae," he shrugged. "We need a marriage and a child born of Irvine and Keith blood to keep the peace. As long as he is kind and respectful, I dinnae care what else he does. Elizabeth has nay allusions of love, so I dinnae think she will care a jot."

Somehow, Robert was not so sure. No wife wanted her husband to keep a mistress. Aye, it was common enough with arranged marriages and something most women had to endure, but he did not suspect she would simply accept such a fate, though he admitted she was a mysterious lass. However, he knew Alex was not like most men. He would suffer his loss before he betrayed his wife or risked offending the Keiths. Though he had known Elizabeth for only a day, he felt a repressed pain radiating from her. She held her head high and kept her back straight to show strength, but he saw sadness in her honeyed eyes. And why he should care bothered him almost as much as the thought of her suffering.

Sighing deeply, William slapped Robert on the shoulder and walked to the door. "I must awaken my sister and tell her the news. She will marry Alex on the morrow. I love Elizabeth, ye ken. She means the world to me. I dinnae like what she must endure, I assure ye. But, we both grew up kenning our duties. I risk my life in battle against the enemy, and she gives her life in marriage to an enemy." He walked past, his last words lingering like some unspoken warning.

The Irvines had better treat his sister well, or there would be hell to pay.

BREATHING PAINED HER. How could something she did so effortlessly every day, suddenly take all her concentration to avoid suffocating on her reality? As if being forced to marry an elderly man had not been bad enough, being told she was being traded from father to son as if she were no more important than a trade between a fishmonger and a baker. Then, she was informed that she had to leave her home and everything she had ever known to marry a man she had hardly exchanged words with in her life. Now, she was awakened by her brother to be warned that her marriage would take place on the morrow. There would be no preparing and no opportunity to get to know her husband before he left for battle.

A tear rolled down her cheek and Elizabeth swiped it away with the back of her hand, wrapping her wool arisaid around her snuggly as the wind beat against her face. Standing on top of the battlements, Elizabeth could see the forested area surrounding the castle to the east and the stars glowing brightly overhead, even if clouds did float by to stifle their light intermittently. It reminded her of something her mother used to say. Just as the light of the stars would be temporarily dimmed by the clouds, so too would the light of her life be temporarily dimmed by her troubles, but just as the wind comes to move away the clouds, so too would better days.

If only her mother and father were here to comfort her now. William had done his best, but he didn't seem to see beyond her duty anymore. Was she to wear black to her wedding? She was still in mourning and, either way, she was afraid of insulting the Irvines, her new kin. How was she to marry on the morrow?

Clenching her hands around the itchy wool fabric, Elizabeth felt herself shake with dread. She would be strong and show no weakness at the ceremony but, tonight, she was crumbling like the walls of an ancient abandoned fortress. Once strong, but now too weak to stand. Allowing a sob to drift in the air, Elizabeth slid her back down the cold stone walls of the parapet, feeling their chill sink into her spine.

Her eyes would be puffy and red when she walked down the aisle, but there was no stopping the flood of tears rolling from them, threatening to pull her under. Clutching her rosary, Elizabeth said a silent prayer for strength and wisdom, all the while wishing her mama was with her now.

"Elizabeth?" Hearing her name on the wind, she gasped and clutched her throat, popping her eyes open to look around the wall walk. At this hour, surely everyone else was in bed.

A tall dark figure walked toward her slowly and she squeaked in terror, huddling into a protective ball, clutching her rosary against her chest. "Who are ye?" she croaked. A demon sent from hell to torment her, just as they say her mother was tormented? She said she saw dark images and had visions. Everyone thought she was mad and evil, but Elizabeth always knew her mama was simply gifted. She, however, did not envy the gift of speaking to the dead and certainly did not wish to be troubled with it now.

"'Tis Robert. Are ye all right?" When he kneeled down beside her, she could make out his features and released a breath of relief, until mortification set in and she wiped her eyes before scrambling to get to her feet. "Easy now, lass," he murmured as his hands rested on her elbows to help raise her to a stand. "Why are ye out here in the cold when ye ought to be sleeping?"

His voice was gentle and concerned, yet she felt ire rising defensively. "Ye try to sleep after being awoken by yer brother telling ye that war is coming again, I must marry a stranger on the morrow, a man who made nay attempt to get to ken me in the one day he had a chance to, and then my kin and new husband would leave for war the following day? Aye, I tell ye, 'tis hard to sleep after such news."

He nodded his head in understanding and pursed his lips. Even with a short dark beard, she could see his dimpled cheeks and they were rather endearing. Why did he care more about her feelings than either of their brothers?

"'Tis the verra same reason I am up and about now. I will be leaving with them after yer wedding. Scotland never rests. Always a battle to fight. Always a man seeking to take what isnae rightfully his. But I cannae relate to having to wed a stranger or being taken away from my kin. So, for that, I am sorry."

Sending Robert a side glance, she tried to figure the man out. "Why do ye care so much about how I feel? Nay other man ever has. My brother treats me kindly, but even to him I am but a pawn in the games of men."

"Am I not also a pawn?" Robert asked. "Arenae we all?" He shrugged and turned to look over the parapet wall, signaling to the forest. "This land isnae ours. Our family was gifted this land by The Bruce during my grandfather's time. This forest is royal hunting land. We are tasked with maintaining it, as well as protecting the village, resolving disputes, being called upon by our king or our cousin, the Earl of Mar, when our swords are needed for another man's gain. I will fight in the war. I dinnae stand to win any land. I gain the opportunity to protect my land from a man who would see it burn, so that our king can continue to hunt... or our king's uncle, since James has been captured for all these years. We are all pawns, lass. Even our king, who rests at the mercy of the English. Life isnae about freedom of will. 'Tis about survival and honor."

Standing beside him and looking down at the forests Robert spoke of, Elizabeth nodded and felt herself relax a wee bit. He was right. Life was not easy and almost nobody had control over their own life. If the worst thing she must endure is marrying a handsome, kind man she would never love while she became the Lady of Drum, then she supposed it was not much at all, if it fulfilled a life-saving peace treaty.

Still, her thoughts had whirled all night and now was her only chance to make this right. Sighing, she turned to look at him. He was similar to his brother, but his eyes were darker, as was his hair. He seemed to be instinctively astute and astoundingly philosophical. "What if we could have peace and prevent yer brother's unhappiness?" she asked carefully and eyed him warily.

"How so?" His gaze locked on hers and her breath caught in her throat, Tilda's words of warning repeating in her mind. Mayhap falling in love with the wrong brother would be the right thing, after all, if she were prone to believing herself capable of such a thing.

"I must marry an Irvine son to create peace. Does it matter which son I marry?"

Robert stilled and she saw a puff of breath escape his lips. "I... I dinnae ken, but I assume so, aye. Yer brother would wish ye to marry the eldest, so ye would be the Lady of Drum."

"Even if the eldest son had a lover?" she asked carefully. Did Robert know about the bairn? She assumed not if Alexander didn't, still he did seem rather perceptive.

Shaking his head, he just shrugged and sent her a look of pity that made her stomach sour. She did not want anyone feeling sorry for her; that was not what this was about. "I'm afraid yer brother is aware of Alexander's previous relationship and is prepared for it to continue. He believes it willnae bother ye, but I see it does. I ken Alex well enough. He willnae do that to ye."

"The only thing that bothers me is their unhappiness. My brother is right about me. I dinnae seek his love, nor he mine. This is a marriage of convenience and I care not if he carries on with Mary. It's only... the situation is a wee bit more complicated than that... and I had thought... mayhap if I were to marry a different brother, Alex and Mary can be together and nay hearts shall be broken."

"And... ye suggest which brother, my lady?" His brow rose and her breath caught once more. He was stunning. There was no way to pretend otherwise and if she married Alexander on the morrow, she would always be attracted to his brother, which felt more sinful than a rosary made of pearls. "Reginald isnae ready to take a wife. He is much too frivolous."

Heart quickening in her chest, Elizabeth felt chills run down her spine. She did not want to appear wanton. This was entirely about helping Alex and Mary. Right? Right. "I was suggesting ye, Robert. Ye are only five years older than I and I havenae seen any signs that ye have a lady... I mean, not that I have paid attention... 'tis just that..." A blush crept up her cheeks, heating her skin and making her feel like a bloody fool. "Oh, this isnae coming out well at all. I am not suggesting this for any other reason than kindness for them. But, if ye didnae wish to marry me... I—"

Placing his finger on her lips to still her speech, Robert tilted his head and squinted into her eyes, sending her a wee smirk that made her wish to swoon and tingles to shoot throughout her body. This was not a good reaction to have to her potential brother by marriage. "Elizabeth. Has anyone ever told ye that ye talk too fast?"

With his finger still pressed against her lips, she slowly nodded. She had been told just that very thing her entire life, especially when she was nervous. "'Tis not that I dinnae wish to marry ye specifically. 'Tis that I dinnae wish to marry anyone, in general. Alexander is the eldest. 'Tis his duty to wed first, 'tis his name on the marriage contract, and 'tis his title that shall give ye rank. I care for my brother's happiness, but he kens his responsibilities and a marriage to Mary was never going to happen. He is the heir, now the laird. He must marry a lass from another family for border security. He has kenned this his entire life and any promises he made to Mary were irresponsible and he kens that."

"Oh." That was a very long rejection. "Ye could have simply said nay." She rolled her eyes and huffed in frustration. Somehow she felt a stinging in her heart, like any chance for a marriage beyond duty had just slipped through her fingers. Somehow, with Robert, she sensed a connection, like they could not only secure peace, but truly be content. Mayhap love was a ridiculous expectation, but attraction would be welcome in her marriage.

"Elizabeth, I wish ye understood that I am not saying nay because I dinnae find ye... bonnie." Robert cleared his throat and looked back toward the forest. "We have our responsibilities, and this is yers, my lady."

He found her bonnie? Somehow, that thought lifted her spirits somewhat, even if she was doomed to marry his brother instead. But he was right. It had been worth mentioning, but never possible. "Verra well. I will marry Alexander in the morn, become Lady of Drum, secure peace between our clans, and take good care of the castle and yer people while ye fight. And I'll pray in the chapel nightly that ye all return to us with all yer limbs."

Chuckling, Robert bowed his head and looked at his left arm. "I appreciate that. I almost lost this limb in a battle against yer brother once. Were ye praying I would keep it back then, I wonder?" he asked with a handsome smile. She was enjoying the ease with which they spoke and how quickly they were able to change the subject.

"Aye, I was. I always pray that nobody is killed or harmed on either side. I ken it is a ridiculous request, for death is inevitable in war, but I still do pray for it. We are all people, simply doing what we think is best for our own people. In the end, who is the wrong? Both? Neither?" Elizabeth shrugged and clutched her arisaid around her shoulders tighter as a gust of wind blew past them. Robert was looking quizzically at her and she wondered if he thought she was daft. Mayhap she was.

"I have never met a lass like ye. Ye are young, yet ye seem to understand the world in a way verra few do. And ye are brave. I ken this is hard for ye, but ye can do it, and Alex will be a good husband to ye, and if he isnae, I shall box his ears." Robert smiled widely and put his arm out to her.

Laughing for the first time in a while, Elizabeth linked arms with him and allowed him to escort her back into the tower where it would still be frigid, but the wind would not threaten to blow her away. "Not if William runs him through first," she giggled, descending the stairs, heading toward her chamber.

As they reached her chamber door, Robert released her arm and bowed slightly. "Then I will make certain Alex is forewarned that his treatment of the Lady of Drum shall always be honorable." His dimples flashed once more, this time in the light of a flickering sconce on the wall, and Tilda's warning from earlier rang in her ears once more.

Clearing her throat, Elizabeth sobered herself and nodded politely, then stepped into her room, removing her arisaid and climbing back into the warm clean sheets of her bed. Tilda was wrong about one thing. Robert Irvine had no affections for her beyond a protective brother, but she had been right to warn Elizabeth not to fall in love with the wrong brother. Robert made her stomach flop and her heart flutter. These were dangerous feelings to have in general for any man, but to have them for the brother of her husband would be a sin and a sentence for a lifetime of heartache. She could not allow that.

Admonishing herself for being a daft lass, fancying herself falling for a man she had only known for a day, and simply because he was kind to her, Elizabeth flipped over onto her side and closed her eyes, demanding herself to get some rest and to stop behaving like a fool. There was no such thing as real love, not outside the old pages of a book, and there was no time for such a thing even if it did exist. Men fought wars and women raised babes to grow up and fight more wars. It was a depressing thought, but a sobering one.

Any idea of romance she had harbored for even a moment died upon the edge of sleep and reality as she floated willingly into the nothingness.

CHAPTER FIVE

T HE IMAGE OF Elizabeth crying on the wall walk had kept Robert up for much of the night. She held her head high when others were around, but privately, she was vulnerable and lonely. Somehow, he felt slightly privileged to have been witness to the more private side of Elizabeth, the side nobody else saw and hoped he had been of some comfort to her the night before.

She had asked to marry him. That had contributed to his sleeplessness as well. Where his mind should have been on war, it had been on his brother's bride. He would need to avoid the lass as much as possible. The feelings she stirred within him were dangerous and inappropriate for a sister by marriage. There was no denying her beauty, but many women were beautiful. There was just something more to Elizabeth, something deeper that he felt drawn to. Still, he had been honest last night. If he could choose a wife, he supposed one like her would be preferred, but he was not looking for one, nor could he legally marry her. And it was just as well. He never wanted a wife he could love. Love made men weak. Look at Alex. He was more miserable than ever. Nay, Robert would marry as befit his clan and he would hope she was comely enough to share a bed with at night, yet dull enough to bear no true love for. It was better that way.

When Elizabeth approached the chapel with her brother by her side, her brilliant blue damask dress caught the rays of the sun, as did the gold threading throughout. It had a wide neck and long flowing sleeves with a belt of gold around her slim waist. Her pearl rosary rested snuggly between her ample breasts, and she touched it from time to time – a nervous habit he had picked up on already. It was clear the item meant more to her than just prayer beads or a piece of jewelry, and he found himself disappointed he had not bothered to ask about it the night before.

Blue was the traditional color of innocence and Elizabeth looked every bit the virginal blushing bride with a tinge of pink in her cheeks and a proud smile on her lips. Apparently, his talk had done her well, for gone were her tears and before him stood a confident woman. Nobody would ever believe she had been sobbing atop the battlements the night before or requesting to marry a different brother. He wanted to be happy, but somehow seeing her appear happy as she approached Alex made his stomach lurch.

"Alexander got a wee bit fortunate, aye?" Reginald leaned in and whispered into Robert's ear.

"To be forced to marry a woman he doesnae ken?" Robert grumbled.

"Dinnae pretend she isnae a beauty, Brother. Even ye, with yer serious disposition, have a good set of eyes. Ye can hit a target from two hundred meters away, yet ye cannae see that our brother's bride is built for sin?" Reginald waggled his brows and Robert scowled at him.

"Ye disrespect yer brother and yer sister with yer words. Shut yer trap, or I shall shut it for ye and ye willnae like my methods." An unexpected instinct to protect Elizabeth gripped at his gut, making his stomach clench. Why was he feeling this way? Mayhap because now that Elizabeth would be kin, he felt the need to keep her safe from anyone who would besmirch her honor, even Reginald... especially Reginald, who did not have a good reputation with the lassies and seemed to run his mouth over-freely.

"Och, who pulled yer trews into a bunch this morn?"

"Ye did with yer disrespect. Do ye want the Keiths to hear how ye speak of her?" Robert whispered to his brother just as Elizabeth walked past, the scent of roses following in her wake. She made no eye contact with him, simply looked straight ahead at Alexander while keeping a steady grin on her face. He knew it was for show, but he was glad she had been able to pull herself together in time.

Alexander had the decency to smile in return, bowing to William before taking his bride's hand and facing the priest in front of their chapel's entrance. The ceremony began but Robert was too distracted with thoughts of war preparations to focus. How were they all to celebrate with a feast tonight when there was so much to do? Yet, this marriage added a strong ally close to their border who would help them defend against The Donald's army.

Vows and rings were exchanged but nothing else really registered in Robert's mind until he saw his brother and Elizabeth walking away from the chapel holding hands and smiling as the crowd of villagers, castle dwellers, and Keiths clapped and cheered before dispersing. The air was thick with tension and he knew their men were chomping at the bit to get to practicing in the lists and preparing for the journey. The celebration would continue tonight but, for now, it was time to focus on other issues.

"I feel bad for that poor lassie. What a wedding day she gets, aye? Everybody shuffling their feet, anxious to be on with their day, instead of the all-day celebration she deserves." Robert recognized the elderly woman speaking as the blacksmith's wife, Ida. So, it was not just he who had felt the itch to be away from the ceremony, though mayhap he had different motives.

"Och, well, she is a noblewoman and 'tis her duty, is it not? She gets to live in the castle, and be Lady of the Castle, does she not? We get to marry for love if we are fortunate in the village, but we slave the day away. I dinnae feel so bad for the lady, if I do say so," a younger woman heavy with child replied as she rubbed the aching arch of her back. "I will work 'til the day I give birth, then be expected to be back on my feet the next day. She has it easy, I say. Besides, the laird ain't so hard on the eyes, aye?"

The conversation faded as the two women walked back toward the village along with the rest of the folks and the warriors were already walking toward the armory to gather weapons.

Following his men, Robert thought on what the women said. He supposed they were right. Everyone played a role. Everyone had hardships. In the end, Elizabeth's situation was much more ideal than many others, including his, for he was off to war in the morn.

"Robert? Are ye coming or what?" one of his men hollered at him as they walked past and dispersed from the chapel.

Nodding his head, Robert looked away and watched as Elizabeth slowly walked back toward the castle with Alexander, wondering why he was constantly so concerned about the lass. He had his own concerns. Everybody did. She was not his wife to protect and, for some reason, reminding himself of that only made him angry.

He was a bloody fool. He could think all day about why he was so damned protective of the lass, but he was afraid if he thought about it too hard, the truth would surface, and he was better off not thinking about it… or Elizabeth.

Shaking his head and popping his knuckles, Robert followed his men, determined to forget all about the marriage, Lady Elizabeth of Drum, or the fact that she was now his sister.

THE KEEP WAS filled with her kin, new and old, yet Elizabeth had never felt more alone. Staring into the crowd, she scanned the room wishing she was part of the crowd below the head table, not sitting next to a husband she didn't even know. Once again, she was placed between Alexander and Robert, neither of them paying her much attention. Somehow, the thought of having Robert's company had made her feel like she would survive this feast, yet he had seemingly decided she was no longer in need of his companionship. Humiliation clawed at her. She had been a fool to even mention her plan to him. Now, he would not even speak with her.

Hands folded in her lap, Elizabeth looked down at her trencher of pheasant, carrots, and onions in a savory sauce, but her stomach was too tied up in knots to manage a bite of food. The bedding ceremony would be expected soon, and everybody would watch her ascend the steps with her husband, like a prized bull about to inseminate a cow, if he could be bothered to so much as look at her, she mused. Nay, she was not looking forward to any bit of it. Now, if it was with Robert...

Gasping at her own lewd thoughts, Elizabeth clutched her rosary and looked about, hoping nobody noticed the sudden blushing of her cheeks. What thoughts! So what that he was handsome. He looked like her husband. So what if he had been the only person to consider her comfort and feelings since arriving at Drum. Alexander was laird and much too busy, so naturally it fell on the younger brother to take on the responsibility. That's all she was to anyone in the end. And clearly, by the way Robert made certain to turn his back slightly toward her as he laughed with the woman seated on his left, he felt his duty was over now that she was married.

Well, she was nobody's responsibility. She could take care of herself, this castle, and all its people while the men were gone, and she yearned to prove as much. Elizabeth Keith, now Irvine, needed no man to comfort her, especially out of some false sense of duty.

Indignation roiled and she pursed her lips, knowing herself well enough to keep quiet, lest she say exactly what was on her mind. If they did not wish to speak to her, it was well and good, for she felt the same way. All Elizabeth wanted to do was get this over with. Alexander left on the morrow and she would have some time alone to adjust to life here at Drum.

The anxiety was getting to be too much. There were jogglers and minstrels, all there to entertain the bride, groom, and their guests. But nobody paid much mind and she was certain everyone was more concerned about what the impending battle would bring, as was she.

Mary was conveniently missing from the festivities, as she was from the chapel, though Elizabeth could not blame her. Leaning in close to Alexander's ear, Elizabeth whispered softly, interrupting his seemingly important conversation with a balding man beside him, who she remembered as his uncle who served as the castle's steward. "I am sorry to interrupt, but I ken ye have to leave in the morn and hoped we may retire?" Speaking the words carefully, she hoped she did not sound wanton, for it was not the bedding she was anxious for, but to be over with it and asleep within the hour.

Turning from his uncle, Alex looked at her strangely, scanning the room, no doubt for Mary. The frustrated sigh that escaped her could not be withheld, nor did it go unnoticed. "Aye, I suppose we should." Now, an unladylike snort came from her, but fortunately the minstrels drowned it out, though she was certain Alex, and mayhap Robert, heard it.

"She isnae here, *Husband*." Elizabeth rolled her eyes and stood up from the head table, done with this entire sham. She was not at all concerned with his relationship with Mary, but could he at least focus on his duties while at his own wedding?

A flush covered his cheeks and his eyes grew wide as he started to stumble on his words and blabber incoherently as he stood up beside her. The room started to cheer and shout bawdy words as men smacked the tables and women whooped and hollered. Elizabeth wished to disappear behind the screens, but it would do no good to avoid the situation. Best to push through.

Taking her hand, Alex helped her down from the head table and over to the spiral staircase where he guided her up to the third story where both their rooms were. She presumed she would be sleeping in his bedchamber this night, which made her stomach clench and her breath catch. Brave though she was, Elizabeth had heard too many horror stories from the lassies of her clan about the pain of the first time, and the childbirth that eventually would follow.

Approaching the door to his chamber, Alexander continued past and stopped in front of hers, pushing the door open, where the fire was already lit and Tilda waited within, a strange look on her face. Was she to get ready in her rooms first and await his return? Her blue damask dress was heavy and, suddenly, she felt a sweat break out all over her body. Taking a deep breath, she tried to calm her nerves.

Before she could open her mouth to ask questions, Alex planted a brotherly kiss on her forehead and stepped back, putting his hands on her shoulders. "As ye ken, I leave on the morrow. I dinnae feel right bedding ye, then leaving."

Something that felt like humiliation mixed with relief washed over her body, sending chills up her spine. "Ye dinnae mean to... to..." Words escaped her. Never had she expected this.

"When I arrive home from battle, we will... consummate the marriage. Until then, I leave ye well, Wife. I dinnae wish to plant a seed in ye if I willnae be around to father a bairn." Little did he know, he was already father to one bairn in the castle.

"But... the sheets..." Elizabeth stuttered, trying to process all that he was saying.

"Yer maid has taken care of that," Alexander looked over at Matilda, who shrugged in the corner, looking as shocked as Elizabeth felt, but she gave a small nod of affirmation to him before he looked at Elizabeth once more.

"Is this about Mary? I dinnae mind, Alex. I ken this isnae a love match."

Shaking his head, Alexander smirked at her for the first time, giving her a look of respect. "Robert did say ye were a keen one. Ye will do well here at Drum, and Mary told me ye spoke with her. Ye are a good woman, Elizabeth. But this isnae about her. I am yer husband now and she kens that. Nay, this is about what I said. I willnae burden ye with a babe until I am certain I will be around to raise it. Until then, my wee wife, I bid ye farewell, until I return."

Smiling softly, Elizabeth finally felt what she had hoped she would all along. A mutual respect for her husband. He was preoccupied as a laird and it was not his fault that they had to marry in a hurry before he left for battle. He had sacrificed more for this marriage than she had, for he had given up love. When he arrived home, she would speak with him about his relationship, let him know she was not bothered if he continued it in private, so as not to embarrass her. But now was not the time.

"My thanks. Ye are a good man Alexander Irvine. I am honored to be yer wife and vow to do my best for Drum and yer kin. I shall work well with Mary. She is a good lass. And I wish ye well and will pray for ye every day until ye return, I vow."

Nodding slowly, Alexander picked up her hand, gave it one soft kiss, then turned on his heels and walked back to his chamber.

Still trying to process everything, Elizabeth stepped into her own chamber and looked at Matilda for answers just after she shut her door. "What just happened?"

"Ye married the only man in Scotland with any honor left, is what just happened."

"I suppose ye are right. I am just confused. What does he mean about ye taking care of the sheets?"

Holding up a vial, Matilda shook it and raised her brows. "'Tis the blood of a swine. He asked me to smear it on the sheets so nobody would suspect the marriage wasnae consummated. He didnae want yer marriage questioned, nor did he want ye embarrassed when the ladies doing the wash run their mouths."

Turning around so Matilda could undo the laces of her heavy dress, Elizabeth sighed as she felt fresh air flood her lungs once more. When her dress and slippers were removed, she walked over to her bed and plopped down on the mattress, allowing her feet to dangle off the edge, pondering the night. "I dinnae ken what to say, but I am relieved. Is that bad?"

"Nay. Ye dinnae ken the man, husband or not. It isnae unusual to feel anxious. But now ye can rest easy, Lizzie... until he returns."

"There will be nay rest, Tilda. I have a castle to run and people to care for now. Not to mention all of our kin are heading off to fight the enemy."

A sense of dread gripped her as she watched Tilda pour a few drops of blood onto the white linen sheets before shoving them aside. Climbing under the covers and allowing Matilda to tuck her in, she wondered how much more blood would be spilled before she saw her husband once more.

CHAPTER SIX

T HE DAWN CAME before Robert had had an ounce of sleep. Too busy loading supplies and helping Alexander ready the men for their northern journey, they expected to meet up with Mar close to Harlaw, only a twenty-mile journey. Easily achieved in a day upon a horse, it would take two to make it with the army, as some men were on foot and carts carrying supplies would slow down their progress.

Scouts had already been sent to the north, ordered to look for signs of the approaching enemy. They had to head off The Donald before he reached Aberdeen and made good of his promise to burn it down for what he considered revenge for past deeds done, none of which the Irvines were guilty of. However, their clan's connection to the Stewart king, his uncle who was currently serving as regent, and their cousin Alexander, Earl of Mar, who was also a Stewart, apparently made them common enemies of the Highlands. So be it.

Farewells were made by the men who had a lass to console, but Robert simply sat upon his horse and bit into a juicy apple, watching the women sob as their men saddled up. Alexander said a brief goodbye to his new wife, who was standing in the outer bailey looking as regal as ever in her forest green dress, brown hair plaited over one shoulder. Her face was neutral, showing no signs of emotion as Alex gave her what appeared to be a chaste kiss on the lips before walking away, his armor bearer in his wake.

Briefly, Robert considered the sort of kiss he would give to his wife if she was as bonnie and intelligent as Elizabeth. It most certainly would be more than a mere peck, but he shook those thoughts off and turned his horse away just as he saw her eyes lock on him from across the courtyard. Robert did not have a lover, nor did he need one. Romance led to love and love led to marriage, which led to bairns and more responsibility than he cared for. Aye, he had had many lovers, but none who did not understand that his duty was to the Stewarts of Scotland and he went where he was needed and fought who needed to be fought without any concern over returning home to a lass or a child.

Summer in Scotland was mild and refreshing, yet traveling out in the open sun for hours, rays beating down upon his flesh, caused him to sweat. But, he had traveled in worse and would take the summer's heat over the winter's chill any day. Leading the men at the front with Alexander and Reginald, Robert realized that his elder brother was much quieter than he usually was on the way to a battle. His frivolous brother usually never showed signs of worry or stress, but since Father's death, Alex seemed perpetually plagued by worry.

"Being laird has turned ye serious," Robert finally said, breaking the long silence.

"'Tis not so much being laird, but being married," he grunted.

Reginald scoffed and rolled his eyes. "Ye are a spoiled lout, ye ken that? She is the bonniest lass I have ever seen and ye got to share her bed last night. There nay need for a frown and if she is such a burden, I shall gladly take her off yer hands."

"Haud yer wheesht," Robert warned, scowling at his brother. "Ye have nay respect, do ye?"

"On the contrary, I respect her, or at least parts of her, verra much."

Alex slowly turned his head and narrowed his eyes at their young-er brother, who was known for his handsome looks, sharp wit, and loose tongue. "I didnae lie when I said I would run ye through, Reg."

"All I am saying is ye need to stop yer frowning and appreciate yer good fortune. Father didnae leave me such a bonnie bride."

Staying silent, Robert breathed deeply and looked ahead. They were about midpoint now. Drum Castle was just about ten miles south of them and it had taken more than half the day to travel this far. There was no point arguing with Reginald. He wanted a fight, even thrived off it, and Robert refused to feed into his younger brother's foolish games. He sensed that Alex felt the same, and only threatened him out of husbandly obligation, though he did not seem as bothered to hear his brother speaking of his wife as mayhap he should, for having bedded her the night before. He wasn't sure why his stomach tightened into a knot at the thought of them together, or why it soured his mood more than the fact that they were headed for battle.

Holding up his left hand, Alexander stopped and the scores of men behind them and he did the same. Robert pulled on his destrier's reins and the well-trained war-horse stopped and shook her head, snorting slightly in defiance, if only to let Robert know that she listened because she wished to, and for no other reason. That's what he loved most about Fodla. She was as fierce and determined as the goddess she was named after, yet reliable and always ready for a fight.

Pointing to the stream just east of them, Alexander hopped off his horse and wiped his brow. "We rest for a wee bit. Water yerselves and yer horses," he shouted to the line of men behind them. Turning to Robert, he jerked his head, signaling for him to follow, away from the other men. Dismounting, Robert allowed Fodla to wander toward the stream while he followed his brother over to a large stone protruding from a small mound of grass, surrounded by yellow and purple wildflowers. Sitting warily on the stone, Alex ran his hands through his dark hair and looked up at the sky. "My mind is heavy, Brother."

"Aye?" Robert already knew as much, but he stepped closer and leaned against the tree, enjoying the support on his lower back at least for a short while until he would be on the road once more.

"Aye."

Wind blew past Robert, causing his linen tunic to billow slightly, cooling the sweat slicking his chest. It was refreshing, yet something foreboding slithered up his spine. He was not certain what his brother had on his mind, but already he knew he would not like it. "Battle weary already?" Robert asked, ribbing his brother and earning a weak smile.

"I am weary of much. I miss the days before Father passed, before I had responsibilities coming out of my arse, lands all over Scotland to manage, titles, peace treaties. I ken I was born to be the heir, but having to take on a wife, a war, and a lairdship all at once is a grand burden."

"Alexander..." Robert had to say it. Mayhap he should not, but he could not understand and wanted an answer. "Elizabeth is... quite bonnie. I ken ye love Mary, and Elizabeth kens as well. But is it so bad being married to the lass? Surely ye can grow to love her."

"Have ye ever loved a woman, Rob? Truly loved her?"

Shaking his head and taking a deep breath, Robert shrugged. "Ye ken I havenae."

"Then ye cannae understand what it is to lose her, even to the bonniest of lassies." Alexander rubbed at his short beard and Robert did the same. It was a nervous tell they both inherited from their father and was usually followed up with a request.

"What do ye need from me, Alex? Anything. Ye ken I am yer friend, not just yer brother."

"I do ken. And I do have a mighty favor. Should I fall in battle—"

"That willnae happen." Robert pushed off the tree's rough trunk, feeling the sudden scratch of its bark against his back. He did not want to hear such talk from his brother. "Ye have fought many battles and survived. Ye are one of Mar's best knights."

"I am fallible, and I am mortal, and I have much to lose should I die. I need to make certain my affairs are in order should the worst happen."

"That willnae happen, Brother. But I already ken I am next in line as laird. I already ken all the lands and all yer responsibilities. Ye neednae worry about any of that."

"That isnae what I am worried about. Our peace with the Keiths is fragile. It wasnae so long ago they set an Irvine lad on fire, if ye remember."

Cringing and feeling his stomach churn, Robert swallowed, remembering the horrifying day and details acutely. How he wished he could forget the traumatic day. The screams. The cries. The smell of burned flesh. The retaliation. The Keiths had paid dearly for their sins, their cattle slaughtered and their fields burned. It had been a bloody road between the families, and peace was much needed. An heir must be born soon to make the bond stronger. "I pray nightly to forget," Robert whispered.

"Me, as well. 'Tis why my marriage to Elizabeth is so verra important. We have ended a feud and gained an ally. If I die, I cannae have the fighting continue. Ye must marry Elizabeth instead. It is in the marriage contract that the next brother in line will marry her, should the other perish. Ye will take over my entire life, Robert, even my name. Ye ken 'tis a tradition for the laird of Drum to be named Alexander."

Aye, he knew this, yet had not ever truly considered it a possibility. A name was just a name. He could sign his brother's name on documents and still remain himself in private. But, to marry his widow? That was asking too much, and though Robert found Elizabeth to be a beautiful and pleasant woman, marriage was not in his immediate plans. "Ye want me to marry yer wife? Are ye mad?" Head spinning, Robert propped against the tree once more, feeling like a horse had just crushed his chest. "Ye ken I dinnae wish to marry for a verra long time, and certainly not to my sister."

Alexander scoffed and waved his hand. "She isnae yer sister. And if I am dead, she is just my widow."

"Dinnae speak of yer death with such ease. Ye arenae going to die and I willnae marry Elizabeth."

Standing from the rock, Alexander straightened his back and grew serious once more. "If I die, ye will. Ye need to. Ye have nay choice. I told ye, 'tis in the contract. Peace depends on it. Give me yer word. I require it, as yer laird."

"Och, dinnae pull that shite on me, Alex." Robert sighed, knowing he had no choice but to comply. If it was worth peace between their people, and contracted, then his fate was sealed. "All right. Ye have my word. But 'tis unnecessary, for ye willnae die." Spitting on his palm, he put out his hand for Alex, who did the same. They shook on it and sealed the agreement. "I will let Reginald ken."

Shaking his head, Alex began to walk back toward the men, then paused and turned around. "Nay. I will tell him. 'Tis better coming from me. One more thing, Robert, and 'tis just as important to me, if not more so. Ye must take care of my Mary. I am worried about her as it is. If I shouldnae return, promise me ye will make sure she is always taken care of."

"Ye neednae ever ask such a thing, Alex. Mary is important to us all. She is family and will always be cared for," Robert vowed and followed his brother toward the river, desperately in need of some cool, refreshing water and a moment of quiet for his pacing thoughts. He always knew he was the spare to the heir of Drum. He always knew there was a chance tragedy would strike and he would have to step in, especially with Alex being knighted last year in France and having strong loyalties to Mar, ever at the ready for a fight. But it had never occurred to him that he would need to take over his brother's wife and discussing Alex's potential death had shaken Robert more than he cared to show. Never had they sat down and talked about anything so important, nor had they ever had to.

"Where is Reginald?" Alexander asked, shielding his eyes against the blazing rays beaming down on them. It was a midsummer's day and a beautiful one at that, but very little shade was to be found on this road heading north.

"He went into the forest that way, with a group of men," a man pointed. "He decided to hunt for some game while we were stopped. Said they would catch up to us."

Sighing, Alexander scratched his beard and looked at Robert, clearly stressed. Obviously, he had wanted to get this off his chest as soon as possible, but it was going to have to wait. "We need to continue on. He kens the way." Alex approached his horse and Robert did the same, mounting Fodla quickly and guiding her away from the river, back toward the dirt road. "Harlaw is about ten miles north of here and if we dinnae break, we will be there by nightfall."

Alex and Robert rode side by side, yet neither man spoke. Alex seemed to be focused as he looked straight ahead, and Robert simply had swirling thoughts of battle on his mind and how much more he had to lose than any other man. Many men had brothers that may fall, and he always had to worry for all his warriors, especially Alexander and Reginald. But of all the men in their train, he was the one who would need to give up everything he knew to take over his brother's life, should he fall.

Shaking his head and squinting his eyes into the horizon, Robert took a deep breath, feeling the air in his lungs and an ache in his heart. Protecting his brothers was always a priority, but now, it was an absolute necessity. Alexander would not fall in battle. Robert would not allow it.

SITTING ALONE ON a rock, Robert stared at nothing in particular. Morning dew clung to green blades of grass, reflecting the light of the rising sun as its rays stretched over the Harlaw horizon. So much beauty surrounded him in the new light of dawn, yet all he could truly see, feel, smell, or taste were the horrors of the day before.

Mayhap if he stared at that one blade of grass, so new, fresh and bright, he could forget the many other blades just over the hill that were still drenched in blood. Not just blood of the enemy, but blood of his kin. So much death. The acrid scent of it wafted on the wind, reminding him even from a distance that there was no escaping the horrors that awaited on the other side. More war. More blood. More death.

When they reached Harlaw the morning before, the Irvines and Keiths were met by their cousin Mar and his army of three thousand men, less than half the men that marched toward them from the north. The Donald had a reported ten thousand men, and from what Robert had seen on the battlefield as they approached, before the slaughter began, he had to agree that the army had been massive, yet they were ill-prepared and untrained.

If nothing else could be learned from Red Harlaw, as the men already referred to it, it was that numbers meant very little. Mar's army consisted of warriors, knights, armor, and superior weapons while the poor bastards fighting from the Highlands had crude swords and no armor to speak of. They had been but commoners made to believe that the will of powerful men was worth dying for. And, they had.

But it was not only them who lost lives. Even important men, knighted men, can fall. Closing his eyes, he willed himself to forget the moment. To stop repeating the images in his mind. The battle had nearly been over. Men were either dead or exhausted and it had been impossible to tell who had won the day, for it felt like a loss all around. But they had survived. The three brothers of Drum had lived through the slaughter.

And then, a man had pushed through the line. Red Hector of the Battles Maclean, the leader of Donald's army and a hulking man with a vendetta to fulfill. Robert took a shaky breath, trying to calm his pulse and roiling stomach. He felt as if he would be sick once more but was certain he had already vomited up every organ he had.

While the Highland army attacked in one line, Mar's army had been split into three, keeping the knights in the back as reserve. That meant that the very best men were the last on the scene and Maclean was determined to fight the best, hacking his way through crowds of men, seemingly not caring who he felled, friend or foe. That's when it happened. Everything was still as clear as the River Dee on a summer's day in Robert's mind. Every detail. Though he wished to forget, he knew it would plague him for a lifetime.

Alexander saw the infamous warrior approaching, covered in blood while wearing a sadistic smile. The man had been mad with bloodlust and wandering the field for his next victim. Alexander saw him first, and before Robert even had a chance to turn around, the two men were locked in combat.

Every second had been torture. Alexander had fought and defeated many men in his life, but just being a few yards away and being unable to do aught but watch and pray his brother survived had been excruciating.

Robert watched as Alexander's blade ran through Hector's chest and breath filled his lungs for the first time in what felt an eternity. His brother had killed the mad bastard and survived. Until the moment the dying man used the last of his reserved energy to push his blade through Alexander's heart.

Everything had happened in slow motion and Robert was certain he had let out a wail that shook the heavens. Even now, he relived the moment over and over, torturously. He and Reginald had run over to their brother, tried to stop the bleeding as Alexander faded before their eyes.

Feeling nauseous once more, Robert doubled over and clenched his belly. His brother was gone. He lay on the field at Harlaw along with thousands of other men. It wasn't supposed to happen this way. Alexander was strong, powerful, intelligent, and always full of light. He was the one who had always guided Robert and Reginald, and now… he was no more.

Bile rose in his throat and he spit it out, wiping his chin and cursed his stinging throat with its repressed pain. There had been no clear winner of the battle and despite the death of his brother, fighting was meant to continue now at dawn.

Taking a breath, Robert walked back to his men, finding Reginald sitting beside where they had temporarily laid Alexander's body. Neither of them was handling this well, but Reginald was only two and twenty, the spoiled third brother who never had much more to do than chase skirts and fight in skirmishes. Life had not been full of trial for him. He had trained beside them on the lists, but never had to fight in any major battles. Now, here he was, staring blankly at a body covered with an Irvine plaid, and Robert had nothing to say for comfort. There was no comfort. No calming the grief. Yet still, the battle was unfinished, and Alexander would want them to fight on.

Walking over to his brother, Robert put out a hand and helped Reginald to his feet. "He wouldnae want us to wallow, Reg." The words burned in his throat. Unshed tears stung his eyes.

"Aye, he would. He was too self-important to not want a display of grief," Reginald chuckled and Robert forced himself not to smile.

"Mayhap so," Robert nodded, slapping Reginald on the back. "But he would wish us to wallow after the battle was won," he corrected.

"Aye. Now that, I believe," Reginald sniffled and gripped his belly, clearly feeling the same loss and pain Robert was.

Every part of Robert ached, not just his heart. Fighting had taken its toll on his body as it had every other man. Nobody had the strength of body or heart to continue this fight as they were surrounded by the bloodshed of their kin, yet none of this could be in vain. There was no giving up and no turning back. If they lost, The Donald's army would continue their march south and burn Aberdeen as promised. It could not be allowed.

"Reg. I need ye to stay back."

"What?" His brother tilted his head and furrowed his brow.

"If I die next, ye are all that Drum has left," Robert forced through his cracked lips and aching throat.

"So ye wish me to stay back like a coward? Nay! I wish to fight!"

"I ken ye do, but think what will happen to our people should we both perish. Uncle's daughters and their awful husbands will come and one of them will be laird. Father would roll over in his grave!"

Reginald went silent, but Robert could see his jaw clenching with frustration. Robert knew his brother wished to avenge Alexander, as did Robert, but there was more in life than vengeance and the man who killed him also lay dead in this field. When vengeance was used to fuel a war, nothing good ever came from it.

"Men! Gather around me!" Mar shouted and everyone turned to face their leader who was also covered in blood, despite having been covered in armor during the battle. The blood he wore was not of the enemy, but of the kin they had moved off the field all night. "It appears The Donald retreated during the night, coward that he is. Even with an army thrice our size, they fled in fear, kenning we were the greater force!"

Men shouted and whooped, both happy for the victory and to not have to fight any more. He doubted any of them had much more fight to give. Though he was relieved not to fight, this felt like no victory at all. They had lost their laird, their brother, their best friend. But he had died to protect his people and his land, just as Robert knew he would have wanted, though it did not make the pain of his loss hurt any less.

Though the battle was over, there was much to do. Bodies had to be burned to prevent disease from spreading, for there was no way to bring them all home. Reluctantly, Reginald and Robert approached Alexander's body, now covered with several Irvine plaids and, once more, Robert held back the wail wanting to escape from the depths of his soul. "We cannae burn him."

"Nay," Reginald whispered, looking down at the pile of plaids, swallowing hard. "He must be buried. It is cruel to leave the others to burn, though we have no choice. But, not Alex. Not the laird."

"There is a kirk a few miles from here. Order the men to put Alex on a cart. Before returning home, we will see him properly buried."

Storming away, Robert gripped his throbbing temples and allowed the tears to flow once more before hardening himself to the reality that stood before him. He was now Laird of Drum, and, whether he liked it or not, he was contracted to marry his brother's wife. His beautiful, intelligent, stubborn widow.

CHAPTER SEVEN

THE SCENTS OF rosemary, garlic, and onions floated on the breeze as Elizabeth kneeled into the soil, determined to remove all the weeds that threatened to consume her new garden. At Castle Dunnottar, her garden was the very best place to escape and find some peace, and Drum's garden had quickly become the same.

The feeling of the cool earth in her hands soothed her soul, which she needed now more than ever as she waited for any news of the battle. It had been a sennight, not so very long where battles were concerned, except that it was only twenty miles away. Already, she had made it her goal to learn the names of all the staff, find her way around the castle, and had been given a hearty blessing by Mary to take over the herbs, fruits, and vegetables, a task she was not as keen on as Elizabeth.

"Ye have worked wonders in here!" Startled, Elizabeth gasped and dropped her trowel, looking over her shoulder to see Mary hovering over her with a smile. Her red hair flowed freely and she truly was glowing like an angel.

"Och, ye scared me," Elizabeth laughed and stood up, wiping the dirt off the knees of her tattered blue work dress. "Ye look happier than I've seen ye in days. How's our wee bairn doing?" Elizabeth placed her hand on Mary's slightly rounded belly and smiled. "Has he quickened yet?"

Mary sighed and put one hand on her belly, as well. "Nay, not quite. The midwife says he may in a moon or so, and that it will feel like wee butterflies in my stomach. Seems surreal and I cannae wait. But, aye, I am happy. My sickness has abated and I heard news that the men were seen approaching from the distance." A sadness fell over her face and she looked up at the bright blue sky overheard. "Though I suppose we await the same man."

"Mary. Ye ken I only await news that everyone is well and that the enemy has been chased away. Aye, we await the same man, but not in the same way. I will say my public greeting to him, and ye may say whatever it is ye wish to say to him in private. Ye ken I dinnae mind. Ye carry his bairn after all."

"How does that not bother ye?" Mary looked at her oddly, tilting her head. "Ye say it so casually. I would be blinded by jealousy if another woman carried my husband's child."

Elizabeth snorted and waved Mary away. "Because ye are in love with him. I suppose I would care if I had feelings beyond duty toward the man. Nay, it doesnae bother me, except that I feel responsible for keeping ye apart. I truly did try to change our fates."

"Ye did? How?"

Chewing her lower lip, Elizabeth sighed and wondered if she was saying more than she should. Offering herself to Robert and being rejected was not her finest moment in life. "After ye told me about the bairn and I found out my marriage was to happen immediately, I was atop the battlements, sobbing like a wee child. Robert found me and comforted me. It had crossed my mind that if I were to marry Robert, ye could be with Alex and I would still fulfill the peace between our clans. Only, he informed me it wasnae possible. The marriage contract was already signed, and I was meant to marry the laird, not the second brother, not that such a detail would matter to me. Furthermore. I felt like I was replacing ye as acting lady of the castle. I like ye, Mary. Ye and Robert are my only friends here at Drum and I cannae stand that my arrival has ruined yer life."

Mary's bonnie lips turned downward as she listened to Elizabeth and before she knew what was happening, her new companion had her locked in a stronger embrace than she could have expected from such a wee lass. "Ye are a good woman, Elizabeth. Ye havenae ruined my life. I ken that Alex and I could never have married. We wanted to run away to be together but he is the heir. It is an impossible position and if he didnae marry ye, he would have married another. I am only glad it was ye, because ye make this tolerable for me."

Shouts rang out and the sound of horse hooves traveled through the air. "The men are back!" Mary gasped and released Elizabeth. A sinking feeling gripped at Elizabeth, almost as if she were drowning from a sudden lack of air. Gripping her rosary, she prayed all the men returned safely, though she knew it was an impossibility. Picking up her soiled skirts, Elizabeth ran toward the commotion, just as anxious to greet the men and hear the news as all the others in the castle and surrounding village. All work ceased as the crowd formed in the outer bailey, the tension palpable.

The horses kicked dirt up into the air creating clouds of brown dust that surrounded her. Covering her nose, Elizabeth fanned the air in front of her, trying to see through the crowd, getting on her tiptoes to watch as dozens of horses came to a stop.

"Let the Lady of Drum through so she can greet the laird!" an older woman's voice rang out and Elizabeth almost forgot who she was. As the lady, she should be in the front, awaiting her laird and husband. People parted for her, making a walkway that somehow made her feel uncomfortable and more visible than she wished to be.

Hands gripping the fabric of her skirts so nobody could see them shaking, Elizabeth watched as the men came to a stop. She needed to see her brother. Never had she suffered more than she had this past sennight, praying nightly for the souls of her kin, for the Irvine brothers, but especially for her brother. Life simply would cease to matter if he was no longer alive.

Spotting him upon his horse near the front, there was no way to control the relief coursing through her mind. "William!" Everything else faded away as she shouted for him, running toward his horse as he dismounted and put out his arms before wrapping her in his warm, familiar embrace. He was covered in a layer of dirt, but he was alive and whole. "Oh, my brother! How I feared for ye!"

She felt his breath heavy against her ear, out of breath it would seem, and when he did not relent on his grip, the frigid fingers of dread climbed up the nape of her neck. "What is wrong? What is it?"

Pushing away from him, she looked at the men, so many fewer than had left a sennight ago. Her stomach sank when she saw the crestfallen faces all around. This was not the look of victory. Was the enemy approaching to burn them down as promised?

Mind in a whirl, she registered Robert and Reginald's faces, briefly wondering where Alex was, assuming he may have stayed back with some men to hold off the enemy. "Where is my husband, William?" Looking over her shoulder, she saw Mary behind her frantically scanning the crowd, wringing her hands together nervously. Women had begun spotting their loved ones and racing over to them while many stood around in angst, looking for men who left but had not returned. Never had a sadness fallen over Mary so heavily as it did watching tears fall from the faces of lovers and widows, watching the moment their entire lives changed forever.

"He fell, Sister," he whispered, not wanting anyone else to hear him.

Gooseflesh rose over every inch of her body and her hands instinctively moved to the rosary around her neck. "What? N-nay. That cannae be." Tears slid down her cheeks and anguish slashed at her heart. She may not have loved her husband, but she knew a lass who did, and Alex was a fine man and would have been a fair husband.

"He saved many of us, Lizzie. Ye would have been proud of yer husband." She fought the frown attempting to form on her face and did her best to keep her composure, if only so the others awaiting news could not fully read her features.

Robert stepped forward and walked past her, as stiff as a statue come to life. He did not acknowledge her whatsoever as he addressed the crowd. "It was a long, bloody battle." His voice was monotone and emotionless, drained of all energy. "We have lost many good men. By the end of the day, there was no clear victor, but on the morning after, The Donald's army had retreated. Victory is ours."

The crowd cheered, but so may wept for the faces missing in the crowd and whispers began to circulate as everyone wondered where their laird was. Robert held up his hand to ask for silence, and all the voices died down. "Aye, we have won, but at a great price. We lost our laird, my brother."

The crowd gasped and a few wails filled the air, but none more painful than the one she knew came from the woman carrying his bairn.

Turning around, Elizabeth saw Mary frantically pushing through the crowd, desperate to escape while terrible wails of grief were wrenched from her body. Not knowing what to do, Elizabeth followed, determined to help in any way she could.

Now that she was a widow, she would likely be sent back to Dunnottar and await instructions to marry once more to some other laird of some other clan in need of an alliance with the Keiths. But all she could think about now was consoling her friend as they wept over the same man and what his loss meant to each of them.

WE LOST OUR laird, my brother. Those were not words Robert had every wished, or expected, to have ever said. Arriving without Alexander felt like arriving without one of his limbs. He was whole by all appearances but, inside, he felt a gaping void of emptiness. He was laird now, not an honor he ever wanted, for the only way it would have ever come to pass was in the face of such tragedy. He would usually ask his elder brother for advice, but now he was the elder. Once more, his stomach recoiled and he stormed off into the keep, not ready to discuss anything more than he had said. It was only midday and he had only just arrived but, already, he felt overwhelmed by all that must be done and his lack of will to do it. He knew Drum inside and out, as he did the village and its people. He was certain of his abilities. Yet, he was unsure of his current emotional state.

In the distance, he saw Elizabeth turn and run off, pushing through the crowd with tears in her eyes. She seemed truly distraught over the loss of her husband. Did she realize she was to marry Robert in his stead? He assumed she must be aware, for it was apparently written in the agreement. But, there was too much to be done and Robert had no time to worry about having to marry his brother's widow. The contract stated that he would become known as Alexander, as well. Taking his brother's name, title, wife... everything. He would lose all that he was, everything he ever wanted, because of a cursed contract.

Where did one go after arriving home from battle without his brother? What did one do? Feeling lost and destitute, Robert decided nothing would get done properly until he rested. Most certainly, there were missives awaiting the laird in the solar, but they could wait one more day. All Robert wanted was a hot bath and a few hours of sleep before the evening meal, where he was sure to be expected to comfort his people.

Walking up the stairs to the second floor, Robert walked past Elizabeth's chamber door, pausing when he heard voices from within. Pressing his ear to the door, he strained to hear, only picking up a few words that made little sense to his already addled mind.

"What to do… the bairn… nay father…" High-pitched wails hit his ears and he cringed at the pain in her voice. A bairn? Could Elizabeth already be with child and somehow know within a sennight's time? He knew naught of such womanly things, but it appeared to be the case. No wonder she was so distressed about his passing. Of course, she was a kindhearted lass and would cry for her husband regardless, of that, he was certain. But being with child and finding out the father had died would make any woman hysterical.

Raising his fist to the door, he contemplated knocking, but he would be of little use to her when he could hardly function himself. He smelled like sweat despite a quick dip in a loch on his journey home, and his legs threatened to give way beneath him. Though he was whole, he had suffered many bruises and more than one minor wound that would need to be tended to by a healer as soon as he was washed up.

"Will be well… figure it out," clips from another voice said. He assumed the other woman was her maid, Matilda, trying to comfort Elizabeth as best as one could at such a time. Deciding there was naught more he could do for the lass, he decided to continue walking the few steps past the laird's chamber, which would, cruelly, be his soon enough, and down two more doors to his own chamber.

Throwing his door open, the draft of the room hit him hard, having not been used or heated in a sennight. He could not care. He was too tired to complain. He was even too tired to call for a maid to prepare him a bath. Pulling his sodden, ripped tunic over his head, he looked down at the slash wound across his chest, angry and red with infection. Touching it, he flinched and hissed in pain.

A sudden knock on the door caught him off guard and he stumbled toward it, unsure who would be visiting at this moment other than Reginald who would never bother to knock. Mary stood before him with her puffy red-rimmed eyes and his heart sank to his toes. In his own grief, he had selfishly not thought of how this news would affect her. She deserved to have found out before the crowd. "I am so sorry, Mary."

Nodding, she lowered her head and sniffled, wiping a tear from her eye. "I am sorry, too, Robert. I lost the love of my life, but ye lost yer brother."

"Aye." It was all he could bring himself to say and, thankfully, she did not seem to expect much more. "Can I help ye with anything?"

"Oh, nay. I only came to check on ye. And I can see ye are in need of some care," she said, eyes locked on his wound. "'Tis a wee bit infected, but nothing a bath, some salve, and clean bandages cannae fix."

"Mary. Ye dinnae need to tend to me. I want ye to go rest."

"But, ye need a bath…"

"Aye, I do. Can ye not ask someone else to prepare it while ye rest?"

Nodding in resignation, he saw her breathe deeply, apparently inwardly relieved to be forced to rest. He knew she liked to stay busy, but she was hurting and needed time to herself. Turning to leave, Mary shut the door behind her and Robert sat in the chair near his hearth and groaned as every muscle in his body screamed in pain.

He must have dozed off, for what felt like a split second later a few young male servants came through carrying the small wooden tub while a line of chambermaids came through his door carrying buckets of hot water. Once the tub was filled and fresh linens and soap had been left for him, everyone left the room. He thanked them and scratched his head, wondering why none of them stayed to bathe him as usual, yet he did not mind. He could very well clean himself and preferred the privacy.

Removing his muddy boots and then his trews, Robert looked down at the steamy hot water and sighed, more than ready to soothe his sore muscles and clean the filth off his body. Stepping in, he sank all the way down, wishing the tub was roomier, but feeling better already. Closing his eyes, he let the steam crawl up his face and the heat soak into his limbs.

After a few moments, he began to feel himself slip into unconsciousness, flashbacks of the battle flashing through his mind in slow motion. Blood. Shouting. Death. Alexander lying dead on the battlefield. A knock on the door made him jump up quickly from the tub, knocking him out of his living nightmare, yet leaving him disoriented. Before he could speak or process that he was still at Drum Castle, still in his chambers, the door opened and an angel walked through the door in a green surcoat with eyes the color of the wheat fields glowing golden in the summer rays just outside the caste walls. Was he dead? Was this heaven? Or was she here to carry him away?

Those golden eyes grew wide and lush pink lips opened as her jaw dropped and some heavy object she was holding fell with a clatter to the floor, snapping Robert back to reality.

"Elizabeth! What are ye doing here?" Robert asked, still feeling like he was caught in a world between the Harlaw field and reality.

"I... uh... came to tend to ye. Only, I didnae ken who I was coming to tend. Mary said all the other chambermaids and healers were busy tending to the other... men." Gulping, she looked down his body, then back up once more, rooted in place before all his senses came back to him and Robert realized he was still standing up in the tub.

"Shite," he grumbled and picked up the linen draped over the edge of the tub, hiding himself from her stunned gaze.

"Oh!" Elizabeth closed her eyes and turned around, realizing she had been gaping at his nude form. "I am sorry!"

"I can wash myself, my lady, but thank ye." Sitting back down in the bath, he grabbed the soap and the rag, wondering if she had any intention of leaving. He was aroused despite himself and could not allow her to notice, or risk embarrassing them both. But it had been too long since he had been nude in front of a woman and even longer since one gaped at him the way she had, the bonnie blush creeping up her cheeks. Aye, she was a beautiful woman and the man in him wanted very much for her to bathe him, or better yet, remove her clothes and...

Robert cursed under his breath. She was his brother's widow. Aye, he would eventually marry her, and sooner than expected now that he knew she was with child. It would be best if nobody else knew, so he could claim the child if necessary. Still, she was not his, not yet, and lusting over his brother's wife felt more sinful than the images of her naked, wet breasts pressed up against his chest and her hand gripping his...

"Are ye going to leave?" he groaned, now catching himself staring at her slim waist and curvy backside.

"Nay." Turning around, she looked at him once more, letting out a long breath when she saw him covered by the water in the bath. "I saw that wound on yer chest. It needs healing and I am a skilled herbalist."

"I vow ye saw more than just my wound," he whispered to himself.

"I... I didnae!" she stammered, turning red once more, clearly filled with indignation. Bending over to pick up the item she had dropped a moment ago, apparently a basket full of healing supplies, he noticed her ample bosom pressing against her bodice. It strained to conceal them, but they were larger than two heads of cabbage and he wondered what they would look like in the palms of his hands.

She stepped closer now, placing the basket next to the wooden tub as she got down on her knees to better view his wound. If he was not careful, she would get a better view of his bollocks, as well. He was stiff as a rod now and having a hard time concealing the evidence and watching her bent over running her fingers in circles around his wound while on her knees was not helping, Lord help him. He was a bastard for reacting this way to her. He had kept his attraction for her in check before, but something about returning from war, having been surrounded by thousands of men, and knowing that he would soon wed and bed the lass had him yearning for her flesh and a chance to feel something pleasurable once more. That was all this was. He did not feel romantic toward the lass. Nay, he just wished to lay her down and... do what his brother did to get her with child.

That was it. His arousal was gone and now he was thoroughly disgusted with himself and his thoughts. She carried his brother's child. He was a disgrace. Alexander would run him through for his lewd thoughts and he would deserve it.

"The wound is infected, Robert, but doesnae need stitches. I can us some herbs and balms to heal it." Placing the back of her hand gently on his forehead, he finally tore his gaze away from the water and looked at her face, now so close to his. She had wee freckles dotting her nose and the apples of cheeks, and this close, he saw flecks of green mixed with gold in her irises. She smelled of something fresh and floral, mixed with earth and herbs, like she had been working in the garden just before. Plaited brown hair was draped over one shoulder and he wondered why her gentle touch felt so soothing to his hot skin.

"Ye are a wee bit warm, Robert."

"'Tis the hot water and the steam," he replied softly. And his unfortunate attraction to her, he thought to himself.

Her eyes locked on his and he saw her pupils dilate. She licked her lips nervously and nodded. "Mayhap. We will keep an eye on it. May I have the linen?"

Furrowing his brow, Robert looked down at where he had very intentionally held the linen to hide his cock and bollocks. "I am not so sure ye want me to remove it," he said carefully, and she blushed once more.

"'Tis nothing I have never seen before, Robert." Elizabeth raised a brow at him, and he stared at her silently like a daft fool, unsure if she was referring to a few moments ago, her time with his brother, or with other men from Dunnottar Castle. Either way, the thought of her with other men, especially his brother, was sufficient enough to turn his mood sour.

"Fine. Take it." He shoved the cloth into her hands, soaking her bodice slightly, but scowling and looking away. It wasn't jealousy, he told himself. How could it be? It was simply disturbing to think of his brother lying with her, and disappointing to consider how many other men she may have lain with. She was a woman of ten and eight years, after all. Still, he did not want a wanton wife that would cuckold him in the future.

"Somebody is in a foul mood," she said, making a tsking sound that only irritated him further. She was bonnie, aye. But suddenly, he wondered if she would always grate on his nerves with her stubbornness and wit.

When Elizabeth wrung the hot water carefully over the wound, Robert hissed and clenched his teeth. It stung like bloody hell, and more so when she took a fresh cloth from the side of the tub and patted the area dry. Shuffling through her basket, Elizabeth pulled out a jar of salve and opened the lid. Scooping out a glob of it with her fingers, she carefully dabbed it over the wound and though it hurt, he had to admit that she had the soothing touch of a skilled healer.

"I am not in a foul mood. I am sore all over. I am tired. I am in pain. And I have lost my brother," he ground out, feeling his usually cool temperament starting to boil over. He did not want to show his anger to Elizabeth and he was not sure why she made him feel like he could say so much, when he would usually hold it all in. It was like he was a volcano ready to explode and she was the beautiful land surrounding it, about to be decimated by the heat of his rage.

"I ken, Robert. I am sorry." Her voice was so soft and genuine, yet he still wished to shout at her. Why was he so angry with her?

"How many men have ye been with, lass?" There. That was the truth of it. He was jealous, damn it all. He was to marry this woman and she freely admitted to having seen naked men before? Had she no morals? What if the child she carried was not even Alexander's? That would explain how she already knew that a bairn grew within her. "Are ye wanton?" He gripped her wrists and Elizabeth gasped, nearly falling forward into the tub.

"How dare ye!" Jerking one hand free, Elizabeth smacked him across the cheek, the sting of her wet palm making a sound loud enough to wake the devil. His head snapped to the side, but he kept his mouth shut, clenching his jaw, knowing damned well he deserved her ire. He was being a bloody arse, taking his grief out on her. "Ye can tend yerself, ye... awful beast!" A tear ran down her cheek and he knew himself for the bastard he was, but there was no time to apologize before she was out the door, slamming it so hard the floor shook.

Well. That was one way to warm his future wife to him. Sighing, he shook his head and frowned. She did not deserve such treatment, even if he was angry about her comment. He had a right, he told himself. She was to be his wife. No man wanted a whore for his bride. Still, that was not what she had said, and for all he knew, she was referring to having seen him naked just moments before.

The evening meal would occur soon, and he still wished to get some rest. Jumping out of the tub, he dried off and pulled the sheets back in his four-poster bed, anxious to feel the soft cool sheets against his flesh. He still ached but felt slightly more soothed. He hoped he could sleep after insulting Elizabeth as he had. At the meal, he vowed, he would apologize to the lady for his cruel treatment of her. No matter what, it had been uncalled for.

Then, he would think of a way to tell the woman that she was now contracted to be his wife and pray she did not smack him across the other side of the face.

CHAPTER EIGHT

"PACK YER BELONGINGS, Tilda. I suspect we leave on the morrow," Elizabeth wasted no time saying as she stormed back into her chamber, shaken by her encounter with Robert. He had been so kind to her before and now… well. He may be grieving the loss of his brother, but he had no right to treat her that way, nor speak to her as if she were nothing but a whore.

She had seen him naked. Fully nude. Something inside her clenched in a rather desirous way, making her wonder if she was, indeed, wanton. She had never seen a nude man and he was mighty well built. It had caused inappropriate thoughts to consume her mind, making her turn red and go hazy in the brain. Oh, as a lass of ten and eight summers, she had thought about the pleasures of the flesh on enough occasions, but she had been rather successfully sheltered by her father, and then by her brother. She knew very little of the facts and suspected Matilda would have had that conversation with her the night before her own wedding to Alexander if they had known in advance that she would marry him so swiftly. Now, everyone assumed she had been wedded and bedded, everyone but Matilda and Mary, who Elizabeth confided in. And Robert, well, he thought she had lain with the whole of Dunnottar Castle, the lout.

Thankfully, his treatment of her had erased any inappropriate thoughts that had temporarily addled her senses. Robert was much like what she considered most men to be, after all. Cruel, arrogant, and disrespectful because she was a woman. Scolding herself for ever believing he could be her ally in this place, she stormed over to the large armoire where her dresses were all hung carefully with care and sorted by color, thanks to her extremely organized maid and friend. Grabbing several in her arms, she yanked them down and tossed them on top of her bed.

Matilda cringed and crossed her arms. "I spent much time on those! What do ye mean we are leaving?"

"My husband is dead." Stopping in her tracks, the words sank in and hit her straight in the heart. How could she say that so bluntly? Clasping her rosary, Elizabeth took a deep breath and plopped on the bed beside her dresses. "Tilda. I am eighteen years old, have been betrothed to one Irvine, married to another, widowed within a sennight of the marriage, and have now been brutally insulted by another Irvine man. There is naught for me here at Drum. Our contract has been fulfilled. Keiths and Irvines fought peaceably beside one another in Harlaw. The alliance stands. I shall head back to Dunnottar and await further instruction from my brother, as I am certain he has more plans for me." Rolling her eyes, Elizabeth plopped back on the bed and hugged her silk pillow.

"I suppose ye are correct. But I didnae think it was expected for us to leave right away." Tilda furrowed her brow and sat beside Elizabeth on the bed, stroking her mistresses' hair. Elizabeth's eyelids fluttered as they tended to do whenever her hair was stroked. Her mama used to do that and it always calmed her, as Tilda knew. Exhaustion hit her like the waves of the ocean that crash against the cliffs of her home and, more than ever, she wished to see them from her window once more. "Who insulted ye? Reginald? I vow, he is a loud-mouthed man but he doesnae mean half of what he says."

"Robert. I was told to tend to his wound, but when I arrived he was... bared. Completely."

"Oh. I bet that was quite a sight."

"Ye're not helping, Tilda! The point is that he refused to let me tend to him and I told him it was nothing I hadnae seen before... which was, quite honestly, a lie. I just wanted him to trust me. Instead, he took me for a whore and asked if I was wanton."

Gasping, Tilda stopped stroking Elizabeth's hair and touched her arm instead. "I am sorry, Lizzie. But he is in pain emotionally and physically. I am certain he didnae mean it."

"Mayhap not but he said it nonetheless. It doesnae matter. I have nay reason to speak to him ever again. I wish to pack up and leave this place. I dinnae belong."

"Ye do. I wish ye saw that. All the people love ye, especially Mary. I dinnae ken how ye turned yer husband's pregnant mistress into a friend, but ye are verra loved here."

"Without a husband, I have nay place here. 'Tis not my home."

With a long drawn out breath, Matilda stood from the bed and drew the covers shut around Elizabeth, blocking the heat from the hearth. "We will do what ye wish, my lady, if yer brother allows it. We will discuss it with him on the morrow. For now, rest before the evening meal and mayhap ye will feel better."

Shaking her head and closing her eyes, Elizabeth curled up into a protective ball, reliving the scene with Robert once more and wondering why his ill opinions of her hurt so much. "Nay. I willnae go to the meal. I am too sick to my stomach to eat and dinnae wish to sit at the high table with that man. I wish to simply sleep until the morn and leave at dawn."

Tilda did not respond. All Elizabeth heard was the soft click of the door and she knew her maid had left, but she also knew she had been heard. She would close her eyes and get some rest, for tomorrow would be a long day of travel.

Still, she could not help the tears that slid down her face. Tears for the husband she lost before she truly got to know him. Tears for the people she had grown to love in such a very short time. Tears for the loss of a man she once respected, who truly had never existed.

Romance, love, chivalry. It was all a glorified falsehood written by poets to entertain the fancies of ridiculous women. None of it truly existed, at least not for her.

BOTH SEATS TO his right were empty at the head table. One was supposed to be the laird's seat, but he was unable to bring himself to sit there. It did not feel right. Leaving it vacant felt like the proper thing to do. Still, the void felt wider than ever as he was forced to accept that his brother would no longer occupy his spot at the head table, never fill the great hall with the sound of his laughter, never spar with him in the lists. He was gone.

Knots pulled at his stomach, for more than one reason. The other vacant chair was a reminder of how abhorrent he had been to Elizabeth. The lass had done naught to him but attempt to tend his wound, yet he had released a venom filled with rage, grief, hatred, and an inexplicable jealousy. He was usually a master of his own emotions, but today, he had lost control and he wondered how much of it was the loss of his brother and how much that Elizabeth affected him in a way he could not fathom. Either way, he felt her absence keenly.

Was she mourning her husband or simply avoiding him? Either way, the constant jabber of his cousin, Sharice, bored him to tears as she sat at his left and picked at his trencher. "Ye ken, my father told me that that there is a man in the village who claims to have seen a goblin once and…"

What in hellfire was she talking about? She had been speaking of a midwife just a moment ago and now she was on to goblins? He loved his cousin, but she was spoiled and rather daft at times. Popping his knuckles beneath the table, Robert couldn't stand it anymore. He needed to find Elizabeth and apologize for his treatment of her. It was not at all like him to disrespect a woman and he hated himself for the pain he had caused her. It had been evident in her eyes. He deserved the slap she gave him and more.

Standing quickly from the bench, Robert looked at Sharice and forced a smile. "Interesting tale, indeed," he said, not having heard anything she said about goblins. "I apologize, but I must retire. 'Tis been a taxing day and there is much to be done on the morrow."

Stopping her chatter, Sharice frowned and grabbed his hand. "I am sorry, Cousin. I ken I talk too much and too fast when I am nervous. I only mean to distract ye from yer pain, not bore ye to tears." She smiled and squeezed his hand, warming his heart.

"Ah, Sharice. Ye are a good person. I apologize. My mind is elsewhere."

"I ken that. I feel terrible for Lady Elizabeth. She seems truly distraught over her loss."

Nodding, Robert thought of the conversation he overheard earlier on the other side of her chamber door. No wonder she was so distraught, being with child and losing her husband. She must worry what was to become of her, having no idea her fate was to marry him, the very bastard who insulted her. Aye, he owed her a visit and an apology.

Squeezing Sharice's hand in return, he released it and walked away from the table, feeling the eyes of the entire room on him, though everyone pretended to go about their business. Aside from the toasts made in Alexander's honor at the beginning of the meal, everyone had decided to celebrate his life, rather than mourn his death. Alex was never one to mope about and would want the entire castle pissed drunk and passed out, rather than crying and sulking. Robert had attempted the same, but after one cup of ale, his stomach rejected everything.

There would be no joy for Robert, but life had to go on and Elizabeth deserved to know where she stood. He would simply have to marry her as soon as possible and attempt to pass the child off as his own. It was still possible at this point. Yet, he would not let on that he knew of the bairn, for it was not a conversation he was meant to hear. When she was willing to tell him, he would listen. Until then, things had to be sorted.

"Robert, wait." The sound of her brother's voice caught him just before he made it to the first step up the tower. Turning around, he saw the man whose eyes looked so much like his sister's, approaching him swiftly.

"William," Robert greeted stiffly, wondering what he had to say.

"My sister's absence is unnerving. 'Tis not like her to disappear, even if she is grieving."

Robert bit his lip, not wanting to admit to her brother how awfully he had treated his sister, yet he would rather take the fall, than have her brother displeased with her. "I am afraid I have something to do with that. We had... words, this afternoon. She left rather displeased with me. I dinnae think my company was welcome tonight, and I cannae blame her."

Tilting his head and narrowing his eyes, he saw a small smirk slide across William's face. "So, that red mark across yer face is courtesy of my sister, aye?"

Placing his hand on his cheek, he grimaced, not having known he still wore the evidence of her ire. "Aye."

Chuckling, William shook his head. "She is a spirited lass. Doesnae accept what she doesnae wish to. Yet she accepts much without a fight, such as being passed down from father to son... to son. Ye must have truly crossed her."

"Aye. I did. I was just about to apologize to her."

"Smart man. Dinnae cross my Lizzie. She willnae accept it, nor will I."

Hearing William's warning clearly, Robert nodded. "I assure ye, I will never mistreat yer sister." Again, he thought to himself, feeling worse than ever yet deciding William need not know the rest of the details. He'd had enough fighting for a lifetime.

"Good. Make sure she is aware of the contract. 'Tis yer burden as laird and future husband to bear the ill tidings. I have already done so twice and dinnae envy ye the task."

"I already mean to tell her. It shall be done." Nodding, they went their separate ways as he turned and took the steps up the second story two at a time, determined to be done with his tasks of apologizing and telling her the news of her fate.

Reaching her chamber door, he knocked gently three times but, after a moment, knocked hard when no answer came. Opening the door slowly, the rusted hinges creaked, but nobody stirred within. The hearth fire burned low, allowing a wee bit of light to illuminate his way as he walked in.

Looking around, he saw her armoire doors wide open with nothing inside. Had she taken off? Heart jumping into his throat, he stepped quickly toward the four-poster bed and slid the curtains open quickly. A woman screamed from within, pulling the covers up to her neck, eyes wide in terror.

"Elizabeth. I am sorry. 'Tis just me, Robert."

"Why are ye here?" she demanded, anger ringing clearly in her voice. "Ye think me a whore and wish to try yer fortune? Piss off, Robert Irvine. I am nay man's whore and shall never touch ye!" Rolling over, she faced away from him and he felt himself smile. Her brother was correct. She was a wee feisty thing when crossed.

"I am sorry about what I said earlier, Elizabeth. It was cruel and unnecessary."

"And none of yer business, at that!" she spat, looking over her shoulder to scowl at him.

Clearing his throat, he mustered up the courage to say what it was that truly needed to be said. "I am afraid that is where ye are wrong, my lady." Looking at the other end of the bed for the first time, he saw all her dresses thrown into a pile and frowned. "Why are ye packing yer things?"

Sitting upright in the bed, she still clutched the sheets to herself and looked at him. "I am leaving."

"Ye are? When?"

"At dawn."

"Oh? Aye? And William kens this?"

"Nay, but he must ken I cannae stay here without a husband. I am no longer needed here. I will return to my home and be forced into another advantageous marriage, nay doubt. Speaking of my brother, he will run ye through if he kens ye are in here. Ye had better leave."

Her words were short and full of annoyance. She truly had gone from respecting him, to despising him. "I apologize for our conversation earlier, Elizabeth. I wasnae myself. 'Tis nay excuse, but 'tis the truth. And… yer brother already kens I am here."

"What?" Eyes bulging and jaw dropping, Elizabeth shifted away from him, clearly not trusting a word he said. "He would never allow ye in my chamber. Ye are a lout and a liar!" Panic flashed in her eyes and she stiffened, eyes darting around the room like a trapped animal. Did she think he had come to force himself upon her? Disappointment churned his gut that she would think so little of him.

"Elizabeth! Calm yerself! I am not here to harm ye. Aye, he kens I am here. I have important information for ye."

"Why would he send ye to tell me anything?" Robert stared at her, wondering if he even needed to say it, wondering if he sat silently long enough, if she could piece it together without his help. Slowly, he saw horror wash over every feature and her eyes grew even wider. "N-nay.

Nay."

"Is it really so bad?" he asked, feeling hurt and rejected. It was only a sennight ago that this lass cried on top of the battlements, begging him to marry her. Now she looked as if she would rather jump off the same battlements than be his wife. "Ye wanted this not so long ago, aye?"

Snorting, Elizabeth flung the sheets away from her and jumped out of the bed, pacing back and forth with wee bare feet exposed and her linen night dress illuminated by the low light of the fire. He hair was plaited on both sides, hanging over her shoulders, but panic consumed her. "I wished to marry ye so Alexander and Mary could be together, so I could fulfill the peace agreement without ruining lives! Only, ye made it perfectly clear that marrying me wasnae to yer liking! Now, I am supposed to go from one brother to the other? A brother who so verra clearly wishes not to marry me, who thinks me a wanton woman?" Scoffing, she flung a long golden-brown braid over her shoulder so it hung halfway down her back... which brought his gaze unwittingly to the perfect curvature of her rounded backside.

Shaking his head, he looked back up at her face, wishing she did not look so disgusted. "I apologized already, twice now. I shouldnae have said that."

"It isnae that ye said it. 'Tis that ye think it. Dinnae deny it."

"What I think of yer past deeds means naught, Elizabeth. I only expect that when we are married, ye will only share yer bed with me and nay other. And, I vow the same."

"Share yer bed? Ye presume much, do ye not?" Stopping her pacing, she turned to look at him. He wasn't sure if the fire in her eyes was a reflection from the hearth or the manifestation of her distain for him, but either way, it was time to make this lass understand the facts.

Standing up from the bed, Robert walked toward her slowly. "Aye, I do expect that when we are wed, we will share a bed. That doesnae mean ye will ever have to do aught ye wish not to do. I shall never force ye, but I do hope, in time, ye will forgive me and trust me as ye once did. I am not an arse, despite my previous behavior." Stepping closer once more, he saw her back stiffen as she pushed her shoulders back, trying to make her wee height look more intimidating than it was.

"Why? Ye made yerself clear. Ye dinnae want me. The contract is fulfilled. I vow my brother will never allow violence between the clans again. Just let me go home."

Shaking his head, he stepped closer once more, knowing she was much too stubborn to back away. "Do ye want me to tell ye that I want ye? Is that it?"

"What? Nay! Of course not!" She crossed her arms over her chest and turned away from him to watch the low flames in the hearth flicker.

Grabbing the poker, Robert bent over to throw a new log on the fire, jabbing at it until it slowly grew red and caught aflame. "The contract isnae fulfilled. It was written that should Alexander die, I would take over everything. His name, his title, his lands... and his wife." He didn't turn to face her. He was too afraid to see the disgust on her face. Never had he thought to have a wife who hated him, not that he didn't deserve it after his actions earlier, but the woman set his mind to spinning. He couldn't decide if he should kiss her to prove that he wanted her or continue to keep his distance. She was his brother's widow and carried his child, aye. But he knew there had been no love between them and no lust either. It was one night of consummation that resulted in a child, and naught more, or so he told himself. It was the only way to survive such a situation.

"Well. I never expected love or romance in my life, but I do say that is the most breathtaking proposal I have ever heard." The sarcasm in her voice was thick and he could not blame her. "I am once again naught but a pawn. I dinnae want this. I have done my duty. William will understand. I will simply explain to him that I am done marrying the Irvine men and wish to go home. He will allow it. He will honor the peace."

"William has no more say in this than we do. 'Tis a binding contract, written by the church and agreed upon by the regent. They need Lowland clans to be at peace. We have enough war with England and the Highlands. This contract was made to ensure our clans unite and it willnae be complete until ye bear a… child." He said the last word slowly, waiting to see if she would confess to already carrying the necessary heir of the Keith and Irvine clans. Instead, she stiffened and looked away.

"Anything can be renegotiated," she said firmly. "I will speak with him on the morrow. We shall fix this. I ken ye dinnae wish to marry me. Ye made that clear and I dinnae wish to marry ye either. I cannae even stand to look at ye, to be honest."

"Ye wound me," Robert said with a bite in his voice. The lass knew how to throw an insult. "I didnae wish to marry anyone, is what I recall saying. I also recall saying that it wasnae my choice, due to the agreement. Well, now that same agreement says we shall marry. I never said I didnae want ye, specifically, Elizabeth. Ye ken ye're a bonnie lass."

"So, ye do want me?" Narrowing her eyes and crooking her brow, she dared him to respond. It felt like a trap. There truly was no correct answer for such a thing. Should he tell her just how much he wanted her body? How she made him feel when she stared at his cock earlier? She would be frightened of him. But if he said he did not want her at all, she would be angrier and more hurt than she already was. There had to be a better response.

Scratching his jaw, he put the poker down and walked toward her, putting his hands on her shoulders, realizing how much shorter she was than him. "Elizabeth. This is a confusing time for us both. We dinnae need to figure out how we feel about it all at this verra moment. Ye are a kind, intelligent, and witty lass. Ye are hard-working and loyal. All wonderful qualities for a wife. And aye, ye are verra beautiful. I would be daft to believe otherwise. But, ye are my brother's widow. Ye have to understand that I cannae feel pleasure in this, because it means my brother is dead. But if I had to choose a wife, I would choose one just like ye." *And because ye carry my brother's child, I cannae let ye go.* If only he could say those words aloud.

"One just like me… but, not me." Her voice trailed off and she gripped her stomach. He wondered about the child within and why she didn't want to confide in him, but she would have to in due time. "I will speak with William in the morning. Good night, Robert." Walking away, Elizabeth headed toward her bed and climbed back under the covers, pulling the curtains closed around her. That was a dismissal if ever he had one.

He knew there was no more left to say. Neither of them had asked for this. She may speak to her brother in the morning, but that only meant he would speak to him on the lists first. Her brother could not be allowed to make decisions without knowing all the details and one thing was for certain, whether Robert wished to marry her or not, he would not allow his brother's child to grow up at Dunnottar or anywhere else, never knowing his family. Nay, she carried an Irvine in her womb, and that child would stay here at Drum.

CHAPTER NINE

"I AM SORRY, Elizabeth. There is naught I can do."

Staring at her brother, Elizabeth stomped her foot like a child and balled her fists. "Ye are Laird of Dunnottar and Marischal of Scotland! Of course, ye can do something! Meet with Robert in his solar and draft a new treaty that says we will remain allies!"

"It isnae so simple, Sister. And I think ye ken that." He gave her a look that confused her to no end. Why was everyone acting like she kept a secret or knew something that clearly she did not know?

"I dinnae ken that," she said like a child once more, mocking his voice and rolling her eyes. "I am done being passed around the Irvines! Robert doesnae even want to marry me! Even Alexander, who had a mistress, was more agreeable than he is!"

William crossed his arms and pursed his lips. "Ye ken about his mistress?"

"Och, ye think me a cursed fool. I kenned it right away. I am a woman. We see more than ye daft men do."

"Listen, Elizabeth. I see ye are angry and I dinnae blame ye. 'Tis not fair that ye have been passed around, but nobody could have expected so much death. There is naught I can do, and after speaking with Robert this morn, I am inclined to have the ceremony as swiftly as possible."

"What?" Indignation swarmed Elizabeth. How dare Robert speak to her brother before she did, and so easily sway him in his favor. Most importantly, why was Robert pushing for a swift marriage? "Ye cannae mean that. I want to go home, William."

"Ye are home, *Lady* of Drum."

"What did he say to ye?" Defeat hit her, leading to despair. "I cannae understand. He doesnae wish to marry me. I ken that much. So, what could he have said?"

"I think that is for ye to tell me, and ye may in due time, when ye are ready. But for now, we move forward. Ye will marry Robert in three days, and he will take the name of Alexander and be laird. Ye think the man wanted any of this? If he must make sacrifices, so will ye." William leaned in, kissed Elizabeth on the forehead and patted her head as if she were naught more than a wee, confused lass.

Cursed men! Always making the rules. Always telling her what she must do. Fine. She would marry Robert, nay... Alexander, as he will be called, in three days. She could not understand the rush, and her brother seemed to believe she knew something that she did not. But, no matter. If she was doomed to be that man's wife, she may as well get it over with. No sense in dragging any of it out.

She may not have a choice in any of this, but she was not going to allow Robert to speak to her brother on her behalf! Turning toward the keep's door, she stormed through and into the blinding light of the inner bailey, cupping her hand over her eyes and lifting her heavy green skirts with the other. Men and women milled about, managing their daily work and greeting her as she moved past. Forcing a smile on her face, she responded, never wanting to appear stern or too busy to greet the people yet determined to reach the lists and give Robert a piece of her mind.

The sounds of fighting men and clashing swords grew closer with every step and she rounded a corner, stopping in her tracks at the sight before her. Aside from a linen wrapped around his chest to guard his wound, Robert was bare-chested and sparring with a man, every lean muscle on his abdomen and arms flexing with every move. Sweat glistened on his tanned skin and his trews clung seductively to his powerful backside and thighs. She had seen him nude the night before standing in the bath, a sight she had not been able to successfully erase from her mind, no matter how hard her better senses tried to forget it. But, seeing him now, moving with so much strength, skill, and powerful grace as he wielded his sword and deflected blows made her feel those strange stirrings all over again. What was it about Robert that made every inch of her feel needy for something she could not explain or describe?

She was angry at his meddling in her life and wished to shout at him and smack him once more, yet seeing him out here also made her wish to be laid down in the field and kissed senseless while he was still half-undressed. Mayhap she was a wanton lass, after all. Still, he had no right to say such things, judge her, then pull her brother aside and talk him into a hurried wedding. Why would he want such a thing anyway?

"Robert!" Elizabeth called to him and stormed forward, waiting for the perfect moment when his sparring ended so he wasn't caught off guard and sliced in half. She did not need another death, especially since his would likely require her to marry Reginald, which scared the wits out of her.

Turning to follow her voice, she was taken aback at the wide grin across his face as she approached, his dimples flashing at her. Heart in throat and pulse racing, Elizabeth did her best to appear unaffected by him. "Why are ye smiling? Because ye ken ye beat me to speaking with William?"

He shrugged and sheathed his sword as he began walking toward her, meeting her on the edge of the grassy field, away from prying eyes and ears. "I spoke with him for reasons of my own. Ye cannae escape the agreement, and due to yer condition, I would think a hurried ceremony was best for all."

"My... condition?" Putting her hands on her hips, she scowled when his gaze roamed down her body and back up to her face. "See anything ye like?" Elizabeth said with a bite in her tone. She did not appreciate being stared at and did the best she could to cover her large breasts, knowing men could not help but stare, but Robert was being rather obvious and it bothered and excited her all at once.

"Elizabeth," Robert said placatingly, putting his arms up in the air. "Ye will be my wife in three days. I will be yer husband. We should be honest with one another. Do ye not agree?"

"Aye, I do. And I will honestly tell ye that I find ye to be a lout!"

"And I find ye to be headstrong and opinionated," Robert retaliated, crossing his large muscular arms over his sweaty chest. His linen wrap was showing a wee bit of blood through it and she winced.

"Who is headstrong? The woman who doesnae want to marry her dead husband's brother? Or the man who still trains with an open wound on his chest?"

"I have fought in worse conditions."

"And men may not prefer a woman with opinions, but I have never learned to keep them to myself. My father indulged my mother, and my brother and I grew up in a home where women were heard and respected. I cannae be any other way, or settle for less."

Smiling again, Robert nodded and winked at her. "I feel the same way. My father indulged my mother, as well. I believe he may have been the only man in Scotland disappointed to have three sons and nay daughters to dote upon."

"Oh." Shocked by his response, Elizabeth looked at him sideways. "Why did ye not respect my wishes about this marriage then? Why did ye go to my brother?"

"Our wishes are of no concern in the matter of our marriage, Elizabeth. I made that clear. 'Tis done. We will marry in three days. There is naught ye can do. I simply had some important business with yer brother."

"Ye both act as if I carry a secret I willnae share." Elizabeth took a deep breath and looked around the castle, then toward the gates leading out. If her brother and Robert thought they could force her into a third marriage, they were daft. She did not know what they had discussed, why they treated her oddly all of a sudden, nor why they rushed the wedding, but she would hie her arse back to Dunnottar with or without her brother's help. There was no way she was marrying Robert after the way he'd spoken to her, even if his sweaty chest made her want to swoon.

"Ye ken I love ye, but this is madness! I willnae be involved. Ye can be killed out there!"

"I would rather die than marry that lout!" Elizabeth proclaimed, stuffing extra clothes, hygienic supplies, and rations she had snuck out of the kitchen earlier. Night was approaching and with the sun going down, everyone would be distracted and preparing for the evening meal. By the time they realized she was no longer in the castle, she would be on her way back to Dunnottar. It was a long journey on foot, but she was done caring, done doing what was bid of her by controlling men. Mayhap marrying Robert would not be so bad if he did not think so ill of her.

"Ye dinnae truly believe that. Nor should ye believe ye will make it home without help, or that yer brother willnae simply beat ye there and drag ye back by yer pearls." Matilda crossed her arms and shook her head. "I shouldnae do this, but if ye insist on going, I need to come with ye. Besides, there will be naught left of me when yer brother finds out I let ye go."

"If we both disappear, it will be obvious I left. I need ye here to cover for me," Elizabeth said over her shoulder and she quickly plaited her hair.

"Ye arenae thinking clearly. I am telling ye. William will simply drag ye back and make ye wed Robert."

Stopping, Elizabeth squinted, deep in thought, an idea forming that would end all her troubles. "Not if I am already married."

"What?" Matilda squeaked and threw her arms up in the arm. "Who in the bloody hell would ye marry instead of Robert? And is being married to him so bad that ye would risk all to avoid it?"

"I didnae believe it would be bad a sennight ago, nay. But after the way he treated me, I willnae be so shamed. I dinnae deserve such treatment, nor do I understand why he and William wish to rush the wedding. I will ask Patrick to accompany me. He has a horse and ye ken he fancies me. He will agree to marry me. If I make it clear 'tis a marriage of convenience, he will understand and not expect more. We grew up together. I can trust him."

Snorting, Matilda rolled her eyes and cringed. "Ye really have lost yer mind. Patrick has been in love with ye since ye were a wee lass. Aye, he will marry ye, but he will want more than convenience. And William will run him through for abandoning his army, stealing away his sister, and threatening to destroy the tentative peace between clans. It willnae work, Lizzie. Please see reason. Please?"

Sighing, Elizabeth calmed down and slowly walked toward her friend, a small smile on her face. "I am seeing reason, Tilda." Grabbing her companion's hand, Elizabeth gave it a reassuring squeeze. "'Tis the only way. I shallnae marry Robert."

Pursing her lips, Tilda nodded, finally understand that Elizabeth would not be persuaded otherwise. "I have one request. Please. I will stop my blabbering and allow ye to be a fool, if ye take but one suggestion from me."

Looking out the window, Elizabeth saw the sun falling further over the hills in the horizon. Soon, she would lose her chance to flee. "What is it, Tilda? Do be quick."

"Ye're a bloody fool if ye think ye can do this alone, and even more if ye think William willnae run Patrick through, making ye a widow three times over and dragging ye back here. But... if ye marry someone else, it will solve all yer problems."

Raising a brow, Elizabeth looked at Tilda. "Who?"

"Reginald, obviously."

"Robert's younger brother? That's absurd."

"Is it? He is an Irvine so it will still keep the peace, prevent ye from marrying Robert, and Reginald is just frivolous enough to go along with it."

The more Matilda said, the more sense it made, yet she knew even less about Reginald than she did about Robert. However, though Reginald was handsome, he did not affect her the way Robert did, which could serve to be her benefit. He would be incapable of hurting her the way Robert had and would not expect much from the marriage. She had seen enough to know he preferred women and drinking, which was fine with her. Elizabeth did miss Dunnottar, but she would also miss Drum and its people, especially Mary, if she were to go. In the end, Tilda was correct. William would simply make her return. Mayhap this was her best chance at avoiding Robert.

"Are ye doing all of this simply to prove a point, I wonder, or simply out of denial?" Tilda asked and stepped away, staring at the fire burning in the hearth.

"What point would that be, exactly, and what would I be denying?" Elizabeth snapped. This situation was feeling out of hand and she considered if she was being irrational. But when she closed her eyes and remembered the ache in her heart and the anger in her veins after Robert insulted her virtue, she hardened herself to any feelings of doubt. She was still as virtuous as the day she was born, not that it was

Robert's business at all… except that it was as her betrothed. Still, Tilda had a point. If she refused to marry him, at least marrying an Irvine would keep the peace and prevent her from marrying a man so very capable of hurting her irreparably.

"Denying that ye are already half in love with Robert and ye ken that he can destroy ye, so ye will do aught to avoid love. But instead, ye choose a marriage based on revenge and spite, to prove that ye are in charge of yer own life. But… are ye? Seems to me ye are avoiding being controlled by yer brother and Robert, yet ye are now being controlled by yer own stubbornness."

"That is ridiculous! I ken I'm not in control of anything! Aye, I do refuse to marry him and if this is the one decision I ever make on my own, then I will do so gladly. And, I am not half in love with him or anyone! He was my friend. He was kind to me and comforted me. Then, when I was most vulnerable, he insulted me and made me feel lower than anyone ever has. I dinnae love him, Tilda. I loathe him, I vow!" Stomping her foot and balling her fists, she realized she was shouting and showing too much emotion for a lass not half in love.

Matilda raised her brow and shook her head, folding her arms the way she did when she knew she was right. Sighing, Elizabeth began pacing the room. "Ye want to hear that I have feelings for Robert? All right. I do. Or, I did. I had believed him honorable and kind." Throwing her hands in the air, she stopped and turned to lean her head against the wall. "I ken he still is honorable and kind, despite his words. He apologized and I ken he is stressed and saddened by his losses. I ken he made a mistake and he is sorry for it. Still, that is partly why I cannae marry him. He… he can break me, Tilda. I dinnae want that. I dinnae wish for love. Love hurts in the end. No love story has a happy ending, Tilda."

"So, ye will base yer decision on old stories and poems written solely to make ye cry? That is absurd, Lizzie, even for ye."

"I saw what losing Mama did to my father. Great love comes to an end and the price one pays is deep. I would prefer to work hard and serve my people and die in my bed an old woman. No man shall mourn me and I shall mourn no man."

Sighing in resignation, Matilda shrugged. "Ye are determined." Elizabeth sighed, feeling a tug at her heart. She was walking away from something she knew could be a real connection. However, there was always a chance that love would not be reciprocated, and that thought scared her more than anything. Losing a husband whom she loved may destroy her someday, but if she was loved in return, she would have memories to last a lifetime. But, if she was not loved, she would spend a lifetime pining for a man, a love, a life, she would never have. And that reality was too scary to consider. "Aye, Tilda. I am."

Nodding her head, Matilda walked over to the door and opened it, looking over her shoulder. "I will take care of everything. Trust me." She left the room and shut the door, leaving Elizabeth chewing on her bottom lip nervously while clutching her pearls. In her heart, she was not at all as confident as she pretended to be, but hearts were best kept out of life's greatest decisions, especially those involving men, vows, and the rest of her life, even if that logic seemed mad, even to herself.

CHAPTER TEN

R OUNDING THE LAST step of the spiral staircase, Matilda looked around the great hall, deciding to head through the kitchens. It was midday and the nooning meal would begin soon. But for now, the room was empty aside from a few lassies from the kitchen preparing the tables with linens and clean plates. Waving to one of her newer companions, Matilda skipped happily behind the screen and into the kitchen where chaos reigned as the main cook pointed and shouted instructions while stirring a huge pot of stew. It smelled wonderful and Matilda's stomach growled.

Elizabeth was her dearest friend in the world and she loved her like a sister. In fact, they were nearly the same age. Only Matilda, having grown up in the working class, seemed to have a better grip on reality than her counterpart. Aye, Elizabeth was well-educated, intelligent, hardworking, and knew her role as a noble-born woman well. She understood it was her task to marry where told, but even Matilda could understand Elizabeth's frustration at being tossed around like a bit of meat in the name of peace.

Though she truly thought Elizabeth's plan to marry someone else was addled and doomed to cause trouble, she had offered to help for one reason: she knew her mistress well enough to know that once she had an idea, she followed through and no amount of reasoning would persuade her. There had been no chance of Matilda allowing Elizabeth to run off with Patrick back to Dunnottar. Patrick was a lovesick fool for Elizabeth, but William would kill the man for his role in her deceit, risking her life and the peace of their people.

Nay, Matilda had needed to think quickly and Reginald was the only choice, for now. But Matilda had a plan. She knew Elizabeth had feelings for Robert, even if she was too afraid to admit it and, worse, too afraid of being hurt to marry a man she actually could love. It was slightly preposterous, yet the sobs of Elizabeth's father after the death of his wife had rung through the halls of Dunnottar, teaching a young Elizabeth that love was best avoided at any cost.

Slipping through the back door of the kitchens and into the court-yard, Matilda walked toward the lists, knowing the men would be ending training to eat a meal soon enough. Her blue linen skirts rustled in the tepid July breeze and she covered her eyes as the rays of sun blinded her after leaving the grim light of the castle.

Spotting Reginald sauntering like a peacock beside Robert, both shirtless and drenched in sweat, Matilda sighed and admitted to herself that the Irvine lads were indeed quite handsome. Though Reginald seemed to think much of himself, there was something about him, a vulnerability and an overall sense of loyalty for his family that she knew would come in handy for her plan. If only he would agree.

"Reginald!" Matilda bounced on her heels and waved her hands in the air to catch his attention. She was a slight lass, smaller than most, and tended to get lost in the crowd, so Matilda had learned to be louder than most to compensate. A smile slid over Reginald's lips, and she knew he was a man who enjoyed the attentions of women. Mayhap it would be slightly harder to convince him of her plan than she suspected.

Slapping Robert on the back and walking in her direction, she did not miss the look of confusion on Robert's serious face as he continued toward the keep.

"My fair Matilda. What can I do for ye? 'Tis not every day such a bonnie lass calls out to a man."

Waving his words away, she tried to remind herself that despite his frivolity and carefree manner, he was second in line to the lairdship. "I dinnae believe that for a moment. I believe ye are surround by bonnie lassies nearly every time I see ye. However, I do, indeed, have something ye can do for me."

"Oh?" He raised a brow and shifted his stance and she shook her head, trying not to blush. This was not quite how it was meant to go, if she was to convince him to marry Elizabeth.

"How do ye feel about yer new Lady of Drum?" she asked slowly and linked arms with him, slowly pulling him away from any prying ears. Clearly, this was not the question he had been expecting, based on the sudden furrow of his brow.

"I dinnae ken what ye mean. She is a fine lady and takes care of Drum and its people well, as far as I can see having been away fighting a battle most of the duration of her time here."

Nodding, Matilda licked her lips and looked away for a moment, trying to decide how to approach this sensitive subject. "How does Robert feel about her?"

"How do ye mean?"

"Does he fancy her? Find her bonnie? Wish to marry her?"

Reginald looked sideways at her, unsure of where this was going. "I dinnae ken how to answer that without getting Robert into trouble..."

"So, he doesnae want to marry her?" Matilda could not help the accusation and insult in her voice. Elizabeth was the kindest, bonniest lass and worked very hard for her people. She would make a fine wife and deserved to be wanted and respected.

"'Tis not that, exactly." Reginald stopped mid-stride and looked at Matilda, scratching his short dark beard. "He isnae ready for marriage.

He had nay intentions of marrying anytime soon. And with him becoming laird and the bairn on the way—"

"Bairn? He has a bairn coming?"

"What? Nay. Elizabeth does."

Matilda snorted and shook her head. "I can tell ye with great certainty that she doesnae."

Reginald shifted again and grunted. "Robert heard her crying in her chambers about Alexander's bairn after he died."

Realization dawned on Matilda and she could not help but tilt her head back and laugh wildly until tears streamed down her cheeks. "Robert believes Elizabeth is carrying Alexander's bairn? Och, nay! That was Mary he heard crying! She is having his child!" Slapping a hand over her mouth, she cringed before speaking again. "Ye cannae tell a soul. That wasnae my secret to tell."

"I vow not to speak a word. I prefer to stay out of all of this. 'Tis a shame. I ken Robert has feelings for Elizabeth. He has from the start. He just needs more time to warm to the idea, yet his belief that she is with child caused him to hurry the marriage, so he can raise the child as his own."

Excitement brewed deep in Matilda's belly. Robert cared for Elizabeth and she cared for him as well, yet both were too stubborn to accept it, both preferring a stale life of duty over the risk of love. Her plan just may work after all… if she could get Reginald to agree.

"Reginald. I sought ye out for a reason. Ye seem like the sort of man who prefers a wee bit of adventure and scandal. I have one for ye if ye want to help give Robert and Elizabeth time to accept their feelings for one another."

"This sounds like the verra situation I attempt to avoid," he said lowly. Yet somehow, Matilda sensed his own excitement and she knew she had found her match in mischief-making.

"I doubt ye've had such a situation arise…"

"Oh? And what situation is this?" he asked, moving closer to Matilda and pulling her into the shadows.

"I need ye to marry Elizabeth. Tonight."

"Are ye mad?" he asked, pulling back slightly.

Not caring if he was the laird's brother or not, she swatted his arm in protest. "Mayhap a bit. I'm mostly concerned for my mistress, and Elizabeth was planning on running away to avoid marriage to Robert."

"He isnae so bad. In fact, he is likely the best husband she could find in all of Scotland."

"I ken that, and she cares for him, but he insulted her honor when he came back from battle and her bruised pride refuses to relent. She willnae marry him. Mostly, she is afraid of a husband she can truly love. She believes love is the ruination of lives." She rolled her eyes, but the look on Reginald's face told her he was truly listening to her mad scheme.

"Robert is afraid of the verra same. I ken he cares for the lass. He says he doesnae wish to marry his brother's pregnant widow. I believe he is simply jealous that it isnae his bairn."

"Then do ye not see? She needs to marry an Irvine son to fulfill the peace between clans. She refuses to marry him, and he claims to not wish to marry her. They belong together but dinnae ken it. We need to make them see."

"How does marrying Elizabeth solve that? She will be bound to me for life. They may realize they belong together eventually, but she will be my wife and I willnae be made a cuckold with my own brother, even if my marriage is for convenience."

"That is why this will work. It will be a false marriage, Reginald, only she must never ken that. She would never agree to this deception, so she must believe it to be true. Once Robert breaks from jealousy, ye will admit to a false wedding and they can be together."

"And her brother, William? Will he not wish to kill me?" Reginald asked, still looking at her as if she had lost her mind. Perhaps she had, but she had to make this work. She had to keep Elizabeth here at

Drum, close to Robert. It was a risky idea, but her friend's future was at stake.

"Aye, he may wish to, but he willnae, not unless he wants more bloodshed between our people, and he doesnae. He will accept it if Elizabeth is happy."

"And if they never fall in love? If they truly despise one another and he never cares I married her? Am I to remain secretly unwed to her forever? 'Tis a wee bit too risky, Tilda. Even for me. The lass is bonnie, I will give her that. But I am not one to settle on a lass. I prefer my freedom."

"Trust me, Reginald. I ken Elizabeth loves him already. She will regret marrying ye soon enough." Matilda winked and bumped him in the shoulder.

"I dinnae ken if I should feel offended or not. But aye, I will do it. For my brother, as strange as that seems. I only hope he forgives me in time."

"I will tell Elizabeth ye agreed to the marriage. She will meet ye at the chapel at twilight. Yer job is to procure a false priest, mayhap a man from the village that will do it for a few coins and one she will likely not recognize. Can ye do that?"

"Believe me, lass. I am not the only man in this castle willing to seek out trouble willingly. I will find a man and we will be there."

"Wonderful!" Throwing her arms around Reginald's neck, Matilda squealed with delight that her devious plan was coming together. Elizabeth would be angry with her when the truth came out, but she will also be glad to be free to marry Robert and forgive Matilda's plotting. She was certain of it.

"I VOW THIS is the last Irvine brother I shall ever stand up at the altar with," Elizabeth whispered into Matilda's ear. Shocked that Reginald had seemingly agreed to wed with her in Robert's place. She was even more shocked he had been able to find a clergyman to marry them on such short a notice. A traveler passing through, Reginald had told them.

Wearing the same damask dress she had worn for her marriage to Alexander, Elizabeth couldn't help but feel slightly apprehensive about her decision. William would most assuredly be displeased with her, but that was precisely why this had to occur immediately before anyone could object.

After making certain Reginald understood this to be a marriage of convenience, Elizabeth decided to move forward with her plan. She felt none of the sparks she felt when she looked at Robert, no tightening in her belly or the excitement of something more, which was precisely what she wanted. He would be free to do as he pleased, and she would run Drum until Robert married a woman of his choosing. Someday, they would need to consider a physical relationship solely for the purpose of having a child, but that thought only made her stomach sour, as did the thought of Robert someday marrying and having heirs. His wife would have more of a duty to create heirs than Elizabeth did. Still, it would be expected eventually. For now, she simply needed to be done with this ridiculous ceremony and get on with her life.

Walking toward Reginald who stood calmly in front of the chapel with a short, rotund man Elizabeth had never seen, she sent him a shaky smile and stopped when she reached him. Nodding, he put out his hand and smiled back reassuringly. Elizabeth was not at all certain what Matilda had said to convince the man to marry her, and she knew that her friend could be quite convincing, just as she convinced Elizabeth to stay at Drum and marry Reginald.

Something did not sit well with her. This situation felt wholly wrong and extremely permanent, only she had no choice but to marry an Irvine. And of the two available men, Reginald was the one who had not insulted her, even though he had also lost a brother. Deciding to hold on to her anger at Robert, Elizabeth took a deep breath and steeled herself to do what must be done.

Mind spinning and on the verge of fleeing altogether, she felt Reginald grip her hand harder as he began to recite his vows. She tried to remember them, tried to properly repeat them, but knew she was sputtering over every word and feeling close to passing out. Just before she protested that this was a mistake and she should never have gone along with it, she heard the strange clergyman declare them husband and wife and stood as still as a statue as Reginald leaned in and swiftly, almost chastely, placed his lips on hers and pulled away, looking at her with a look that told her he knew she was already regretting her decision.

But, it was done. And because there was no love between them, he appeared unmoved or hurt by her lack of affection. "My lady wife. 'Tis late and the castle will awake in a few hours. Allow me to escort ye to yer chamber so ye can get some rest. Ye appear ashen."

"I dinnae feel well," was all she could muster with a nod of her head and allowed Reginald, her new husband, to walk her toward the castle entrance, through the bailey, and into the keep. Just as they approached the stairs, a noise made Elizabeth start, her heart pounding in her chest as she struggled to breathe through her rising panic. Was Reginald going to hold true to his word of keeping this arrangement chaste for now, or would he attempt to bed her, after all?

Approaching her door, Reginald stopped, pushed the door open for her, and bowed his head in a gesture of dismissal. "I bid ye a good night, Wife."

Relief flooded her so swiftly, she nearly lost her balance, leaning against the cold stone frame of her door, reveling in the chill of the surface against her back, seeping through the fabric of her gown. "Do ye not fear my brother's anger?" she asked before stepping inside, wondering why Reginald seemed so cool and calm about the entire events of the night.

"Nay. What is there to fear? Ye needed to marry an Irvine brother, and now ye have."

"Aye, except I'm rather certain he expected me to marry Robert, as he is laird and the contract said I would marry the next in line."

With a shrug, Reginald leaned against the other side of her door and looked at her intently. "Mayhap. But it doesnae matter now, does it? He and Robert can work that out. If Robert is angry I stole his wife, he may fight it, using the contract as reason enough, but ye said yerself that my brother has nay interest in ye, and ye have none in him, aye?"

"Aye," she whispered, nodding and feeling like a bloody liar and a fool. She could not very well tell Reginald that she married him solely because she knew she would never love him. She may not believe in romance and love, but certainly there were things better left unsaid.

"Then they shall both be pleased. Robert for having evaded a bride he never wanted, and yer brother for ye marrying a man who ye chose." His words stung, but she did her best to hide the pain. To know Robert never wanted her, to hear the words from his brother's lips, solidified her belief that this was for the best. There was no happiness to be found if she fell in love with a man who did not care for her. Suddenly, her stomach plummeted, making her feel nauseated with tears threatening to spill. She had to go before he caught a glimpse of her true anguish.

"Good night, H-Husband," she croaked, the words feeling foreign and forced on her tongue.

"Rest assured that by the time ye awake on the morrow, I will have this all cleared up and ye will have nothing to worry over." Kissing her forehead the same way Alexander had done on their wedding night, Reginald spun on his heels and walked away. Leaving her alone just as she wished.

Yet she wondered if this was all her life would ever amount to. Husbands who had no interest in her and gave only polite kisses. But, is that not what she had wished for?

CHAPTER ELEVEN

"Ye are jesting."

Reginald shook his head and shrugged. "Nay, I am not. I married Elizabeth last night."

"Surely ye jest. Ye stole my bride?" Robert chuckled and shook his head, putting his quill back into the ink bottle and setting aside the missive he had been writing. Reginald was always up to some game, but Robert could not figure out what he hoped to gain by such a lie. "Ye are hoping I will play my hand and admit some undying love for the lass, show a raging jealously, and prove some belief ye have that I care for her. Like I said before, I shall marry the lass because I must, and for nay other reason. And I shall do so in two days' time, with the hope of passing her unborn child off as my own."

"And, I am telling ye that ye neednae worry over wedding her, for I have done so already. Now, ye are free and ye can never say that I am a bad brother again." Reginald smirked and leaned against the wall, crossing one foot slowly over the other and searching Robert out for a reaction, but Robert knew Reginald was playing at something, he just did not know what.

Folding his hands together and placing them slowly upon his desk, he met his brother's gaze and decided to test his brother's story. "Oh?

Who was yer witness?"

"Tilda."

"Who was the clergyman?"

"Father Arnold, from the village." Reginald did not bat an eyelash as he stared Robert down, answering all the questions swiftly and without hesitation.

"What did Elizabeth wear?"

"Ye mean during the ceremony, or during the bedding? They were much different in nature, I assure ye."

That comment made Robert clench his fists, but he bit his lip, doing his best to prevent falling prey to his brother's baiting. "To the ceremony." Robert had to speak slowly to hide the quaking of his voice. His pulse quickened and he wanted to knock his brother out simply for using his future bride in some ridiculous falsehood.

"She wore the same dress she wore to her wedding with Alexander. Dark blue damask."

"And ye have proof of this marriage then?"

"Aye." Reginald stepped forward and tossed a rolled-up piece of parchment at Robert, who caught it midair and slowly unfurled it, expecting to see a blank document. Instead, he saw what appeared to be a signed wedding certificate.

"Ye have gone to great lengths to trick me, Reg. But enough is enough. And I dinnae have time for yer shite anymore."

"Do ye wish to speak with Matilda? Or better yet, my bride? I am more than certain she will explain the situation to ye. In the end, I did this for ye, Brother. Ye didnae wish to marry her, and she didnae wish to marry ye. All she cared to do was her duty, marry an Irvine, and keep the peace. Ye made it clear to her more than once that ye didnae want her. I made it clear that I did." He shrugged and started to walk away, but Robert had had enough.

Standing swiftly from his chair, it nearly toppled over as he rounded his desk and grabbed his brother by the collar. "I have had enough of this," he said through his teeth. "Aye or nay. Did ye marry Elizabeth?"

"Aye."

It took all his willpower, all his training as a warrior to keep a cool head, to slowly release his brother without hitting him square in the jaw. Clearing his throat, Robert stepped away and walked back to his desk, sitting down slowly. Inside, he ached worse than he ever thought possible. It was as if he had been kicked in the gut by a horse, as if someone had reached in and ripped his heart out. He could not understand why Elizabeth, who had asked him to marry her once not so long ago, would be so determined to avoid a lifetime with him now that she was able. Aye, he had been an arse to her the day he arrived home from battle, but he had apologized and she had been clear before that she did not want a romantic relationship.

Nor had he… until he laid eyes on Elizabeth Keith from Dunnottar Castle. Mayhap he did not want to admit it to himself from the very beginning because she was destined to marry his brother. Afterwards, feeling any sort of excitement over the prospect of marrying her had felt horribly wrong, because that would mean facing the reality of his brother's death and he was already surrounded by the memories of their childhood laughter ringing down the cold halls. Reality had already swallowed him whole, evidenced by the pile of missives he had to respond to, and the fact that he had been meant to marry his brother's widow.

In his determination to control his feelings for Elizabeth, he had inadvertently pushed her away… right into the arms of the wrong brother. Still, pride would not allow Reginald to get the best of him. Mayhap it was a habit of a lifetime, but the brothers had always preferred to show physical strength over emotional weakness.

"Well, then I suppose I should thank ye. One less problem in my life." He clenched his fists beneath the desk so Reginald could not see the evidence of his anger. "Would ye mind bringing her and William into my solar so we can all discuss this and the contract that ye two so blatantly disregarded. I suppose we will have to write up another."

Squinting his eyes, Reginald shifted and crossed his arms. "That's all ye have to say? Ye arenae mad?"

"Och, I am mad. I am mad I must now deal with William's wrath and pray he doesnae see this as a slight against his sister, her now being married to the last brother and not the laird. I am mad that ye dinnae tell me and that we have a wedding ceremony planned for two days hence, and I suppose everyone will be surprised by who the groom will be at the reception feast. But, 'tis done. As usual, ye've gone and done what is best for ye, and left the mess to me to clean up. Please send yer bride in." Looking back toward his papers, he shooed Reginald toward the door, doing his best not to throw everything off the surface of his desk and punch the stone wall behind him, or worse, his brother.

Was he truly so terrible that Elizabeth would do this? Reginald left and Robert hopped out of his seat, pacing his solar as the hearth fire popped and wind blew through the small window slit. It was true he had no wish to marry any time soon, but Elizabeth was all he could ever want in a wife and any feelings he had repressed before now floated to the surface, overflowing and making him feel sick with both envy and the sense of rejection. He was not a jealous man. This emotion was new to him and he found he despised it greatly.

After several minutes of taking deep breaths and doing his best to control his temper, his solar door flew open with a very angry William standing in the entrance. "Ye rejected my sister? Gave her to yer brother?"

Stopping in his tracks, Robert stared at Reginald once more, sending him a look that promised an arse kicking later and rubbed his hands down his face, growling in frustration. "Nay. I did nay such thing. I only just found out about this. 'Tis why I sent for ye. I had plans to marry her and ye ken this."

"Did ye tell her ye didnae wish to marry? Ye called her wanton?" William strode in looking as angry as a bull ready to gut him with his horns.

"Aye. I did say those things. And one of them is true. I apologized for the other already. It was directly after our arrival back to Drum and I was vulnerable and she came in to bathe me and—"

"What?" her brother asked. "Ye bathed him?"

"Aye. I bathe many men, Brother. 'Tis part of running a household, lest ye forget." Elizabeth crossed her arms and flared her nostrils, ready for a fight and Robert wanted nothing more than to take her in his arms, shake some sense into her, and kiss her until she could no longer breathe, showing her how badly he truly did want her, even if he had not felt able to tell her before. But he could never have her. She had now lain with both his brothers and would bear Alexander's child while Reginald raised it. Holy hell! This was a disaster. Of all the women in Scotland to feel this way about...

He felt Elizabeth's gaze on him and he looked in her direction, noticing the way her small fingers tangled in her skirts and she nibbled her lower lip between her teeth. The honey gold of her eyes showed so little of what the woman was truly thinking.

"Well, what now? I can run him through and make my sister a widow once more," William scowled and stepped toward Reginald, who did not bother to flinch.

"Will!" Elizabeth scolded and gripped her brother's arm. "I sent Matilda to ask him to marry me. He did so to save the peace, for I refused to marry Robert and planned on running away if ye made me. Because of Reginald, I am still here at Drum. Robert made it clear he didnae wish for a wife, especially me, and though I never wanted love, I certainly require respect."

Robert narrowed his eyes at her, wanting to tell her that he not only respected her, he had strong feelings that would one day be love had they ever had an opportunity to grow. Instead, she had insulted him. Mayhap this was for the best, if this was how Elizabeth behaved. After all, she had asked him to marry her before her wedding with Alex, and now she did the same with Reginald. Perhaps she was a wanton after all.

Deciding to let that thought fuel his resolve, he simply nodded and decided to move on. "What's done is done. She chose an Irvine brother, and I wish them well. I have other matters to attend to, including a newly written peace contract between our clans, if we still have it."

William stared at Reginald, his jaw visibly flexing before he looked at his sister and shook his head in disappointment and anger. "As ye said, what's done is done. Elizabeth has done all that has been required of her, her entire life, and I suppose she has once more."

"I wasnae a requirement. I was her chosen husband, lest we forget." Reginald took her hand in his and kissed her palm gently. Robert wasn't certain if Reginald was trying to see which man would kill him first, or if he truly loved Elizabeth as well, so instead he walked toward his desk and stared at the fire once more, imagining his hands around his brother's throat.

"Verra well. The two newlyweds may go about their day. We will continue on in here until we have an agreement made."

"Robert?" He stiffened at the sound of his name coming from her lips. He was not sure what she had to say, nor if he wished to hear it, but out of respect for his new sister, he turned and faced her, raising a brow. "Thank ye for understanding."

Nodding, he folded his arms behind his back and faced the fire once more, making it clear that they were dismissed.

"Come, Wife. There is much to be done today and we shall celebrate our union in two nights' time with both our clans in attendance. It shall be all ye deserve." Robert rolled his eyes at his brother's sudden new affinity for politeness. Reginald had always been a man of sweet words and many women, but doting was a new trait of his and Robert did not find it becoming.

Once the door shut behind him, he turned to look at William, whose face was blotchy with what Robert assumed was an even mixture of anger and confusion. He could relate.

"Ye rejected my sister."

"Nay, I didnae."

"Ye made her feel unwanted."

"Aye, I suppose I did, though that hadnae been my intention," Robert admitted and pointed to the other chair by his desk.

William slowly sat and eyed Robert. "What had been yer intention?"

Pausing, Robert tapped his fingers on the solid oak of his desk and pondered how best to answer. He supposed he had done enough lying to everyone, including himself. Best to tell at least one truth for the day. With a sigh, he tilted his head back and groaned. "William, she is yer sister. I dinnae ken how to say all I am thinking."

"Do yer best, but call her a wanton once more and ye will be saying it through bloody lips, aye?"

"That was a mistake. She had said something... never mind. It was wrong and I apologized. I do regret it, though I dinnae think she will ever forgive it. Truth is, she is my brother's widow and he is dead. Ye ken yer sister is a good lass. I would be a fortunate man to be her husband. But being her husband means my brother is..."

"Dead," William said, deadpan, with a nod of understanding.

Swallowing his pain, Robert nodded. "Aye. 'Tis difficult to embrace a marriage that is only possible because he fell in battle. I took my pain and anger out on her and it was wrong. But the truth is, I would have gladly become her husband. I simply had a hard time accepting that truth."

William's eye's widened and he leaned forward in his chair. "Ye care for her."

There was no use in denying it, and at least one person in the world should knew the truth. "Aye. I do. I tried not to. It felt wrong. But, I do. And now, she has married my brother." A cynical laugh escaped him, and he shook his head. "So, shall we call a peace between our clans? Things didnae occur as intended, but they seldom do."

William regarded him for a few moments in silence, and Robert wasn't sure what he was thinking. "Aye. The Irvines and Keiths are one, even if it did come about in an unexpected way. Let us rewrite this cursed contract and go to the buttery for a few mugs of yer finest ale."

"I couldnae agree more," Robert said with a huff and picked up his quill. Having to write a peace treaty was something he rather enjoyed as Laird of Drum. Knowing it was because his brother had stolen his wife was far less enjoyable.

NEWS OF HER secret marriage spread quickly throughout the castle, and Elizabeth assumed it was due to her new husband, who had no issue talking about his new bride. Working in the kitchens with her hair pulled back into a kerchief, steam from the new loaves of bread crept up her face, making her feel flushed. Yet the hard work was keeping her more than occupied. Her mind had not stopped spinning since her meeting with Robert several hours ago. He did not seem to care that she had married his brother, which was just as well and only solidified her belief that he would never have felt for her the way she had felt for him. Marrying Reginald had been the right decision, she supposed. He was kind and humorous, not ashamed of her, and felt like a companion, which was all she required.

"Say it isnae so."

Mary's words drifted to her ears over the sounds of pots banging and Cook's shouted commands. Turning around, Elizabeth locked eyes with her friend and blew a dangling hair away from her face. "I did what I must, Mary."

"I thought ye and Robert would be perfect together. I have kenned him all my life. He is a good man and will be a fine husband and father."

"Perhaps, to the right woman. I simply wasnae it. He has no interest in marriage, nor being with me."

Mary looked at her suspiciously and put her hands on her hips, the roundness of her belly starting to show through the linen of her dress, especially when she had an apron tied around her waist. "Ye said ye didnae want love or romance in a marriage, so why would any of that matter?"

Turning around, Elizabeth moved the cooling loaves of bread onto a large wooden tray and placed them across the kitchen with the other loaves. "I dinnae."

"Then what is the problem?"

"There is no problem. I needed to marry an Irvine, and Reginald was more willing to marry than Robert. So, I chose him. Robert doesnae seem bothered in the least. On the contrary, he seems rather relieved. So ye see, all is well." Her stomach clenched for the hundredth time that day. Despite being surrounded by the savory scents of bread and stew, Elizabeth had been unable to eat a bite, her stomach choosing to protest in agony instead. What was done, was done, she reminded herself silently, also for the hundredth time.

"Ye dinnae expect me to believe such hogwash. I ken ye care for him, Lizzie. It makes no sense."

"Mayhap it is precisely for that reason I chose Reginald. Neither of us want more from this. There is no expectation, no deeper connection."

"No risk of being hurt."

Elizabeth looked at Mary and began to walk to the garden. She did not need to be questioned about her decision and nothing could undo it, even if she wished to, not that she did. The fresh air of the afternoon cooled her sweat-slicked skin as a gentle breeze brushed her neck. The kitchens were hotter than the pits of hell, she vowed. Yet, the Lady of Drum Castle helped where she was needed. However, all was prepared for the nooning meal and the men would be gathering soon, ready to devour their food.

Everything in the castle had felt chaotic with the preparations for her wedding feast. All she wished to do was hide in her chamber and not come out for as long as it took for everyone to forget she existed. As of now, she seemed to be all anyone could think about, or worse, speak about. And, not all the words had been kind. Many were angry at her and Reginald for sneaking behind Robert's back. Most felt sorry for their laird, mistaking his stress over the death of his brother and becoming a laird as a broken heart. That only made her roll her eyes. They truly did not know him if they believed him to be saddened by her actions. Robert had proven more than once that Elizabeth was an obligation and not one he wished to manage.

"So, ye arenae going to speak to me, now?"

Her mind had been wandering all day, and Elizabeth seemed to forget what she was doing every few moments. "Och, I am sorry, Mary. I just have a lot on my mind. How are ye feeling?"

"I have been feeling ill in the mornings, but well otherwise. He is growing. I wish his father was here to watch him grow." The watering of Mary's eyes made Elizabeth feel like a cursed fool. She was so busy feeling sorry for herself that she had not been a good friend.

"I havenae been here for ye. I am sorry." Gripping her hand, Elizabeth gave Mary a sad smile, wondering what her companion would do about her situation. It was not at all acceptable for a young unmarried woman to be with child. She would need to find a husband soon or go to a nunnery, but these thoughts were better left unsaid, as she was certain Mary was aware of the situation.

"Ye have had a lot going on, as well. Ye lost one husband and took another so verra quickly. And speaking of yer husband, here he comes now."

Before Elizabeth could turn around, she felt an arm slip around her waist from behind and quickly turn her around. "Greetings, Wife." Looking up, she found herself in Reginald's arms, face to face with him as he looked down at her with a cheeky smile. Puzzled as to why he was being so affectionate, she stiffened, flinching when she saw Robert standing beside him, a deep brooding look on his face as he stared menacingly at her.

Pulling away swiftly, she cleared her throat. "Greetings. Are ye done with training?"

"Aye. 'Tis time for the nooning. I came to fetch my bonnie bride so we may share our first meal together."

Robert grunted and stormed off toward the keep, his bare back glistening with sweat as every muscle bunched with each step he took. Swallowing hard, Elizabeth stood there doing everything she could not to stare at her husband's brother. This was going to be a harder feat than she ever expected, and just because she did not marry the man did not mean she suddenly stopped having feelings for him – only now they were wholly inappropriate and most sinful.

Looping her arm in his, she allowed him to walk her back to the keep in silence, the entire time pondering why Robert seemed so angry if he truly hated her so much. She had thought only to make his life easier by not forcing him to marry her, yet he seemed angrier than ever. Looking over her shoulder, she saw Mary who shrugged and scrunched up her face in confusion. At least Elizabeth was not the only one who was shocked by Robert's behavior.

Entering the keep, her chest constricted with a slight panic as she realized all eyes were on them. Robert was already at the front of the head table, sitting down beside his uncle and paying no attention to anything else, which was preferable to his scowls.

Escorting her toward the table, Reginald pulled out the chair beside Robert, which was reserved for the Lady of Drum. Though she had been acting as such, never had it crossed her mind she would be required to sit beside him at dinner. Until he married, she still maintained the position, so she sat down slowly and turned her body away from Robert to avoid any more unpleasantries, still unsure about the source of his hostility. The thought of Robert marrying someone else and having to see him with a wife every day made any appetite she had worked up vanish, replaced by a cruel gnawing in the pit of her stomach. Why was this so hard? Mayhap she would have been better off leaving Drum altogether.

Using his knife to cut the best piece of meat and place it on her side of their shared trencher, Reginald smiled. "Dinnae worry about my sour brother. He is only experiencing his first feelings of jealousy in his entire life and isnae certain how to manage them."

Elizabeth clutched her pearls and shook her head. "Oh, I wouldnae say 'tis jealousy. Reginald. He hasnae cared for me from the verra start. He was only kind to me because Alex needed him to be. I've been naught but in the way since my arrival."

"That is the most untrue thing I have ever heard. Everybody here loves ye, Elizabeth. The staff ken ye work hard and in such a short amount of time, ye have made Drum yer home and earned their respect." Reginald stuffed a bite of meat into his mouth and she did her best to take a wee bite as well, not wanting to be rude.

Her elbow bumped with Robert's and she flinched, feeling gooseflesh crawl up her body. Why did the smallest touch affect her in such a way? Being so close to him was proving already to be impossible. Her reaction to him was visceral and unexpected, unlike anything she had ever expected to feel in her lifetime. Hoping to be done with this meal and back to her duties, she forced a few more bites, quietly excused herself from the table, and slid as silently as possible past the screens and into the kitchen where she felt mildly more at ease, despite the constant chaos. Chaos was a distraction she understood. Robert, however, was not. Nor was the guilt of feeling this way for her husband's brother, even if Reginald knew their marriage would never be more than convenient. Nothing felt convenient so far, but it had not even been a day, she reminded herself.

Heading through the back, she walked toward the stables, deciding to check on her favorite mare, Aina, who was breeding and very close to foaling. Sometimes just being in the stables with the horses reminded her of childhood back in Dunnottar. She would help groom the horses with her brother and their marshal after long rides across their lands. The wind blowing through her hair had made her feel free as a bird and she longed for that feeling once more. It had been so long since she went for ride all alone.

Walking past a few stables, she turned to her left and opened the gate, petting Aina under her chin with one hand and on top of her head with the other. "Well, hello sweet lassie. How are ye feeling today? Ye look as if ye are ready to give birth, are ye not?" The mare nuzzled deeper into Elizabeth's hand and snorted, making her laugh. She missed the company of horses. They were loyal, yet stubborn creatures and always very intelligent. They could read people. Her mother had always told her a man could be known by the treatment and respect of his horse, and she had found that to be true.

Feeding Aina a carrot, Elizabeth ran her hands a few times through her thick silky mane before shutting the gate once more and allowing Aina to lay down once more to rest. She was almost as wide as she was tall and looked uncomfortable at best.

It was just after midday and though it was nearly August, the weather had turned windy and overcast, creating a wonderful breeze that Elizabeth was suddenly determined to enjoy before going back to her duties. She had left early, so everyone else was likely still finishing their meals, giving her time to seek a bit of solitude and test out a smaller mare she had had her eye on since arriving at Drum.

Walking a bit further into the stalls and looking to her right, Elizabeth got on her tiptoes and peeked over the gate she knew held Fianna, a mare just two years of age appearing to be mild in temper, well trained thanks to the superior marshal at Drum, and the perfect size for Elizabeth to mount easily enough even without a mounting block. Looking at the saddles hanging on the wall, Elizabeth chewed her bottom lips, then smirked, deciding if she was going to go on a spontaneous ride to enjoy the fresh air and open fields south of Drum leading to the River Dee, she may as well ride without a saddle. Her mother would be appalled, but nobody was around to bother or care and she was a married woman now, determined to find joy in anything she could.

Opening the gate, Elizabeth signaled Fianna forward, petting her soothingly before placing the bit in her mouth, sliding on the bridle and guiding her out by the reins. "That's a good wee lassie," Elizabeth soothed and continued to lead her out into the brightness of the low white clouds that caused Elizabeth to squint until she adjusted to the light. Fianna followed and Elizabeth took a moment to feed her a carrot and talk to her soothingly before she was ready to mount. Removing her short leather boots and stockings, Elizabeth set them aside before hopping up with the ease she had learned through a lifetime of riding. Skirts bunched up around her knees, Elizabeth smiled and tugged the ribbon out of her hair, allowing it to blow freely in the wind.

Freedom. It would be short lived, she knew but, for the moment, it was hers. Squeezing the horse's flanks with her strong thighs, Fianna took off toward the wide-open plains, two wild women, thirsty for adventure.

CHAPTER TWELVE

WHEN ELIZABETH ABRUPTLY left the head table, Robert looked over at Reginald, curious why she had fled before the meal was finished. Reginald looked up from his trencher and smiled widely at Robert, causing him to shake his head. Whatever had happened did not seem to concern Reginald at all. Mayhap the marriage truly was only one of convenience. Reginald had made enough comments about Elizabeth's bonnie features and ample breasts for Robert to know he was attracted to her, but beyond that, he could not see any true love match between the two... not that it should bother him either way. Nay, he had been relieved to not require a bride just now, even if it would be necessary to take a wife soon enough as laird, and Elizabeth was the only woman he could have ever truly been happy with. None of that mattered now, and he was relieved to avoid any romantic complications.

Speaking with his uncle about more of the lands he needed to manage and the tenants who still owed for the season, Robert's head was beginning to ache. The wedding was to take place tomorrow afternoon, followed by a grand feast, but now it would just be a feast and it would not involve him at all, freeing him from any involvement other than attendance, which still felt like burden enough. Word had caught his ears that Elizabeth had been hard at work in the kitchens, helping to prepare for the feast, which was most unusual for a bride and he found he rather respected her desire to work hard and help as needed, never worrying about getting her hands dirty. She was running Drum quite well, though once he married, she would be replaced, not to mention she would be having a wee bairn by next fall, which would surely slow her down for a while. Was that why she left so quickly? Mayhap something was wrong with the child?

"Where did Elizabeth rush off to?" Robert asked his brother, doing his best not to sound overly concerned, but it was Alexander's child, after all, and he felt responsible for its care and wellbeing as an uncle and laird.

"Why do ye care?" Reginald said calmly, poking at the last big chunk of meat on his trencher.

"I was only curious. She seemed in a rush."

Shrugging, Reginald looked up. "I dinnae tell my wife where she can or cannae go. She is free to do as she wishes."

Robert rubbed his beard. "Why did ye marry her? I ken ye dinnae wish to marry any more than I did. Do ye love her?"

Sputtering on the large gulp of ale he had just taken, Reginald pounded his chest and coughed until his face turned red. "I have been married to the woman for less than a day, and ye think I am in love with the lass?"

"Then why did ye take her from me?" Robert growled, then clenched his jaw shut, knowing he was not doing well to hide his emotions. The words came out of his mouth so quickly, he cursed himself for being a jealous fool.

Crooking a brow, Reginald snorted. "Did I? Ye said ye didnae want a wife."

"Nor did ye," Robert shot back. "But, I was contracted to wed with her and my last promise to Alexander was that I would make sure Elizabeth is cared for."

"Aye, and she is. I vow to take *verra* good care of her." He waggled his brows and slowly sipped his ale without breaking eye contact. Robert pursed his lips and took a deep breath, doing all he could not to cause a scene and start a fight in the middle of the keep. "Is that what this is all about? Yer promise to Alexander?" Reginald added slowly, narrowing his eyes at Robert.

"Aye," Robert shot back, believing that to be a far better response than admitting he was jealous of his younger, arse of a brother.

"Well then, ye neednae worry. He simply wanted peace, and peace has been made. Now, ye can breathe easy, Brother."

"Ye havenae answered why ye married her."

Putting his cup down slowly, Reginald wiped his beard and let out a low belch. "Ye truly wish to ken why?" Robert met his gaze, narrowed his eyes, and nodded once in response. "Because the lass cannae stand ye and begged me to marry her so she wouldnae have to marry ye after ye insulted her. She threatened to run off to her own lands otherwise. Furthermore, she has the verra best tits I have ever seen, and I wished to hear her beg while she laid naked in my bed. That's why."

Belly churning with disgust as his veins flowed with the fire of his rage, Robert swiftly stood up from his chair and caused it to scrape across the floor with a resounding echo just as he swung his right fist with all his might, landing a blow across Reginald's jaw.

Laughing like a madman, Reginald jumped up and threw Robert to the ground, punching him once in the nose as he sat astride him. Gasps from the crowd drifted to Robert's ears, but he did not care. He had been itching for a fight since his return home, and Reginald was always willing to give him one. Never had Robert truly wished to hurt his brother as he did now.

"Eh, the Irvine men like to rough each other up now and again. 'Tis no bother," his uncle grunted to the crowd, no doubt sipping on his ale slowly and staring into nothingness.

But this wasn't any usual fight between brothers. Reginald had taken the only woman Robert had ever truly felt something more than lust for. He and Elizabeth had a connection and even though she was upset with him, Robert thought he had a lifetime to make up for his cruelty to her. Now, instead, he was forced to spend a lifetime watching her with Reginald. And the images his brother put in his head had only driven him to the brink of madness.

"Ye shouldnae speak about yer wife like she is whore!" Robert grunted as he rolled over, pinning Reginald beneath him and getting in another good blow, this time to the nose. "Especially with her condition!"

Jumping off his brother, Robert wiped at the blood he felt trickling out of the split in his lip. Looking down once more at Reginald, he shook his head and said lowly, so only he could hear. "Dinnae disrespect her in my presence ever again."

Storming down the aisle toward the keep's large wooden door, he saw all eyes on him as he flew past, needing fresh air to calm his inflamed nerves. His fists shook as the rage ebbed through him. Reginald had taken Elizabeth in the dead of night, only so he could have his way with her freely and claim it was done for peace between the clans. But Robert had known his brother wanted her from the first moment he saw her, even if only physically. Though marrying a lass just to bed her was a bold move, even for Reginald. He enjoyed a challenge and the chase. Forever was not something he had ever considered. Yet, nor had Robert until he was faced with it.

Shouting curses into the increasingly aggressive wind, he was surprised at the chill in the air. The sun was high and shining through the low clouds as his stride picked up. Reaching the outer bailey, he turned toward the stables, deciding he needed to get away for a while, to ride as hard as he could until exhaustion overtook him, or he could mayhap think straight.

As he approached, he saw their marshal, Finlay, a middle-aged man who had kept the horses for his father for several years, shoveling fresh hay into the stables before looking up to greet him. "Good day, my laird. Care for me to saddle Fodla?"

"Nay, I shall do so myself, but thank ye."

"I can see ye need a ride after another disagreement with yer brother. Ye lads have always been the same." His gaze went to Robert's split lip, but he didn't bother to wipe away the fresh blood. Nodding, he walked into the stables toward Fodla's stall.

"Begging my pardon, Laird. I saw my lady leaving the keep in a hurry and when I came out here to feed the horses and check on Aina, I noticed the stall was open for Fianna and she was missing. I would-nae suspect who took her, only I ken Lady Elizabeth enjoys horses and riding and had asked many questions about Fianna. Took a fancy to her, she did. Now, they are both gone, it seems." The man seemed nervous, as if he was responsible for any of Elizabeth's actions. Robert knew as well as anyone that Elizabeth did whatever she wanted. She may have agreed to the peace contracts and the marriages because she was wise enough to accept her fate. However, when Elizabeth was not interested in following rules, she was bound to do any manner of ridiculous things to avoid them... such as marry the wrong brother in the middle of the night.

"Ye think she has fled?" Robert saddled Fodla quickly and escorted her out of the stables, knowing she was just as anxious for escape as he was at the moment.

"I dinnae ken, Laird. Would she?"

"I dinnae ken, either, but she does seem prone to doing her own bidding, does she not?" Mounting Fodla, he looked down at Finlay and shook his head. "None of this is yer doing. Ye were eating a meal along with yer kin. None of us suspected she would flee. I will track her down."

Pointing to the wall, Finlay looked at the saddles. "She didnae even saddle up, my laird."

An alarming thought gripped at him, causing him to bite back a curse. She was carrying Alexander's child and had decided to tromp through the wild on horseback, and without a saddle. Was she mad? Or was she so desperate to flee back to her lands as his brother had mentioned, that she would take such a risk?

With no time to lose, Robert urged Fodla on, charging through the outer bailey and south, the only area of Drum not covered by forestlands. The main road that would lead to Dunnottar was in that direction, as well as the River Dee. As insane as Elizabeth may seem, he could not believe she would ride through the forest full of boars, deer, and many other predators. She was wild, but not daft.

She had fled directly after leaving the keep and had a half-hour lead on him, so he had to hope she was not pushing Fianna terribly hard, or he would have trouble locating her. Still, he had to find her. Failure was not an option. He could not understand why she would leave now that she was married to Reginald, unless she had already realized in less than a day what a lout he could be. That thought made him smile a wee bit. He did not wish for her unhappiness, but he was a better husband than Reginald and any person at Drum could have told her as much.

Speeding over grass fields of wildflowers, Robert followed what appeared to be fresh tracks where the grass was flattened. The land was dry, so muddy hoof prints would not have been left behind. After an hour of riding aimlessly and finding no sign of the cursed woman, something a darker shade of green than the grass fields caught the corners of his eyes and he pulled on the reins, bringing Fodla to a stop and looking over his shoulder.

Speeding through the field with her chestnut hair blowing wildly and her skirts hiked up to her bare thighs, she was also bare foot and without a saddle, as Finlay had suspected. He had found the woman he had been seeking – only, he had certainly not expected to find her in this state, nearly half-naked and laughing into the wind as she handled

Fianna like a woman who had grown up on horses. Throat constricting, Robert attempted to swallow but the image before him had him rooted in place and speechless. Never had he seen a more beautiful, freer woman. She did not appear to be fleeing at all, for who would flee without boots, or stockings, or a satchel of supplies? Nay she was a wild woman who meant nothing more than to find her escape, an endeavor he could wholeheartedly understand.

And yet, this far past the river, she had put herself and their clan in danger. The Fraser lands were just over the rise and they were a watchful and cunning clan. Neither ally nor enemy of the Irvines, they would still take an opportunity for trouble if one arose and finding the Lady of Drum wandering their lands in a near state of undress would be such an opportunity. She would be taken and held for ransom without a doubt... and mayhap worse.

Relieved he had found her before she found trouble, his heart suddenly pounded wildly in his chest at the realization of just how close she had come to danger. Watching her from a distance, he couldn't help the tightness in his gut, the admiration he felt for the lass, and the arousal watching her created. Her legs were long and lean and her breasts looked about ready to burst free from her bodice. She was his brother's wife and he knew it was wrong to stare at her or think of her is such a way but he truly could not help his physical reaction to her, nor the way his heart leapt and his chest tightened whenever he thought of her. Hell, she had been meant to be his wife. Was it wrong to want what was supposed to be his, what had been taken from him? Mayhap not, especially since Reginald had ogled her while she was meant to be Alex's wife, aye? But, acting upon it in any manner would be forbidden, which would not be an issue since she seemed determined to keep her distance from him, determined to push him away. So much so, that she had snuck behind his back to marry his own brother.

Then, he remembered something that made him suddenly feel like grabbing the lass off her horse and shaking some sense into her. The bairn. Alex's bairn. Urging Fodla forward, Robert raced toward Elizabeth, who still seemed completely ignorant that she was being watched or followed, which only angered him further. She was a smart lass, but she was much too unaware of prying eyes and potential danger.

"Elizabeth!" he roared over the wind as he charged toward her. "Elizabeth! What are ye doing!"

Head turning toward him, her perfectly pink lips parted in disbelief just before she pulled back on Fianna's reins, coming to a complete stop as he reached her side. "R-Robert," she said breathlessly, chest rising and falling as she panted for breath. By the hounds of hell, she was a beautiful woman. Once again, he felt his blood surge. She looked like she belonged here in the middle of a field of flowers, like the fae, and he longed to pull her down from the horse and lay her onto the grass, proving to her what she could have had with him. But, nay.

Shaking his head, he focused again on his disappointment and anger. "What are ye doing?"

"I am riding, of course." Tilting her head up to the sun, he saw the long expanse of her creamy neck and the rise of her breasts a wee bit more over the edge of her bodice. Was there ever another woman made on this earth more lovely than her... his brother's cursed wife?

Scowling, he nudged Fodla forward to bring himself closer to Elizabeth. "I can see that, aye. Verra close to the Fraser border, at that. Ye put yerself in danger! And the bairn!"

Confusion consumed every feature of her face, from her tilted head and narrowed eyes to her downturned lips. "What bairn, Robert?"

"Alex's bairn!" he barked and swiftly dismounted his horse, standing beneath her dangling legs, which only made him want to touch her. He put his hand on her horse's reins and she seemed to suddenly notice how very exposed she was. Grunting, she hopped down from Fianna and landed just in front of him with the grace of a cat and the skill of the finest horsemen he knew.

Gold flecks danced in the irises of her eyes, the sun reflecting through the stray strands of wild waves. She was already close, yet she took one step closer. He refused to step away or back down from whatever spar she wished to have. "Ye think I am with child? And that I would ride so frivolously if I were? Ye think so little of me, do ye, Robert?"

"Aye! I mean, Nay. Aye, I heard ye crying about the bairn through yer chamber door the day we arrived from battle. Nay, I dinnae think little of ye, Elizabeth. But I do think ye are being reckless in yer rebellion."

Stepping closer so that her bare toes rested on the tips of his boots, she straightened her back and stood at her full height. "Ye listen in on my private conversations, do ye? What else do ye think ye ken about me? That I am a wanton lass? Mayhap I dinnae even ken who the father is."

Anger flared in him and he stepped forward, forcing her back up against Fianna who did not budge as she grazed on the wild dandelions in the field.

"I already have made my apologies for my remarks that day. Ye will never forgive them? Instead, ye will sneak behind my back and marry my brother? Ye think me so terrible?"

"I married Reginald because I had to marry an Irvine, and ye didnae seem so inclined to marry at first, until ye suddenly decided to marry me immediately. Wait—ye thought I was carrying Alexander's child, so ye rushed the wedding to pass the bairn off as yer own, aye?"

Robert nodded, realizing both his arms were resting on the horse, effectively pinning Elizabeth on either side, but she was too angry to notice, and he had no intention of letting her go until he had answers.

"Well then, I suppose ye still have time to marry the woman carrying his child, but 'tis not me. And I feel more than ever that I made the right choice, for ye only wanted to protect the child ye thought I carried, not marry me. Now ye may do both."

She quirked a brow at him and he felt his head racing, trying to remember the day he returned home and heard the crying voice through her chamber door. "Then, who is it? Mary?"

Rolling her eyes, Elizabeth put her hands on her hips and grunted. "Of course, it is! Would that not make more sense? Have ye nay idea how this sort of thing works, Robert? A man must actually bed a woman to get her with child."

Robert's heart skipped a beat and he leaned in a wee bit closer. "Alex didnae…"

"Nay, he didnae. Not that it is any of yer business."

Why did he feel a swift sense of relief, knowing she had not slept with both of his brothers? It did not, could not matter… and yet, somehow it did. She was not with child. But, Mary was and would soon need to find a husband before she began to show… though despite Elizabeth's suggestion, he would not be the man to marry his brother's lover. The thought gave him chills up his spine. Why marrying his widow seemed any less bad, he could not fathom, except that Alex demanded he do so, and he had very much wanted to despite his better intentions.

"Will ye leave me be now that ye have yer answers?" Elizabeth tried to push past Robert, but he locked his elbows and pressed even closer to her. He could feel her breath on his face and had to fight his urge to lean in further, to press his lips on hers, to see if she would return his kiss or slap him across the face. He knew that he could not control his feelings, but he could control his behaviors, and he would not dishonor his brother… even if Reginald had dishonored Robert first.

"Not until ye explain to me why ye are out here so close to Fraser lands riding like a wild woman without a saddle or half yer clothing."

"I dinnae have to explain anything to ye! Ye arenae my husband!" she shouted and pushed hard against his chest, huffing in frustration when he did not budge.

"I am yer laird and ye are still Lady Drum. Ye do answer to me, especially about matters of safety! Had ye been spotted on their land, they could have rightfully captured ye and ransomed ye back, or worse. Not all men as are as honorable as the Irvines.

"Och, aye, my *laird*," Elizabeth said with an exaggerated curtsy that he supposed was so perfected, it would work well at the courts of England. "I was riding because I enjoy it and wished to do so."

"Without boots or... stockings?" he asked, stumbling on the last word, images of her long, exposed legs filling his mind with inappropriate thoughts.

Watching her chew on her lower lip, he wondered if she knew what he was thinking. "Not usually, nay. But things havenae been so easy. I ken they havenae for ye, either, Robert. I am sorry for all ye have been through and my part in it. I simply wanted to be free for a wee bit. Free from being told where to be, what to do, how to dress, who to marry. I didnae mean to cause ye worry or risk harm." Her shoulders slumped in defeat, her words softening with every sound until he could hardly hear them, even though they were face to face.

Sympathy consumed him when he saw the defeated look on her face. He had been so buried in the loss of his brother, the battle, taking over the lairdship, being pushed into a marriage, and thinking she was with child, he had not stopped to consider how any of that had made her feel. "I understand."

Looking up at him with her large honey eyes, she looked lost and the vulnerability she tried so hard to conceal was visible once more, as it was the night up in the battlements when she asked him wed with her. "Ye do?"

"Aye. I was coming out here for a ride as well, when I was told ye and Fianna were missing. In fact, I feared ye were fleeing back to

Dunnottar. I chased after ye for over an hour in a frenzy." He smiled slightly, trying to calm her down and soften the mood. Shouting at each other clearly wasn't the answer.

Sniffling, she looked away from him for a moment and he realized she was choking back tears. "I had thought about it. Matilda convinced me to stay and marry Reginald instead. Said it would help everyone. Ye wouldnae have to marry, since I ken ye dinnae want to, and I would still keep peace between our clans and avoid lo—" Cutting herself off, she cleared her throat and looked at him once. "I would avoid a long journey home."

Something deep inside him did not believe that was what she had been about to say, but he was not sure what she meant and now that they were finally speaking calmly, he did not want to question her words, especially when they were so revealing. "Ye chose to marry Reginald for my sake?"

"Aye. I didnae need to be married to a man who would see me as a burden for the rest of his life. Reginald was more than willing to wed with me, so it seemed the right thing to do, to allow ye to choose yer own wife in due time. What happened to yer lip?" she asked, slowly reaching out to touch the pad of her finger to the cracked skin.

Of course, Reginald had been more than willing to wed her. Had she any idea how beautiful she was? How intelligent, feisty, loyal, and all around perfect she was? Nay, she truly mustn't. And, he must have done a fine job of convincing her he wasn't already half in love with her, if she believed she would ever be a burden to him. He was a cursed fool.

"Yer husband happened."

"Reginald hit ye?"

"Aye. But I hit him first."

A frown swept over her lovely face. "Why?"

Shaking his head, Robert sighed. "'Tis not important. Brother's fight. Elizabeth, can we attempt to get along? We did well enough before the battle. I ken things have changed, but I would like to get along with my sister." Saying those words so casually felt like knives in his heart. There was nothing sisterly about his feelings for her. But he could not tell her how he felt, and he could not continue fighting with her all the time. He had to learn to treat her as he would a member of his family, even if it was as a sister and not his wife.

"Aye. I would like that. Mayhap it would make this a wee bit more bearable. Ye ken, I have done all I have ever been told to do my entire life without a single complaint. But after two marriages with Irvine men, I suppose I became a bit rebellious." A soft giggle floated from her lips to his ears and he decided it was a good idea to finally back away before he lost all control of himself and leaned in to taste her for himself.

A look crossed her face when he stepped back and he wondered if it had been disappointment, or simply a trick of his imagination. Either way, it did not matter. She would never be his and he was better off accepting that now and fighting the urge to take her in his arms, press himself against her, feel her warmth, her softness, her...

"Robert?"

"Aye?"

"Are ye all right? Ye are staring at me. Is there a bug on me?" she smiled and he knew she was jesting, but the need to scan her body took hold and he allowed himself one fine glimpse of her all flushed and windswept to save to his memory forever, which sparked an idea.

"Aye, I was only thinking. Mayhap we can make a deal. Ye wish for freedom to ride the lands, but as Lady of Drum, ye are a target to surrounding clans whether ye ken it or not. Allow me to escort ye anytime ye wish to ride, and I willnae limit ye. Is that fair?"

Hesitating, she clutched the pearls around her neck and looked down, deep in thought. "I dinnae wish to burden ye, Robert. Sometimes I wish to ride spontaneously and if ye are busy—"

"Then I shall stop what I am doing to make certain the lady of our people remains safe."

"Aye, my thanks, but, is that not something my husband can do just as well?"

Irritation bubbled to the surface at the reminder of her husband, but he shook it off, determined to keep the mood lighter. "Do? Aye. Just as well? Nay." Robert scoffed and crossed his arms over his chest. "I am the best rider and even he will tell ye so. He stole my bride. The least he can allow me to do is ride with her." Those last words came out so quickly, he had no chance to stop himself and feared he had shown too much emotion.

"If a man never had something, it cannae be stolen from him," she said matter of factly, reminding him that she had never been his in the first place. Though, that was not altogether true. In his mind, for a short while, even if for only a day, she had been his. But when he awoke, she belonged to another.

Nodding and forcing a smile, Robert agreed. "I suppose ye are correct, my lady. Now, have ye had enough romping for the day? Shall I escort ye back to the castle now?"

She looked up at the sky before looking back at him with a grin. "I believe a storm is brewing. Mayhap we should leave."

Sniffing the air, he nodded, smelling that earthiness that surrounds the world just before a new rain, felt the heaviness gathering in the air. "Ye are correct. Any moment."

Just then, the sky opened up and Elizabeth squealed in delight, widening her arms to the sky, spinning circles in the grass with her wee bare feet as her skirts twirled around her legs just before becoming matted down by the fresh droplets falling to the ground like tears of all the men who had fallen at Harlaw. Mayhap they were tears, Alex's tears. Only, Robert knew Alexander would not be crying. Nay, his tears would be those of laughter and irony that his brother should be falling in love with his widow.

"Aye, Alex. I am a bloody fool." Elizabeth continued to laugh and twirl as water soaked her to the bone, her garments weighed down and now plastered to her skin, revealing the sleekness of her body beneath. She was a wonder of the world, and she was his sister.

If he knew how to cry, mayhap he would have in this moment, knowing the tears would be masked by the downpour. But after the horrors of "Red Harlaw", Robert wondered if he would ever cry again.

"All right, my lady. Let us return before ye catch an illness and my brother boxes my ears."

Light as a feather and as graceful as a swan, Elizabeth kicked her leg over Fianna, hiking her soggy skirts up one last time before sending him a wink and peeling off through the fields, back toward Drum.

Robert decided at that moment that any bit of Elizabeth he was fortunate enough to witness – her smile, the creases in the corners of her eyes when she laughed, the way that one curl in front of her head seemed to have a mind of its own – would be secretly treasured and held close to his heart. If she could not be his wife, she could be his proof that love was possible for him, even if unreachable.

Chapter Thirteen

S NEEZING FOR THE third time that morning, Elizabeth sniffled and nodded when Matilda handed her a handkerchief for her nose. "I told ye that ye would be ill come morning. What were ye thinking, dancing in that storm barefoot? Ye caught yer death."

Waving her away, Elizabeth blew her nose and smiled. "I did nay such thing. Ye worry overmuch."

"About ye? Aye, I do." Matilda pulled tighter on the laces of Elizabeth's red bodice, the dress she had chosen to wear for the feast and festivities celebrating her marriage.

Grunting, Elizabeth tried to breath. "Too tight!"

Matilda pulled on them once more and tied them up, stepping away to admire the dress. "Ye look quite lovely, Lizzie. Yer husband will be proud to have ye on his arm."

A lightness had washed over Elizabeth since returning to the castle the day before. She and Robert had argued in that field, but walked away better for it, having a greater respect for one another. She truly did not wish to spend her life angry at the man. And though she only felt stronger for him than ever, at least she was relieved to have avoided unrequited love, as was her goal. Reginald may never love her, but he respected her and gave her freedom, which was all she required.

"I still dinnae understand why ye and Robert were in that field together. That is a mistake. Ye didnae marry him. Ye cannae be wondering off alone with him," Matilda said, making a tsking noise.

"One would never believe ye are my companion and not my mother, Tilda. I ken well. I didnae ride off with him."

"Och, nay. He came after ye. That is much worse."

"He worried I was leaving Drum and would find danger, which I was close to doing. I admit I hadnae considered the borders. He caught me just before heading over the ridge to Fraser land."

"This isnae making me feel any better. Ye have become reckless and I dinnae ken what to do with ye. Marrying the wrong brother, riding off alone, returning soaking wet." She shook her head and bent over to grab Elizabeth's leather slippers, placing them on her feet, which she was mighty grateful for. Bending over with her bodice so tight would be nearly impossible.

"I married a different brother. Not the wrong one."

A rude snort came from Matilda. "I dinnae see ye dancing in the rain with Reginald." Biting her lip and taking a deep breath, Elizabeth decided it was best to stay silent. She need not defend herself. Besides, there had been no dancing in the rain. She could not help it if the storm came on so abruptly, nor if she had been so overcome by its beauty that she reveled in it a wee bit before riding home. She would have been soaked either way.

"Say what ye will, but Robert and I now have peace between us and that is all I need." Another rude sound came from Matilda and now Elizabeth could not bite her tongue. "Ye convinced me to marry Reginald! 'Twas yer idea! Now ye scold me for it?"

"Ye needed to marry an Irvine and ye refused Robert outright. It was the only option." Matilda tugged a wee bit too hard as she began to twist Elizabeth's hair into one of her masterful designs, and she fought back tears of pain, refusing to let Matilda get the best of her.

"I ken I made a mistake, all right?" Elizabeth snapped, fisting her skirts and squeezing her eyes shut. "I should have married Robert. But, I didnae. The truth is that I am in love with my husband's brother, and there is naught I can do about it. I would prefer to make it through this feast and the celebrations without ye reminding me of what a stubborn fool I am and what a mess I have made of my life!" Tears threatened to spill, but she choked them back, refusing to allow her emotions to break down now. She could cry in private later if needed, curse herself all she wanted. But right now, there were minstrels, jogglers, people from both clans, and a huge feast awaiting her in the keep.

Matilda opened her mouth to say something just as a loud knock rapped on the door. "Are ye ready, my wife? 'Tis time for the feast." Elizabeth's eyes widened and she slapped a hand over her mouth. Had Reginald heard her admit to loving his brother? The blood drained from her face as the horrible thought settled.

Looking at Matilda, she mouthed, "Do ye think he heard?" All Matilda did was shrug and walk over to open the door, allowing him entrance. She turned to face him, afraid to see anger or confusion on his face, but instead he wore a genuine smile, as always. Yet he also had a black and purple bruise over his left eye and Elizabeth suspected it was from his argument with Robert, though she had no idea what it had been about.

"Ye look beautiful. The bonniest lass in all of Aberdeen. Nay, Scotland." His gaze shot to Matilda briefly, before looking back at her. Why had he looked at Matilda that way? As if he wanted to say something he could not.

"My thanks. I am ready." Her elation over making amends with Robert seemed to disappear as dread took hold. So many people would be there to celebrate a marriage that meant nothing at all to her. But that was life, was it not? *Not if ye had married Robert.* Her mind kept reprimanding her for being a dolt, but just as quickly, she shook it off once more, trying to focus on the logical reasons she had chosen Reginald.

Placing her hand in the crook of his arm, she allowed him to lead her down the stairs to the very last place she wanted to be, the center of everyone's attention, toward the whispers of the rightfully confused members of both clans.

Soft music filled the room, along with the sounds of idle chatter and laughter. The large hearth behind the head table blazed brightly and illuminated the room along with the many wall sconces flickering as men and women entered the great hall through the front entrance facing the inner bailey.

Elizabeth had to focus on her breathing as she took her first step into the room, feeling fresh rushes beneath her feet and the scents of meat and savory sauces wafting from behind the screens. Her bodice felt tighter than ever and she hoped she would not pass out with every step she took toward the high table. With every second that passed, the voices quieted, and eyes turned in their direction. The people overall seemed pleased with the union, considering it ended their feud, yet curiosity was clearly written on all the faces she passed.

Reginald guided her to her seat next to Robert, who wore what felt like a forced smile and more knots tightened in her belly. They had resolved their issues just the day before, but the tension between them still felt irreversible, like her decision to marry his brother would forever hinder their ability to get along. He tilted his head toward Reginald with a very unnatural stiffness before addressing the crowd. "I present to ye all, the newly wedded couple," he said with little emotion. Those words felt foreign to her ears, like they were meant for someone else. She did not feel like a married woman.

Reginald grabbed her hand and smiled, and she gave a shaky grin back. When the cheers and clapping died off, she sat slowly in her chair, Reginald on her left and Robert on her right. Two seats down from Reginald, her brother sat beside their cousin, Isabella. He glanced at Elizabeth and gave her a reassuring grin, which helped comfort her a wee bit. Still, her bodice felt tighter than ever and she was certain her cheeks were just as red as the fabric of her surcoat. Placing her hands beneath the table to hide their shaking, she accidentally bumped into Robert's knee and flinched, pulling back. "I am sorry."

"No need," he said calmly without looking at her while he cut the meat on his trencher to serve to the woman sitting beside him. Elizabeth had never seen the woman before but her large green eyes and soft blond hair complemented her fair features. The lass giggled when Robert passed a large piece of meat to her and leaned in a bit closer to him.

"Who is that lass?" Elizabeth asked Reginald, leaning in so only he could hear, then placed a small bite of venison into her mouth. The ache in the pit of her stomach made certain she'd had no appetite for several days, but she had to attempt to eat the meal meant to celebrate her marriage.

"That is Marta Gordon, a prospective bride for Robert."

"A... bride?" Choking on the meat, Reginald banged on her back until she successfully swallowed the piece, tears brimming in her eyes as she choked back an embarrassing coughing fit. "That was fast."

Reginald shrugged. "Aye, well, he is laird and we share much land with the Gordons. The match had been in question for years. She quite fancies Robert, as ye can see and the marriage would secure our northern border. She had been an option for me, as well. But, I am happily married now." Winking at her, he popped a piece of meat in his mouth and smiled. "She is a bonnie lass, but not the smartest of them. I suppose it doesnae matter as long as she can run the keep and have some bairns."

Run the keep? This lass would become Lady of Drum if she married Robert. She knew the day would come, but she had not expected it to come so soon. He was supposed to be celebrating his marriage with her at this feast and, instead, he was courting another lass.

Elizabeth knew she had no right to feel angry or jealous, yet the nauseous waves pulling her under made her break into a sweat. She wanted to convince herself that she simply did not want to lose control of the castle, but that was the very least of her concerns. She was afraid of losing a man she never had, a man she could have had if not for her stubborn need to avoid emotions. Now, she was flooded with so many emotions, she did not know what to do with them.

As the meal wore on, Reginald chatted back and forth with her and her brother idly, never anything of consequence, which suited her state of mind just fine. There was no way she could concentrate on greater matters while she heard Marta's soft giggles, whispers, and sweet childlike voice tinging beside Robert, who also chuckled now and then and had, at one point, completely turned his back to Elizabeth.

Matilda was at one of the long rectangular tables laughing with some of the other people from Clan Keith, but kept stealing furtive glances at Elizabeth and Reginald. Once again, her strange behavior was not unnoticed, but Elizabeth was good and well stuck at that table until the festivities wore down. "Have ye noticed that Matilda has been acting strangely? She keeps looking at us as if we have food on our faces."

"I dinnae ken," he said with a shrug and began speaking with her brother once more. Huffing out a sigh, Elizabeth simply folded her hands on her lap under the table and looked down at her half-full trencher, trying to stifle a yawn at her own wedding feast.

"My laird!" A man swiftly came through the door, causing the fires in the sconces to flicker as a draft flew in. Approaching the table was Finlay, the marshal, and Elizabeth sat up straight, knowing only one thing would bring him in to disrupt the feast. "Tis Aina. She is in labor, my laird. I came to fetch ye at yer request."

Standing up quickly, Robert pushed away from his chair and Elizabeth stood up, as well. "I am coming," she said and stepped around

Robert to leave the high table.

Grabbing her arm, he pulled her back. "Nay. This is nay place for a lady and ye should stay at yer own wedding feast."

Jerking her arm out of his grip, she scowled at him. "The feast is nearly over, my husband has been speaking with my brother for an hour while I sit and stare at my food, and I am the one who visits Aina every day in the stables. I wish to comfort her."

Snorting, Robert rolled his eyes and blocked her way. "Ye arenae needed."

"I dinnae ken why ye care so much whether I come or go. Ye arenae my husband."

"Aye, and thank God's mercy for that. Ye are stubborn and willful and opinionated."

Eyes widening in shock at his words before narrowing on him once more, Elizabeth ground her teeth and clenched her fist. So much for their short-lived peace. "And ye are a bullheaded, controlling arse!"

Reginald popped out of his chair and stepped close to Elizabeth, pulling her against him. "Dinnae speak to my wife in that manner!"

"Oh, do shut up!" Robert roared at his brother. "This is all yer fault in the first place!" Marta's wide green eyes looked between the three of them, jaw slack. Fortunately, the lass knew to stay out of it and keep quiet. Mayhap she was smarter than she looked.

"How is any of this my fault? I didnae inseminate the ridiculous mare," Reginald said defensively, but a small smirk played across his face and Elizabeth scowled at him as well. Was this all a game to Reginald? He took nothing seriously, which was half the reason why she decided to marry him, but already his careless mannerisms grated on her nerves.

"I have had enough of the both of ye!" Robert waved them away and stormed from them. Watching him sprint toward the inner bailey with Finlay in his wake, Elizabeth realized the entirety of the hall was staring at the scene. Naturally. They had been loud enough to wake the dead. Some wedding feast.

But, if Robert thought he could command her to stay put like a wee good lassie, he had another think coming. Picking up the skirts of her heavy red dress and taking a stifled breath as the corset pinched into her breasts once more, Elizabeth determinedly stomped her way out of the keep and toward the stables. She would be there when Aina foaled, and nobody, not even her lout of a laird was going to stop her.

HE KNEW SHE was following behind him. He could feel her presence all over his body, creeping up his neck and tingling his scalp like an energy he was beholden to. He had tried to make peace, tried to put it all aside, shove his feelings for Elizabeth into the darkest corner of his heart and court Marta instead. It had been going well until he had to actually speak to Elizabeth.

"Ye dinnae follow instructions well, do ye?" he asked without looking behind him.

"Not when they come from a man with nay sense of reason, nay," she huffed, clearly trying to keep up with his steps.

Spinning on his heels, he faced her and stopped so abruptly, she plowed into him and gasped when he grabbed her arms to steady her. "Ye are the one who makes nay sense, my lady. Why would ye marry my ridiculous brother instead of me?" Robert gave her a small shake and she gripped his waist to gain some purchase.

"I told ye why! I dinnae ken why ye care!"

"I dinnae!" he roared, feeling the blood run to his face. He knew he was acting boorish but the cursed lass drove him mad in every way possible. He wanted to shake her, yell, confess his love, press his lips to hers and lay her down in the stables, lift her skirts and show her how a real man made love to his woman. But, she was not his and that only made him want to shout more.

"Good!" she replied, digging her nails into his side almost painfully. They were so close together he could feel her breasts pressed against his chest. Looking down, he saw them heaving as she breathed, straining against her bodice. How he wanted to pull the string and watch them come tumbling out in to his hands. He would feel their softness and warmth and know even more of her beauty. "Ye have Marta waiting for ye in the keep, so ye neednae worry over me or my husband!" she quipped.

Leaning closer, he grazed his lips so gently against her ear that he would have wondered if she felt it, if not for the shuddering of her body. "Ye are right, Lizzie. I do." Pulling away, he left her standing there, suddenly alone, swerving slightly as if in a daze. Good. Mayhap he gave her something to think about. It was too late to rectify what had transpired. Despite his deep yearning for Elizabeth, he could never have her. It would take all the strength he owned to keep from trying to steal her away, but he was not that sort of man, brother, or laird. She had chosen otherwise and he would have to live with it. Some sick satisfaction came over him when he realized she was affected by him and his touch. That would have to suffice for the moment.

"My laird! She is ready to foal!" He heard Finlay shout from the stables, holding up a lantern to see what was taking them so long. Elizabeth sniffed in frustration and shoved past him toward the stables. Grumbling, Robert followed, knowing he had no control over what she did and having no more time to argue with her.

"The foal appears to be breech!" Finlay grunted, rolling up the sleeves of his tunic and getting on his knees in front of the horse who whinnied in distressed, thrashing her head and rolling her eyes.

"Poor, sweet Aina," Elizabeth soothed, also crouching in the hay and running her hands over the horse's strained neck. "The foal's hind feet are coming. That, indeed, means she is breech. She may be able to birth on her own, but the hips will be the deciding point. We may need to pull its feet to reposition the foal."

"Aye, ye are correct, my lady," Finlay said with a nod.

Robert stepped forward, rolled up his sleeves and looked sideways at her. "Ye have done this before?"

Continuing to caress Aina's neck, Elizabeth nodded. "Aye. I always insisted on being present at the foaling. I love horses and we share a bond. I feel as if my presence is calming to them." Robert watched at Aina's breathing calmed with every stroke of Elizabeth's fingers and he knew she was correct in coming here tonight. She truly was a calming presence to the mare.

"Ye are a remarkable woman, my lady. Drum is fortunate to have ye," Finlay said with a smile.

Clearing his throat, Robert got on his knees between Elizabeth and Finlay, having also seen many foalings but having been involved in none.

"May I ask a favor of ye, my lady? If it isnae too much?" Finlay asked with a shaky voice. "With yer wedding feast happening, I am short-handed out here and there is another horse that is in need of help with a punctured hoof. I hate to ask ye but—"

"I can tend to Aina while ye tend to the other horse, Finlay."

"I am sorry to ask. But, ye seem capable and she trusts ye and I need to tend the other horse before an infection can set in and I—"

"Really. 'Tis all right. If I am in need of ye, I will call for ye." Elizabeth smiled sweetly at Finlay and Robert was even more in awe of her than ever. She was indeed stubborn and outspoken but she was capable and kind, as well.

Finlay left and Robert was struck by how calm Elizabeth was while the foal's hooves protruded from its mother. "All right. Robert. I need ye to soothe her and keep her calm while I attempt to turn the foal, but first..." Reaching around her back, Elizabeth pulled on the string of her bodice, unloosening the garment swiftly before stepping out of her red dress altogether. Naught but a shift was worn beneath and Robert shifted, looking away but not before he saw the impression of her nipples pushing through her sheer white linen.

"Why are ye disrobing?" he asked, doing as she said and speaking softly while stroking the horse's neck. His heart beat hard in his chest being so close to her in a state of undress, yet he knew there must be a reason for her behavior even if it did serve as a distraction to him.

"My bodice as too tight. I told Matilda but she didnae care. It was hard enough to move at dinner, but I cannae birth a foal with such constrictions." He nodded, deciding that made perfect sense and also quite glad he was not forced to wear such things on most occasions. The worst he had to endure were hose and a doublet if attending a royal event which, fortunately for him, was almost never, especially with King James still being held by the English.

Getting up on her knees, Elizabeth placed her hands around the hind legs of the foal, looking sideways at Robert. "Are ye ready? This will cause her distress."

"Aye," he said and swallowed hard, getting closer to the mare and murmuring reassuring words he was certain she could not understand. He felt completely helpless but, for once, it was refreshing to put trust in someone else's hands and allow them to take control.

As Elizabeth started to slowly turn the foal, the mare neighed in protest and began bucking her head and her eyes rolled back. "Is she all right?" Robert asked, feeling sorry for the poor creature. He had seen many foalings but never one such as this and never had he assisted, not that he was doing more than comforting her.

"I am doing all I can... to make sure... she is all right," Elizabeth said panting through clenched teeth and beginning to sweat. A lantern hung on the stall wall but little light was available otherwise. He could see the pained look on Elizabeth's face mixed with concern and sympathy.

Suddenly, the mare seized and made a horrible sound just as the foal came tumbling out, landing on top of Elizabeth. Robert watched in awe as if everything had slowed down before him. When Elizabeth tumbled backward with the foal on top of her, her arms wrapped around the wee thing's bloody body, Robert dove for her and put his hand beneath her head.

"Are ye all right, Lizzie?" He looked her up and down but all he could see were long brown limbs, blood, some sort of slimy coating, and Elizabeth sprawled beneath it all.

Pure joy could be heard in her laughter as she landed in a pile of hay behind her. Staring at her, covered in blood and hair all disheveled, she was still the most beautiful woman he had ever seen. Her excitement was contagious and his heart felt as if it may burst watching her hold the wee foal in her arms. Someday, she would hold a bairn in a similar way, only that bairn would be his brother's, not his. Energy filled the space between them when her eyes, full of wonder, locked with his, gold flecks sparkling in their depths. New life had come into this world, filling the barn with a sensation Robert seldom felt any longer: hope. Hope that he could be happy even if he knew the truth of her feelings. He may never have her for his wife, but mayhap just knowing that what he felt, what he saw in her eyes, heard in her laughter, was more than just the excitement of the moment.

"Elizabeth, do ye love Reginald?" He heard the words come from his own mouth, wishing he could immediately take them back when her laughter died and she sat up slowly, propping herself up on her elbows as the foal began to fumble, trying to stand up on its own for the first time. How could five words make the entire mood shift?

"That is an odd question to ask of me in the moment."

"Is it?"

"Aye. Why does it matter? I had to marry an Irvine, so I did." Licking her lips, she looked away from him quickly, breaking eye contact as she stared at the flames in the lantern "Love was never something I expected to find," she whispered.

"So... ye did find it, then?" An ache in his heart pinched at him and he suddenly felt like the walls of the stable were closing in on him. She loved his brother. Even though he could never have her, knowing she would never love him and never had hurt worse than he expected. What a fool he was to ask such a question and allow her answer to affect him so profoundly.

Elizabeth snapped her gaze back to him and petted Aina softly as the foal continued to wobble and fall on her four new legs. "Aye. I did."

Nodding, Robert closed his eyes and turned away. No longer could he gaze at the only woman he'd ever cared about and listen to her admit to loving his brother. "I am glad for ye." It was true. Despite the heartache of not being the man she chose, not being the man she loved, Robert simply wanted her to be happy. Yet, she never seemed happy when in Reginald's presence. She was not unhappy, either, yet her spirit seemed as dull as a rose that had once shone in the sunlight until being neglected too long.

Hearing shuffling in the hay, he looked over his shoulder and saw her stand up, her linen shift covered in Aina's blood. "I need to change out of this before I put my dress on once more. Can ye... turn around?" Her eyes shifted nervously between him and the floor. He saw her dress tossed into a heap on the ground, covered in hay. If someone came in at this moment, they would wonder what had just happened.

"Of course. I will leave ye now." Bowing his head, he turned on his heels and began to walk away, feeling the keen need for distance between him and Elizabeth before he sinned and took his brother's wife in his arms.

"Robert." Turning around once more, he saw a blush creep up her face in the flickering fire light. "I will need help tying the laces on my surcoat."

"That... I cannae do that, Lizzie. Mayhap I can go back and find

Matilda or another lady, even Reginald. I cannae dress ye."

A frown crossed her face and her brow crinkled slightly. "I ken ye dinnae care for me much, but I am not asking ye for more than tying me up in back. Ye would rather I stood here in the cold alone while ye fetched someone?"

The air felt thick as he tried to breathe. The pit of his stomach clamped and his heart twisted. She thought he disliked her? "If ye want me to help, I shall." Turning around, he stared at the foal instead, who was still struggling to get up on her legs without falling over again and bent over to rub Aina's neck while he awaited.

The sound of footsteps crunching in the fresh hay made Robert stand up quickly and look toward the entry to the stables. The figure of a short, stocky man walked toward him, his features distorted in the shadows. "Evening, my laird," the deep voice said just as a face came into view, then stopped dead in his tracks, mouth agape.

Elizabeth screeched and ran to Robert, hiding her nude form behind him, desperately trying to cover what she could with the fabric of her dress. Realizing what the scene must look like, Elizabeth behind him naked, Aina on the floor of the stables, blood and a foal just beginning to walk. He felt Elizabeth gripping his shoulders, burrowing her face into his back. He did not owe anyone an explanation, yet he felt compelled to protect Elizabeth's honor before anyone believed she would betray her husband. "Lady Elizabeth has safely delivered this foal, but became covered in blood and was simply changing while my back was turned."

"'Tis not my business, Laird." Ewan smirked and put his hands up with a shrug, clearly not believing Robert's story.

Elizabeth gasped behind him, peeking from around his side. He felt her breasts pressing against his back and grit his teeth. How cruel a fate to have the woman he loved pressed against him while nude and he could not see, nor touch her.

"Father!" Elizabeth yelped and buried herself more into his back.

"I… this isnae… I would never…"

"Father?" Robert asked, looking at the man he knew as the black-smith's father, not Elizabeth's father. Ewan blanched and started to slowly back away when he saw who was hiding behind him. "Ewan!" Robert roared, stopping the man in his tracks. "What are ye keeping from me, to be backing away with fear in yer eyes? Why is the Lady of Drum, who is a Keith, calling ye father?" He had no idea what was happening, but he knew deep in his gut that something was off. Elizabeth seemed distraught and nervous in the man's presence and Ewan looked as if he had seen a ghost.

Ewan stuttered something unintelligible before muttering, "He paid me to do it. I needed to feed my family…"

"Do *what?*" Robert demanded, clenching his fists. He did not like secrets being kept, especially ones that seemed to cause distraught to the Lady of Drum.

"He is the cleric who married me and Reginald, Robert. Mayhap Reginald paid him for his service. But I vow, Father, this isnae what it appears," Elizabeth said beseechingly. He could feel her shaking against him and knew how much her faith meant to her. To be caught undressed with her husband's brother must be making her feel like the wanton he had once accused her of being. Shame would always consume him every time he remembered that moment and his cruel treatment of her. He would never forgive himself, for he had lost her in that moment, practically drove her into his brother's arms. And now she was in love with Reginald. Only…

The wheels in his mind continued to turn for what felt like an eternity of silence as anger and relief warred within. How could Ewan have married them legally? He could not have. She was not married…

"Laird?"

"Robert?"

Both of them called to him, knocking him out of his thoughts. "Ewan. I am not done with ye. Go now. I will decide what to do with ye later."

"Aye, my laird." Tipping his head, Ewan scuttled off faster than Robert had suspected the man could move.

"What was that all about? Why was he so frightened?" Elizabeth asked from behind him. He felt her weight ease off his back, heard the sounds of fabric rustling. Keeping his back turned, he stayed silent until she was ready for him to tie her laces.

Feeling a tap on his shoulder, he turned to see Elizabeth mostly dressed, with just her shoulders and back exposed as she held the front to her chest. Putting his hands on her shoulders, he took a deep breath and decided to simply tell her the truth.

"Elizabeth. Ye arenae truly married to Reginald." And, Robert would gut his brother for lying to her and sharing her bed.

CHAPTER FOURTEEN

ER BODY SHOOK both from the chill of the night seeping through the wooden slats of the stables and from her rattled nerves. When the priest who married her and Reginald came in and caught her undressed, she knew he would assume the very worst of her, yet she still remained untouched by any man. Hiding behind Robert had been her only option, yet he felt so warm and safe despite the circumstances.

The interaction between Robert and Father Ewan continued to play repeatedly through her mind, the last bit making no sense whatsoever. Why would Robert say she was not married to Reginald? Even now, as his hands rested on her bared shoulders, his words slowly infiltrated her mind. His grip tightened and she felt him shake. His touch felt like the sweetest sin, the grandest temptation of her life. How she wished his words to be true, to be able to undo her folly.

"Did ye hear me?" His breath, soft and warm, caressed her earlobe, causing chills to run up her neck.

"I hear ye, but I dinnae ken what ye mean," she responded softly, closing her eyes and enjoying the feel of his nimble fingers tugging at the ties of her bodice.

For a long while, all she heard was his deep breathing and she wondered what he was thinking, what he was trying to say that had him unable to speak. Once she felt him tie off the strings, she turned around to face him, looking up at his height and frowning at the look of pain and anger in his glazed over eyes. "Are ye angry at me? I am sorry I put ye in this position... I will explain it to Reginald... he will understand and—"

"Wheesht, Lizzie!" he growled and ran his hands through his dark hair. His dimple showed in the flicker of the light and she longed to reach out and touch his beard, to soothe whatever hurt he felt, yet she somehow, without words, understood that she was the reason for his pain. "Ye said ye love Reginald, aye?"

Looking away, Elizabeth pursed her lips and crossed her arms, missing the warmth of his touch only moments ago. Now he was cold and distant, asking questions she did not wish to answer, appearing ready to punch a hole through the walls of the stables. The foal had long ago found her footing and began to nurse on Aina, so Elizabeth slowly shut the door to their stall, knowing they were doing well and that Finlay would be back soon.

"Ye willnae answer my question."

"I dinnae wish to."

"Why not? Is it so hard to admit ye love yer husband?"

"Nay." She scowled at him, not liking his harsh tone or how he went from tender to aggressive in the span of a moment. Yet, what hurt the most was being so close to him, having felt his touch on her, knowing it was wrong but enjoying it anyway, knowing she can never be his.

"Then why can ye not just say the words?" he barked, causing her to flinch.

"Why do ye care so much if I do?" she shouted back, pushing against the solid expanse of his chest. "Stop shouting at me! I have done naught to ye! Why do ye always become so angry with me? Why do ye hate me?" She felt tears begin to brim in her eyes, but forced herself to stay strong. He did not deserve her tears.

"For all that is holy, ye frustrating woman! Can ye not see it? I dinnae hate ye! I love ye! I love ye so much that I feel ill to my stomach every time I think of ye with my brother! I feel like ye tore my heart out and stomped on it every time I remember that ye chose him over me! And right now, I feel so utterly lost wanting to kiss ye until ye cannae breathe, and kenning that ye dinnae want the same from me! I may not be a perfect man, Elizabeth. I made mistakes and I apologized for them. I didnae want to love ye. Marrying ye meant my brother was dead. I would have come to terms with it and been happy to marry ye, but ye gave me nay chance! Ye ran off with Reg! Ye wee fool. I could have loved ye better than him!"

Now tears ran down her face like a torrential storm, blinding her with their constant flow. Her heart shuddered in her chest and she folded her arms over her stomach, feeling as if she would be ill. "Robert... I... am sorry. I cannae say how I feel without being unfaithful!" Sliding down the wall of the stables, she huddled into a ball, pulling her knees up protectively into her chest. "I have erred gravely," she sobbed into her arms. "For 'tis not Reginald I love."

Taking two large strides closer to her, Robert kneeled down in front of her and placed his hands on her knees. "Who do ye love then, lass?"

Looking up, she locked gazes with him and shook her head. She could not, would not, say the words. She had chosen this path, and Reginald had saved her by marrying her. She would not betray him by confessing her love to his brother.

"Ye arenae married to Reginald, Elizabeth. Not in truth."

Shaking her head again, she sniffled and wiped her eyes. "Ye keep saying that, but I dinnae ken what ye mean. Father Ewan married us. Matilda witnessed it."

"Nay. I cannae understand why and I vow I will get answers, but Ewan isnae a clergyman. He cannae have married ye legally nor in the eyes of the Lord. And believe me when I tell ye that I will make Reginald suffer greatly for having bed ye while ye believed him to be yer husband. What he has done is worth casting him out!" he growled.

"Robert... I am not married?" How could that be? Why? What purpose did fooling her into a marriage serve? Did Matilda know? Thinking back on the last few days and how oddly her friend had been behaving, a wave of sadness washed over her. Matilda knew. Humiliation was a new emotion for her, and it did not sit well in the pit of her belly. Yet relief, somehow, was her predominant emotion. She was not married to a man she did not love, and the man she did love had just confessed to feeling the same for her.

"Robert, I dinnae ken why they did this, but I do ken that Matilda was in on it. She has been acting strangely. Still, there are two verra important things I must tell ye before we do aught else. The first thing is that Reginald hasnae shared my bed. Nor did Alexander. I am a maiden still, I vow it. Whatever Reginald's intentions, he didnae take advantage of me. He has been kind and proper, keeping his distance and behaving rather detached. I simply didnae mind because... well, because the second thing I must confess is... I love ye, as well, Robert. 'Tis ye I fell in love with. None other. I have loved ye since the night ye comforted me on the battlements."

"Ye love me, lass?" Robert said softly and his features smoothed out, years of stress and pain seeming to vanish before her eyes.

"Aye, I do. I was a fool to think marrying Reginald would be the safe choice. I wanted to avoid the pain of love, the pain of losing someone I loved or never having the love in return. I felt like a life of duty was preferable to loving someone until it became a weakness. But, I was wrong. Nothing hurt more than not being able to tell ye how I felt. To believing I would have to life with this pain for the rest of my life. I cannae understand why he did what he did but, right now, I am too happy to care."

"Lizzie..." Robert's blue eyes melted her insides and he leaned in closer to her, placing his forehead against hers. It felt as if her heart would explode in her chest, being so close to Robert and knowing he felt the same way about her. "I love ye. I am sorry I ever made ye feel like I didnae want ye. And I am sorry I insulted yer honor. I am a bloody fool."

"Love makes fools of us all, does it not?" she whispered, then giggled, feeling happiness flow through her in a way she had never felt before.

"Mayhap. I ken I am a fool for ye. That much is certain. I have never been so miserable in all my life, believing ye would never be mine. I am too bloody happy to be overly angry at Reginald. But I vow, we shall get answers."

"Matilda was in on it. She would never hurt me. Something tells me we were set up," Elizabeth sighed and placed her hand on his arm.

Sitting down next to her, Robert scooped her up quickly and placed her in his lap, causing her to squeal and wrap her arms around his neck. "Set up, ye say?" His face was so close to hers and she wondered, hoped, prayed that he would kiss her.

"Aye. It was our belief that we couldnae be together that brought us together in the end, is it not? They kenned we would be drawn to one another through our pain. Tilda is a mischievous lass, but I have never been on the other end of one of her schemes until now. Though I am embarrassed for having fallen into their web, right now, I cannae be angry."

Robert's strong arms wrapped tighter around her waist and she felt something hard digging into her backside. She was certain of what it was and blushed wildly. "I shall never be angry again for the rest of my days if I can hold ye like this every night."

Did a swarm of butterflies just hatch within her belly? She felt as if she might float away. She had come here to birth a foal, had been so angry at Robert in the beginning. Now, she was in his lap with no shift beneath her dress, listening to him confess his love. "What are ye saying, Robert?"

"Elizabeth, I cannae ever lose ye again. I love ye more than I ever thought I could love a woman. Ye are kind. Instead of making an enemy of Mary, ye made her a friend. Ye are hard-working and loyal. Ye came here a stranger and embraced our people. Everyone respects ye. Ye are intelligent and selfless, giving of yer time to visit the horses and help them foal. I have never met a more remarkable woman in my entire life. And, ye are more beautiful than any lass I have or will ever meet. Will ye marry me? I will make certain we have a true clergyman, I vow it."

Laughing, Elizabeth nuzzled closer and kissed him on the cheek. "Aye! I will marry ye, Robert Irvine. Ye were always meant to be my love. I was a foolish lass to ever believe otherwise."

"And I was a foolish man. Mayhap we can be foolish together." Robert chuckled softly then slowly leaned in, bringing his lips closer to hers. Heart pounding and breath quickening, Elizabeth licked her lips and closed her eyes, leaning in to press her mouth softly against his in what would be her first real kiss in her entire life.

When they connected, she felt that same spark of energy she had felt every time their hands had touched, yet it was deeper and more profound, like she finally found where she belonged. His lips were soft and firm and when he deepened the kiss, she allowed him to take control. Waves of excitement flowed through her body, finally being in Robert's strong embrace, knowing he could forgive her for her mistakes and still want to marry her.

When his tongue pressed against her lips, begging for entry, she opened her mouth slightly and reveled in the feel of him. Her tongue slowly danced with his, causing shivers of desire to run through her body as a moan escaped her lips.

Pulling away slightly, Robert pressed his forehead to hers once more and sighed. "I have wanted to do that since the first moment I saw ye arrive on yer horse."

"I have wanted to do that since the first time ye spoke to me," she confessed, feeling herself turn flush from her admission. "I have never kissed a man like that before."

"I am pleased to be yer first in all things. But, we shouldnae tarry here. Finlay will be back and it is getting late. Besides, we need to find Reginald and Matilda. I need some answers and if they arenae to my liking, I will bloody my brother for the trouble he has caused."

His eyes darkened as he stood, bringing her up with him. Bending over, he picked up her ruined shift from the stack of hay and bunched it up in his palm. "I ken ye are angry, as am I. But, before ye resort to bloodying anyone, may I attempt to get answers my own way?"

"How do ye plan on doing that?" he asked, looking down at her and making her shiver all over once more. His eyes looked at her with such emotion, so much love and respect that she wondered how she had never noticed it before.

"I think they both deserve a wee bit of scheming in return, aye? Matilda has been up to all sorts of trouble for years. This time, she has gone too far and I plan to find out why she made a fool of me, and I ken just how to do it."

Robert stepped closer to kiss her lips softly, wrapping his arms around her waist and pulled her close. "Ye are a devious one. I will leave it to ye, if ye allow me to handle Reginald."

"I believe 'tis time for us to teach them a lesson about messing with the lives of others," Elizabeth said with a smirk and wrapped her arms around Robert's neck, kissing him once more before she set off to find her plotting maid.

SNEAKING INTO THE keep through the kitchens, Elizabeth hoped to make it to the tower stairs before being seen by any passersby. She was certain she had hay bits in her hair and she felt odd without her shift on. Though she had done nothing wrong, she felt as if she was a wee lass sneaking into the home before her parents caught her.

"Ye look like ye are up to no good."

Turning around, Elizabeth spotted Mary in the corner of the kitchen nibbling on bits of leftover bread from the feast. The staff had mostly retired for the night and it was otherwise pitch black aside from a few sconces flickering on the wall. Sighing in relief to find her friend, Elizabeth smiled and walked over to her. "As are ye, sneaking around the kitchens in the middle of the night. Shameful."

Swallowing her last bite, Mary squinted her eyes and looked Elizabeth up and down. "Ye look happier than ye have since ye arrived at Drum, and it isnae a coincidence that it happened on the same night ye have hay in yer hair." Crossing her arms, she waited for Elizabeth to respond.

"I was helping Aina foal, 'tis all."

"'Tis all, my round arse," Mary laughed. "Ye are up to something. I ken it."

Sighing, Elizabeth looked around to make sure nobody was near, then pulled her friend even further into the shadows. "If I tell ye, do ye promise not to tell anyone?"

"That ye were cuckolding yer husband with his brother?" Only Mary could say such a thing and not sound at all reproving.

"That is the verra thing, Mary. Reginald isnae my husband. I dinnae ken why, but Matilda and Reginald had the blacksmith's father, Ewan, stand in as a clergyman for our vows."

"So, ye arenae married?"

Elizabeth shook her head. "But I will be. As soon as we found out, Robert asked me to marry him. He loves me, Mary!"

Rolling her eyes and shoving more bread in her mouth, Mary spit out a few crumbs as she tried to speak with a full mouth. "Ye are the only person in the castle who would be surprised by that."

"I think I was so determined to avoid being hurt that all I did was hurt myself more. I am a foolish woman."

"But now ye can make it right. As for me, I have a bairn on the way and nobody." Mary rubbed her belly and sighed, but at least she did not burst into tears as she tended to do. Elizabeth knew they needed to find a husband for Mary soon, but she had no idea who.

"Ye have me and Robert and Reginald. We are yer family now. That bairn will be a cousin to my children someday." Squeezing Mary's hand, she smiled and clutched her pearl rosary. "I vow we will find ye a good husband. But for now, I have answers to pull out of Matilda and I plan on making her feel what it is like on the other end of her schemes."

Shoving the last piece of bread in her mouth, Mary wiped the crumbs on her surcoat and smirked. "I willnae miss this. I am coming with ye."

Together, they walked up the tower stares while Elizabeth filled Mary in on all she knew and how she planned to discover more. When they reached her chamber door, Elizabeth pinched her cheeks to redden them, then rubbed her eyes to make it look as if she had been crying. Opening the door quickly, she heard Matilda squeak in fright as she sat on the edge of the bed wringing her hands nervously.

"There ye are. I have been wondering where ye were. Ye have been gone a long while. I sent Reginald to find ye in the stables and ye were all gone. He said Finlay was with the new foal, and said ye had left a wee bit ago. Where have ye been?"

Inwardly, Elizabeth smirked. This was the perfect set up for her plan and, she was relieved that she and Robert had left before Reginald had spotted them and ruined her fun. Keeping a frown on her face and rubbing her eyes, she felt Mary standing beside her, holding her hand in mock support and she squeezed back. "I am a terrible, awful, sinful woman!" Elizabeth wailed and collapsed on the floor, clutching her pearl rosary with one hand and covering her face with the other. Mary rubbed her back and Elizabeth had to do her best to cover her smile. She was not as skilled a schemer as Matilda, but she was determined to get answers.

"What happened?" Matilda asked and dropped to her knees beside Elizabeth, touching her leg.

"I have done the verra worst thing a woman can do, Tilda. The verra worst. I will surely burn in hell for what I have done. I will be shunned!"

"Nothing ye could ever do would be so bad, Lizzie. Tell me. Did ye... kill someone?"

A real gasp escaped Elizabeth and she looked at her friend, crinkling her brow. "Are ye mad? I would never!"

"Well, good. Then whatever ye have done cannae be so bad."

"It is! I vow I have done something wicked, and yet I cannae regret it, which only makes me more wicked!"

"What have ye done, then?"

"I... I fell in love with my husband's brother! I tried, Tilda. But, I cannae help it." Elizabeth lowered her head once more and pretended to sob into her hands once more, hoping she was being convincing.

"Lizzie... I ken ye love Robert. Everyone kens it. Ye cannae help how ye feel, only what ye do about those feelings."

"That's just it! I have... done something about those feelings!"

Looking up, she was impressed to see Matilda turning white as blood drained from her face. "Oh, Lizzie... did ye..."

"Aye! He confessed his love for me and we just... couldnae help it! And now I have lain with my husband's brother and the guilt will surely destroy me and I will never be forgiven for my heinous sin!"

Matilda went silent while Mary rubbed her back and she continued her performance, hoping it was enough to get her companion to admit the truth and explain herself. If not, her plan would backfire, her friend always believing she was an adulteress when, in reality, she was still a maiden.

"Lizzie... I... I must tell ye something. Something I swear I did only for ye, because ye were too stubborn to face the truth and I had hoped that it would make ye see how ye truly felt. Ye arenae an adulterer because—"

"Because I am not truly married to Reginald." Elizabeth cleared her throat and stood up slowly, calmly, keeping her features as stone-like as possible, crossing her arms. "I already ken, Tilda. I met *Father Ewan*, who is only father to the blacksmith, not a clergyman. Robert was with me. We ken what ye and Reginald have done, but we cannae ken why ye would do such a thing." Anger warred inside. She wanted to shout and rage at her friend, but she needed to know what happened and still, despite it all, trusted Tilda enough to believe that she had meant well.

Sighing, Tilda lowered her shoulders in defeat once she was standing before Elizabeth and nodded. "Aye. I am relieved ye ken. 'Tis been awful lying to ye. I am sorry. Ye were threatening to run away and I couldnae allow it. I had to keep ye here and if ye were too bloody stubborn to marry the man ye loved, I made sure ye stayed here until ye figured yerself out. 'Tis not my fault ye are a stubborn woman, Elizabeth Keith." Now Matilda was crossing her arms and straightening her back, ready to defend her honor in a way that made Elizabeth bite back a chuckle of amusement.

"What did ye think was truly going to come of this. Tilda?"

"Exactly what has come of it, ye ridiculous woman! I had hoped that being married to Reginald and being around Robert, realizing ye loved the man and being unable to be with him, would open yer eyes to what ye could have had! And, ye can! Ye arenae married. Only, I didnae think ye had it in ye to sleep with yer husband's brother. Never did I expect ye to find out this way and torture yerself. I am sorry, Lizzie."

Mary giggled beside Elizabeth and they looked at each other smugly. "Come now, Tilda. I am still a maiden I wouldnae do such a thing. Yer plan did work, as underhanded as it was. I have been miserable and 'tis only been a matter of days. I would never have survived this for a lifetime."

"Oh, well thank the heavens for that. It worked. Reginald only agreed because he also kens his brother loves ye and wanted to drive Robert mad with jealousy."

"It was an awful trick, Tilda."

"It was awful of ye to put me in the position to have to do so, threatening to leave Irvine land unattended. Ye are a daft woman when ye are so stubborn. Is loving a man really so bad?"

"Nay. It is wonderful! And as soon as we discovered the truth, Robert asked me to marry him! We will have to plan it soon, before our clan leaves for Keith lands once more. William will be thrilled."

"William will likely attempt to kill Reginald. That isnae something he will be thrilled about. Lizzie, ye have made a mess of things. The entire castle will be scandalized."

"I care not anymore. I was untouched by both brothers, I vow. I was never truly married to Reginald. I am certain all will be confused, but we shall clear it up and move on. I will nay longer live without Robert."

"I am sorry I caused ye pain. I love ye dearly, Lizzie. I hope ye ken I did this for love of ye, as Reg did this for love of Robert."

Sighing, Elizabeth took Matilda's hand and squeezed it tightly. "I do ken that, aye. I only care about moving forward now. All will be well, for me now anyway. I wouldnae want to be Reginald right now."

"Robert may verra well box his ears," Mary nodded. "These Irvine brothers are kenned for that."

"Oh, nay, I dinnae think Robert will do such a thing. Reginald was only trying to help," Matilda said. "Let us go to sleep. 'Tis been a long night. On the morrow, we will sort everything out."

Elizabeth hesitated, pondering why Matilda seemed so defensive of

Reginald, but decided Matilda was correct. She was happier than she ever remembered being in her life and was ready for this day to be over, so she may wake up in the morn, clear this mess up and make plans to marry the only man she should have ever married in the first place.

CHAPTER FIFTEEN

SPOTTING REGINALD ON the way up the tower stairs, Robert sped his pace to catch up to his scheming brother, wondering where he was heading. He was much too pleased with how the night had ended to be over-angry, but he still was determined to get answers and give his brother what he deserved.

"There ye are, Brother. Just the man I've been looking for." Turning slowly on the stairs, Reginald looked down at Robert who was only a few steps below him and gave him his usual lazy smile.

"Have ye? It seems ye have done nothing but avoid me the last few days and scowl. Here ye are, seeking me out and even with a grin upon yer face. Did yer visit with Marta go that well?" Reginald waggled his brows suggestively and Robert smiled, stepping up a few more stairs to bring himself level with his brother.

"Nay, alas I havenae spoken with her since the meal, but I did run into Ewan from the village."

"Oh, aye?" Reginald kept a straight face, but Robert knew his brother well enough to detect his underlying guilt. Mayhap it was the twitch of his upper lip or the way his eyes shifted to the side for a split second before looking back, but Robert had been able to see through Reginald his entire life.

"Aye. I was quite surprised when Elizabeth called him Father. Even more surprised when she said he was the clergyman who conducted yer marriage ceremony." Robert popped his knuckles, a clear sign that his mood was growing sour. Aye, he was elated to finally have Elizabeth for his own, but he would have married her today had it not been for Reginald's meddling.

"Ah."

"Is that all ye have to say? How about ye explain to me why ye stole my bride from me just to fake a marriage, Reginald? Before I box yer ears and kick yer arse!" Now he was angry. Being face to face with his brother and his smug grin, remembering the way he spoke of his Elizabeth, lying that they had made love. The thought made his stomach churn and his right arm pulled back as his fist clenched and flew toward his brother's nose of its own volition.

Grunting from the sudden and unexpected impact, Reginald stumbled back and up a few more steps to the second floor, holding his nose as blood dripped out. "Are ye mad?"

"Aye, I am mad and right pissed off. Ye meddled in my life and risked losing an alliance! All for what? Another of yer games? Elizabeth isnae a game!" Robert roared and walked up to his brother again, wishing more than anything to plant another fist into his face, but holding back. He needed answers and wouldn't get them if Reginald was unconscious or toothless.

"Ye're a bloody fool, Rob!" Reginald swung back and knocked him on the side of this jaw, causing him to fall back into the corridor. "Ye should have told her how ye felt! I did this for ye!"

Getting up on his feet once more, Robert charged at Reginald and knocked him back against the wall with a thud. With an incredulous snort, Robert pinned his brother against the cold stone wall. "For me, or yer cock? All ye care about is bedding women! I ken how ye looked at Elizabeth! Ye wanted her for yerself! Ye lied to her, tricked her into a false marriage, and then lied to me about bedding her! Why?" He shook Reginald hard, but his brother pushed him back and they began grappling, each man attempting to best the other for the hundredth time in their lives. Sticking a foot out, Robert tripped Reginald and gripped his arms, pushing him onto the ground, before straddling him. "Tell me why I shouldnae knock all yer teeth out this verra moment?"

"Do whatever ye want, ye stubborn arse! But we did this for ye. I kenned ye loved her but wouldnae admit it, and Tilda kenned Elizabeth loved ye, but was afraid of falling for a man who couldnae love her back. Ye are both fools!" Reginald spat. "I wished to make ye jealous, so ye could admit how ye felt for the lass. Apparently it worked."

Before Robert could finish processing what his brother had said and decide to climb off him or pummel him, the door nearest Reginald's head flew open and Robert looked up to see Elizabeth and Matilda standing in their shifts, wool arisaids wrapped around them with their mouths agape in shock.

Another door opened and Mary stepped out, rubbing her swelling belly with a wry smile on her face. "Another Irvine brother fight. 'Tis a shame Alex isnae here to knock both yer heads together." Making a tsking sound, she looked up and saw Elizabeth and Tilda, smiling widely. "I told ye Robert would box his ears."

"What in God's name is all this noise?" a booming, deep voice shouted from the next door down. "A man can get no sleep in this cursed keep!"

"Hush, William!" Elizabeth scolded her elder brother, who crinkled his brow when he saw the scene before him.

"Ye married into the worst clan in all of Scotland, Lizzie!"

"William! I am not married! Now do shut up!"

William's mouth opened, then closed again and Robert understood the man's frustration and confusion. He would have to deal with her brother's ire before he could make things right, but now was not the time.

Stepping forward, Elizabeth's small bare feet stopped before him as she looked down at what must have appeared to be a childish scene. Putting out a hand calmly, she looked at him and frowned, silently begging him to stop with her honeyed eyes.

"Ye're an arse," he groaned to Reginald as he climbed off him, putting out a hand to grab Elizabeth's hand before putting out another to help Reginald off the cold stone floors.

"As are ye," Reginald grunted, wiping debris off his backside and appearing rather embarrassed to be caught in such a position.

"Ye are all arses," Mary chimed in cheerfully from her chamber door. "The lot of ye. Alexander would have enjoyed this scene verra much. Figure yerselves out before ye make a mockery of yer clan."

"Too late for that!" William finally said, and Robert could do naught but sigh and run his hands over his face wearily.

"Ye are an arse, as well," Mary said calmly, looking in William's direction.

"What did I do?" he asked, scratching his head and glaring at Mary.

"I dinnae ken. But all men are arses in the end, aye? Some lassies as well." Looking at Elizabeth and Matilda, Mary shrugged and slammed her chamber door shut.

"Will someone tell me what is going on?" William stormed over to Robert and Reginald, fire in his eyes. "I am regretting this cursed peace between us right now when all I wish to do is run ye both through, and I dinnae even ken what ye did... but I ken ye did something!"

"We all did, William. None of us is innocent in this."

Scowling, William looked at his sister, then glared silently at Robert and Reginald before storming back toward his chamber, mumbling curses under his breath. "Will, wait!" Elizabeth pleaded, following in his wake while clutching to her arisaid.

"Go to bed, Lizzie," he growled over his shoulder. "I dinnae wish to discuss this nonsense right now! I am out of patience with ye! We will talk in the morn!"

"But... I have to tell ye—" The door slammed in her face, and Robert saw Elizabeth flinch before turning around to face him with a frown as she began to move slowly toward him.

"Ye are all mad. See if I ever help ye again," Reginald scoffed and limped away, wiping blood off his lip. Robert wanted to shout that falsifying a marriage with the woman he loved was the worst help he had ever received, but he was weary and sore, wishing only to end this cursed night so he could be with Elizabeth in the morn.

Matilda grabbed Elizabeth's arm before she ever reached his side and dragged her back, slowly shutting her chamber door, leaving Robert alone once more, wondering how everything had become so very complicated. His nose and jaw hurt like hell from his second fight of the night with Reginald, William was ready to simply drag Elizabeth back to Dunnottar, and Robert had to somehow convince the man that he was worthy of Elizabeth, which seemed an impossible feat at the moment. Never had he felt less worthy in his entire life.

The night grew late, but Robert's mind was too occupied to even consider sleeping. Likely, he would be up until dawn, deciding how to best move forward and start his future with Elizabeth. He could not wait to call her wife, finally remove her clothing and see what beauty lay beneath. The thought alone had driven him mad for many sennights. The reality would surely be enough to bring him to his knees in worship. But that seemed a long way off and, for now, Robert needed fresh air and time to think in the still, quiet night.

Turning back toward the stairs, Robert climbed to the top of the tower, letting the familiarity of the battlements soothe his frazzled nerves. The sound of trees rustling in the forest below filled his ears and the cool night air filled his lungs. Ever since he was a wee lad, coming up here to oversee the land had been his favorite place of solitude. He felt safe here, though never had he expected to be the laird of the lands that now surrounded him.

"I miss ye, Brother," he said to the wind, wondering if Alex would ever hear his words. Either way, he felt compelled to speak to him. "Ye left a right mess behind. One widow. One lover carrying yer child. A castle and a title and lands that now fall to me to care for, none of which I ever wanted." Feeling the pain throbbing in his cheek, he knew he would have a bruise. Nothing worse than before. The three brothers were known for a good fight now and then. Without Alex, it was up to him and Reginald to beat the shite out of one another from time to time. He just wished it wasn't because of Alex's widow.

"That isnae entirely true. I mustnae lie. As much as it shames me to admit this now, I coveted yer wife, and I am verra sorry. I loved the lass from the moment I saw her. Had ye lived, I would have done well enough hiding my emotions for her. I would never have betrayed ye and I hope ye ken that. But then ye went ahead and got yerself killed by that bastard, Hector. I was so angry at ye for leaving me. I didnae want yer life and I refused to love yer widow out of spite. I pushed her away until she decided to marry Reginald. But ye must ken that already, aye? Ye probably are laughing yer arse off at us. Are ye not?"

Swallowing down his grief, Robert found his usual spot along the wall, the same spot he and his two brothers had carved their initials into the rough stones as children. Running his finger along the cold ridges of etched memories, Robert sighed. "I have been a fool, Alex. But I plan on making everything right. I am in love with Elizabeth. I thought it was wrong before, but nothing has ever been more right. I should have married her when she asked me to from the beginning. Ye had asked it of me, as well, and I ken ye were jesting, but it would have been best for us all."

"Alex asked ye to marry me?" He heard Elizabeth's voice and his head snapped up. He had been so deep in his thoughts that he had not heard her approach, nor saw her from the side. Hair plaited and draped over one shoulder, she was wearing the same thing she wore before, a simple linen shift with the Keith plaid wrapped around her shoulders.

"The Lady of Drum should wear the Irvine plaid," he said softly with a smile and signaled for her to join him against the wall.

"I didnae mean to interrupt ye in a private moment. I couldnae sleep and thought to come up here."

"Aye, how could ye sleep after the night we had? I am sorry I woke ye in the first place, disagreeing with Reg."

"Ye call that a disagreement? I wouldnae like to see ye truly angry with him then."

Shrugging and chuckling, Robert draped his arm around her shoulders and brought her closer to him, enjoying the feel of her tucked close to his body. "We are brothers. We fight sometimes but 'tis how we move on. And nay, Alex kenned he had to marry ye. He only said that one night when he was sad about Mary. I wanted to marry ye, even then, but it wasnae my right. Once it was my right, I denied it until I pushed ye away and I will never forgive myself."

"Robert, ye need to let that go. I love ye and plan to make ye my husband as soon as possible."

Tucking a stray brown hair behind her ear, Robert felt a warmth flood his insides while he looked at her. "Ye are the most beautiful woman I have ever kenned. I am a fortunate man that ye could still love me after I have been such a bastard to ye." Leaning in, he pressed his lips against hers and groaned in surprise and excitement when she met him halfway, wrapping her arms around his neck and eager to respond.

Pulling away for a moment, Elizabeth licked her lips and searched his eyes, causing him to shift when his arousal became too painful. The way she looked at him was enough to nearly undo him and, having wanted her so badly for so long, Robert was struggling to keep himself together.

"I love ye, Robert. Ye ken that, aye?" she whispered and kissed his lips softly, pulling away once more.

"I do, and I am the luckiest man in the world for it. I love ye more than anything, Lizzie. I cannae wait to make ye my wife."

"Robert..." she searched his features one more time and bit her lower lip in a way that spoke of wanton thoughts and intimate caresses, making him bite back another groan. "I cannae wait either." Slowly, Elizabeth climbed onto his lap and he saw a wee blush creep up her cheeks when she felt the evidence of his desire pressing at her backside. "I want to make love to ye, to be yers here and now, to ken that, when I walk toward ye on our wedding day, that we hold this secret between us." Her arms wrapped around his neck once more and she waited for him to respond, though all he could do was feel her soft warmth, smell her sweet floral scent and all his resistance began to wane with every breath between them.

"I want ye more than anything. Are ye certain that is what ye want? I plan to make certain we are wed within a sennight. I willnae wait longer than necessary to make ye my wife. We can wait if that is what ye want, love."

Shaking her head slowly and shifting in his lap, Elizabeth sighed and rested her forehead against his. "'Tis just that, ye see, I keep getting this feeling... down here," she whispered and looked down the area between her legs, her shift creeping higher and higher up her thighs with every move she made.

"Is that so, lass?" he murmured, knowing he would lose control if she so innocently continued to speak that way, yet he could not help himself from asking further. "What sort of feeling?"

"'Tis hard to explain, but I only feel it when I am near ye, or see ye, or think of ye. 'Tis as if my body wants something it doesnae understand. But I ken what it is and I need to make it go away, Robert, before it drives me mad."

She was driving him mad with her words. Never had he loved a lass before, and never had he wanted to make love to anyone as much as he did her. In the past, it had simply been the need for release, but with Elizabeth, the need to love her, feel her, be one with her, was consuming his every thought. "If I am a fortunate man, that feeling will never go away, Lizzie. That is lust and I feel it every time I am with ye, or see ye, or think of ye, as well, love."

Leaning in, he took her soft lips with his own and felt his stomach tighten with need when she sighed and opened to him, allowing his tongue entry. For a few sweet and torturous moments, that was all they did, explore one another's mouths, nibbling, tasting, and learning the feel of one another. Her hands slowly moved down to his chest, where she pressed one palm flat to his heart and looked up at him with a small smile. "I can feel it beating."

"It beats only for ye, my bride."

"I hope I never live to see the day when it stops. I shall never bear the loss of ye, Robert."

"Ye willnae lose me. Never," he promised and picked up her other hand, kissing her fingertips softly, one by one.

He felt a shiver run through her body and when he looked down, saw her nipples pebbled against her shift, begging for his touch. How he had longed to touch her breasts, see them, taste them. He knew they would taste sweeter than any honey. Hands gripping her waist, he slowly allowed them to move upward toward those perfect round temptations he had been dreaming of since the first day they met. When his thumb gently grazed her hard peaks, she flexed her hips instinctively and arched her back. "Ah, that feels wonderful," she sighed. "I never kenned they could feel that way."

"I have barely touched ye, love," he chuckled, looking at the tie on her shift and placing his fingers there, waiting for her permission. When she nodded, he tugged the bow and loosened the fabric, slowly working the shift down her shoulders until her glorious breasts finally came into his view, her rosy buds tightening when the cold air hit them.

"By all that is holy, ye are perfection." Cupping each breast in his palms, he once again stroked her nipples with the pads of his thumbs, reveling in her soft whimpers of delight and the way her body seemed to move against his without her even trying. If she continued that, he would lose himself in a most embarrassing manner.

Her breathing became shallow as she watched him touch her for the first time, and something about that drove him absolutely wild. "Ye like that, love?" he asked and when she nodded and continued to watch, he decided to lean in and flick his tongue over her erect nipple, pleased when her hips bucked and she moaned lowly. Giving her ripe breast a tender nip, he played with the other nipple before switching sides.

Never had he known a woman more responsive, more innocent yet made for pleasure. She was trusting and passionate and he wanted to see how much more pleasure he could bring her without taking things too far. As much as he wished to bury himself to the hilt within her, he wanted to respect her maidenhood and save the true act for their marriage night and knew he could help give her relief in ways she may not yet understand.

"Make love to me, Robert," she whispered, shifting in his lap, driving him mad with need. Yet tonight would be only about Elizabeth's pleasure. He had waited this long and could wait a few more days.

"Elizabeth, my sweet lass, we will make love on the night of our wedding, but until then, will ye allow me to show ye pleasure in other ways?" Sliding his hands down her body, he rested them on her thighs and fisted the fabric of her shift, awaiting her response.

Disappointment showed on her face, but she nodded and he smirked in response, knowing she would not remain disappointed for long. Running his hands slowly up and down the length of her slim legs, noticing her small ankles and creamy complexion, he gritted his teeth against his restrained need. Straddling his lap with her shift halfway up her thighs, he was so close to seeing that secret part of her he had dreamed about for so long. "Ye are so perfect, love," he murmured, running his hands back up her legs, over her thighs while pushing the fabric up higher. Lifting her backside slightly, she allowed him to raise it up to her hips, exposing her from the waist down, her breasts still only inches from his face. She was glorious and, though not fully nude, she was more lovely than he could have ever imagined.

Placing her plaid on the ground behind her, he instructed her to lay back onto it, and she willingly did as he instructed. "What are ye going to do to me, Robert?" she asked softly, leaning up on her elbows to better see and the curiosity in her voice nearly undid him. She was a temptress and truly did not know it.

Deciding to show her rather than explain, Robert looked down and took in the beautiful sight before him, running one finger slowly over her mound and delighting when she instantly responded, gasping as her hips bucked. Pushing her legs open a little wider, he explored her first with his gaze, wondering how he had become so fortunate a man, to have her love and trust in this manner. Slowly pushing one finger inside her, he watched her face when her mouth opened slightly and a small whimper escaped from her lips. "How does this feel?" he asked, pushing a bit deeper before pulling out and repeating the motion gently, getting her used to his touch.

"It is so... good," she sighed, tilting her head back. "But yet, I still need more. Is that wrong?"

Chuckling, he shook his head. "Nay, love. I am just getting started." Elizabeth's eyes widened at his words and a distinctive blush crept down her neck and over her chest, her bared nipples still puckered and erect. Slipping a second finger in, Robert groaned, loving the soft wet feel of her, the heat. He longed to remove his trews and bury himself deep within her, but knew he had the rest of his life to make love to her, even if waiting felt like his own personal hell.

To his surprise, he looked up to see Elizabeth watching what he was doing, a look of longing in her eyes as he pushed in and out. She was so willing, so eager and nothing could have aroused him more than knowing he was the first man to cause her such pleasure in her life. With his other hand, he found the sensitive nub just above her entrance and gently circled the tip of his finger over it, delighting in her sudden moan of pleasure and the way she pushed her hips down, deepening his thrusts as he continued to move in a rhythmic motion.

Robert could not decide what was more arousing, watching himself pleasure her, or watching her reaction to it as her breath quickened and her head tilted back, hips beginning to rock in tandem with his ministrations. "That's it, my love. Let it go," he whispered, seeing her breasts heaving as her body began to tense around him. She was close to experiencing her first release and he was close to losing his own in a most embarrassing way, but never had he been more aroused in his entire life.

A few low groans escaped her before she collapsed onto her back and lifted her hips, rolling against him, urging him to continue until she cried out in ecstasy and clawed at his arms before collapsing in exhaustion.

Lifting her back up, he pulled her against him and cradled her in his arms, feeling her breaths slowly regulating again, hearing her sighs of contentment. "I dinnae ken what ye just did to me, Robert, but I vow I shall let ye do it whenever ye please," she sighed and rested her head on his chest.

Chuckling, he lifted her chin and stared into her eyes. "Be careful what ye promise, Lizzie. I will tire ye out if ye allow me to do that whenever I please, for I wish to do that every second of every day. And when we are married, I will show ye even more. It gets better than that."

"Impossible," she purred, nuzzling into him, wrapping her arms around his waist as he did the same. He could feel her breasts pressing against his chest and felt so much love, so much tenderness for her. Never had he thought to want only one woman for the rest of his life, but he would never look at another lass again, for nobody could ever be his Lizzie.

"'Tis possible. I assure ye."

When she shifted in his lap, he groaned and pulled back, still dangerously close to losing himself. "Oh, nay, Robert. What about ye? Do ye not want me to… touch it?"

"It?" Robert smiled and kissed her forehead tenderly, sweeping away a few tendrils that were stuck to her sweaty skin. "Och. Aye, of course I want ye to touch it more than anything. But, not tonight. 'Tis late and we have yer brother to deal with on the morrow. If I were him, I would run me through."

"William is protective of me, 'tis true. But I will make certain he understands what happened and how much I love ye. He kens I never wanted love, that I wished to avoid it at all costs. He may never understand what I did, but he will understand why. And when he sees how much I love ye, Robert Irvine, Laird of Drum, he will bless our union. I vow it."

Pulling her linen shift back up her shoulders, he was saddened to lose sight of her perfect round breasts and already could not wait to taste them once more. But the night grew colder and the dawn would arrive soon enough. Once he tied her shift up, Robert wrapped her Keith plaid around her shoulders and slowly helped her to her feet. She was so much smaller than him, yet so much stronger. She had faced her duties with strength, and when she was tired of simply following along, she took her life into her own hands. She was a fighter and he would never subdue that spirit, he vowed.

"I hope ye are right, Lizzie. I dinnae think he will be as easy to manage as ye believe."

Kissing him softly before he walked her back down the tower stairs to her chamber, she shrugged and took his arm. "He will accept it, I ken he will."

"I WILLNAE ACCEPT this!" William roared and slammed his fist down on Robert's solid oak desk, causing Elizabeth to flinch at the sudden outburst. "Ye are driving me mad, Lizzie! What has gotten into ye? Ye married the wrong brother in some act of rebellion when everyone around ye kens ye love Robert! Yer need to avoid love has driven ye insane!"

"I'm not insane, Will. I ken this situation isnae ideal, but—"

"Not ideal? I have been away from Dunnottar for too cursed long! I came to marry ye off, sign a peace contract, and go back to my people! Then war came. Then Alexander died, rest his soul. Then ye snuck off into the middle of the night and married a man I hadnae agreed to, a man not in the contracts and not to be laird. Yet, I accepted it. I wanted ye to be happy! Now ye tell me the marriage was false, ye love Robert, he loves ye, and ye want to marry another Irvine? How am I supposed to explain this to our people, Lizzie! This is absurd!" he spat and slammed his fist down once again.

Robert sat behind his desk with his elbows propped on the surface.

His hands were folded together before his mouth as he listened calmly and somehow kept his composure. It was more than Lizzie was capable of. The hackles on the back of her neck rose in defiance, yet she clenched her fists at her sides and took a deep breath. "I ken this is absurd, Brother. I ken I made it so. Take yer anger out on me, but dinnae punish Robert. We all ken he didnae ask for any of this confusion."

"Och, 'tis not Robert I wish to kill. 'Tis his deceitful brother!" William pointed at Reginald who propped himself coolly against the stone wall of the laird's solar, arms crossed as he looked straight ahead. "Have ye Irvines nay honor? I am tempted to burn our peace agreement and drag Elizabeth back home! And who was that wild banshee shouting at me from her chamber last night?"

"William!" Elizabeth scolded. "That is Mary and she is my friend."

"Mary… as in Alexander's lover who carries his child? She is yer… friend? Ye truly have earned the need to wear that rosary daily, Lizzie, though I dinnae ken if ye use it."

"Haud yer wheesht!" Elizabeth had had enough. William had a right to be upset by the situation, but Mary had nothing to do with this and he could not speak about her companion in that manner. "Mary was in love with Alexander! She is suffering his loss and carrying his child, aye! She has paid for her sins and as for me, 'tis not a sin to be her friend. 'Twould be a sin to shun her, as ye are!"

William had the decency to not respond. Still, he crossed his arms and pursed his lips, unwilling to apologize, not that she expected him to. "I made a mistake. I didnae want to become our father, pining for a lost love every day and ye ken that! But now, I see I have become him, for I do pine, Brother. And I do love. When I thought I was married to Reg, I was miserable."

"Thank ye," Reg scoffed but bit back a smile.

"Ye ken what I mean!" she said at his comment, stomping her foot. "And I thank ye for what ye did. I ken ye and Tilda did all ye did to make me see my mistakes, and to make Robert open his eyes, as well. It worked. We have."

Looking over at Robert, her heart leapt when she saw him relax a bit in his seat, attempting to hide his smile behind his clasped hands. But his eyes sparkled and his dimple flashed, letting her know he was amused and happy she was defending them. She knew he would defend them as well, but William was her brother and this was her mess to clean up. Despite Robert's anger and mistreatment toward her, he had been willing to marry her.

"We are in love, William. And if ye drag me back to Dunnottar, I will simply find my way back here. I was ready to flee home alone to avoid love. Matilda suggested I marry another Irvine to keep the peace and keep me put. Ye should be thanking her and Reginald for doing what was needed to keep me at Drum and from making a big mistake. I am a stubborn lass. I ken this, as do ye. I am marrying Robert, as intended. Peace remains between the clans, the Keiths are all still here to witness the marriage. The only thing that has changed is me."

William's face softened as he took steps toward her, placing his large hands on her shoulders. "Ye have changed. I see that. Ye are willing to risk all for love, when before ye did aught to avoid it. Still, am I supposed to allow Reginald to get away with the trouble he has caused?"

Stepping away from the wall, Reginald put his hands up in the air in surrender. "Ye want to run me through? Ye ken ye cannae, but I will allow ye the first swing."

Narrowing his eyes, William released his grip on Elizabeth and stepped up to Reginald, both men rather equal in height and size. "The first swing?" William asked, a menacing tone in his voice.

"Aye. I will let ye have the first. After that, I cannae be as gracious." Reginald stepped up closer to William. "Ye want to hit me. I ken ye do."

"I willnae fall for yer shite," William growled. "If I hit ye then yer brother will jump in. I've seen how ye Irvines brawl."

"We fight our own battles, mate. I dinnae need him to take ye down." Reginald popped his knuckles and got into a fighting stance. Elizabeth watched the two, wishing they would both knock each other out in one fell swoop and be done with it.

Rolling her eyes, Elizabeth stepped between them. "Ye will have to hit me first."

"That is ridiculous!" Reginald scoffed.

"Are ye mad?" her brother chimed in.

"Ye are both ridiculous and mad! Look at yerselves, grown men acting like wee children. Ye can kick each other's arses another time if ye so wish, I dinnae care! But it willnae change what has happened, nor what will be. I am marrying Robert as soon as possible and I expect the Keiths to be in attendance and it would be bloody preferable if my brother didnae have a fat lip and a black eye on my wedding day!"

Frowning, William crinkled his brow and stepped back, then Reginald did the same.

"As soon as she is gone, I will kick yer arse," William said to Reginald, pointing a finger in the man's direction.

"I look forward to it. I do an enjoy a good arse kicking."

Looking over her shoulder, she saw Robert sitting and staring at her, a look of love on his face that made her heart swell. She wanted to run over to him, sit in his lap and kiss him until she was breathless, but she wanted him to live to see their wedding day, and William would most certainly kill him if he knew what they had done last night.

Just the thought of it made a flush creep up her cheeks and Robert smirked, clearly thinking the same thing.

The door to Robert's solar burst open causing Elizabeth to squeal at the sudden intrusion, clutching her heart when she saw the grave look on Charles' face. It was never a good sign when their outlook or messengers stormed in so abruptly. "My laird! A band of Macleans march this way!"

"Macleans?" Robert repeated, standing from his chair and rounding his desk.

"The man who killed Alex was a Maclean, aye?" Elizabeth asked, feeling herself begin to shake with fear.

Robert nodded and wrapped her in his arms, feeling her quake in his embrace. She was not certain what was happening, but the Macleans were a Highland clan. There was no other reason for them to be here, aside for seeking justice.

"Aye, and he killed Red Hector of the Battles, their leader and finest warrior. They must be here to seek revenge," Robert said calmly, kissing the top of her forehead before releasing her and moving into swift action while she swerved in place, dread sinking in her stomach.

"Reginald, tell the men to armor up and prepare for the worst. William, yer men can back us up or stay within the walls. After all, Elizabeth isnae yet wed to an Irvine and thus our treaty doesnae stand. I willnae expect ye to risk yer men, but it would be good faith for our future as brothers, and as allies."

Elizabeth looked at William, inwardly pleading him to move past the events of the day and do what was right. They may not be obligated to fight, but if peace was ever to truly unite their clans, now was the time to prove it.

"Ye Irvines are naught but trouble." William looked at Robert and paused for a moment before looking at Elizabeth and smiling widely. "Fortunately, so are we Keiths. And we will stand by ye."

Taking a deep breath, Elizabeth watched as her brother and future husband clasped forearms in a form of understanding and felt slightly at ease, until Robert moved toward the door. "Charles! Get all the women and children up into the top of the tower. I will ride out to meet the Macleans to determine their cause for being on our lands. If I need help, I will give the signal."

"Nay!" Elizabeth ran over to him, feeling as if she would be sick. "I willnae let ye go out there alone! I have already lost one husband to them. I shallnae lose ye!" Wrapping her arms tightly around Robert, she inhaled deeply, trying to calm her nerves, taking in his masculine scent and the feel of his hard muscles beneath his beige tunic.

"Lizzie, my love, I need ye to be strong and listen. Ye are Lady of Drum. The women and children need ye. They need yer stubbornness and intelligence now. Trust me and my men to handle this. I trust ye to keep everyone in the tower safe. Can ye do that for me, Bride?"

Swallowing hard, she nodded and gripped his arm. "Dinnae be a fool, Robert. Promise to take a few men with ye. I cannae leave until I ken ye will do that."

"I will be by his side." Turning, she saw her brother step forward and tears welled up in her eyes.

"Thank ye," she cried and hugged her brother hard. "Ye dinnae be a fool either, Will. I cannae live without ye, ye ken."

"I have survived more than the Macleans. We will find out what they want and settle this one way or another."

"I will be with him, as well," Reginald said. "He is my blood and my laird. I will protect him with my life. Besides, I would be a terrible laird. He needs to live to protect his people from my foolishness."

Overcome with more emotions than she knew what to do with, Elizabeth simply nodded and squeezed Reginald's hand tightly, squeaking when he pulled her to him and embraced her hard.

"Ye were my wife for only a few days, lass, but the best wife I shall ever have."

"I ken that isnae true. Ye will have a fine wife one day. Now go. I will be here managing the others." Walking over to Robert one last time, she looked up at him and gripped his shoulders. "I love ye, Robert Irvine. I cannae lose ye."

"And, ye willnae. Not now, not ever. I love ye, Lizzie." Kissing her hard on the mouth, he walked away, Reginald and William following closely behind, no doubt to round up their men before meeting the Macleans outside the walls.

Alone in the solar, she could hear the fire popping in the hearth, voices of men shouting in the courtyard below, and the blood rushing to her head, causing her ears to ring. Panic was not an option. Clenching her fists into her skirts, she fled down the stairs, ready to gather the women and children and keep them safe or die trying, as the Lady of Drum should.

CHAPTER SIXTEEN

"EVERYTHING IS READY, my laird," Charles shouted from atop the battlements, looking down at the surrounding area. "They approach from the west!"

Archers lined the walls, ready to shoot on his command. Armed men on horses were just outside the gates and would stay far enough back to let the Macleans know they were hoping not to fight, but close enough to be seen as a warning. All the women and children were in the tower with Elizabeth while William and Reginald flanked his sides. Drum would not fall on his watch and according to Charles and the other men on guard, there appeared to only be a score of Macleans, which Robert knew either meant they did not come for battle, or more of their men were waiting in hiding and he would assume the latter until he knew for certain.

The Irvine plaid was wrapped around his body proudly, alongside Reginald's and William in his Keith plaid, showing that they stood united. Urging their horses forward, the three men rode out to meet the Macleans before they got too close to the castle walls.

As the Macleans came into view, Robert slowed his horse to a trot, then stopped altogether, dismounting and holding the hilt of his sword, standing proudly as the Laird of Drum and determined to keep his people safe.

"I dinnae ken what has brought ye to Irvine land. But I warn ye, I have both the Irvines and Keiths here ready to fight, and my archers ready to shoot on my command." Looking around, Robert squinted his eyes, searching the surrounding area for any movement in the trees or bushes. But aside from the wind, everything seemed still, eerily so. But the Macleans were outnumbered and Robert's instincts and knowledge of warfare told him this was not an attack, though what it was, he could not guess.

A large blond-haired man with a long beard covering most of his face step forward wearing the green and red plaid of his clan, sword sheathed at his side. Stepping forward, Robert met the man halfway, crossing his arms and making a show of not holding on to his hilt any longer. He would draw his sword if needed, but for now, he simply wanted to read the man and hear him out.

"Ye are the Laird of Drum?" the man's deep voice asked as he crossed his arms, as well.

"Aye. I am now that my brother was killed by a Maclean at Harlaw," Robert replied with warning in his tone. "Ye come to kill me now?"

"My father was killed by yer brother at Harlaw, as well. And, nay. Enough blood has been spilled."

Narrowing his eyes, Robert looked at the man carefully, seeing the resemblance to the man called Red Hector of the Battles. "Ye are Lachlan Maclean?" The man was well-known in Scotland for being almost as brave a fighter as his father, yet of sound mind and not as bloodthirsty.

"Aye."

"Why have ye come all this way, if not to avenge yer father?" Was the man attempting to put him off his scent? The moment Robert believed it was safe, would hundreds of men jump out of the surrounding forest and start an attack? Though he made certain to have men patrolling the forests, if enough men came through and slaughtered them, Robert would not know until it was too late.

Yet, there was no honor in catching Robert off guard in a face to face combat and all he had ever heard about the character of Lachlan Maclean told Robert that he was an honorable man, unlike his father.

Putting his hand on the handle of his sword, Lachlan quickly unsheathed it, causing Robert to jump back defensively and draw his own. He heard Reginald and William do the same behind him. Just as he was preparing to let out their war whoop to his men for backup, he heard a wail from the castle tower in the distance and recognized it as Elizabeth's voice. Could Elizabeth possibly see what was happening from so far away? His name being called drifted on the wind to his ears and he clenched his jaw, prepared to fight and survive, for there was no way he would leave his Elizabeth alone.

His men approached swiftly from the rear, not awaiting the signal as planned. But, clearly, seeing a sword being drawn on their laird and hearing Elizabeth's cries in the distance alerted them to further danger, heightening the tension.

"Think carefully before ye act any further, Lachlan. This willnae end well for ye and yer men, I assure ye," Robert warned, gripping the hilt of his sword tighter and preparing for a fight if needed.

Looking Robert in the eyes, Lachlan dropped his sword on the cool, wet grass at Robert's feet and kneeled before him. "I havenae come to fight. I have come to seek peace. This was the sword my father used in battle. I wish to exchange swords with ye as a symbol of our clans' future peace. No more blood shall be spilled between our two clans."

Standing before Lachlan, Robert crinkled his brow and pondered the situation. He had heard of such exchanges yet had never been involved in one and felt relief flow through him. There had been too much blood shed, too much violence. The Scots needed to unite and look toward their true enemy, the English, not one another.

Getting down on his knee in front of Lachlan, Robert placed his sword down before him as well and nodded once. "Red Harlaw was a disgrace. We all have suffered too much loss. The Irvines wish to move forward peaceably."

Putting his arm out, Lachlan waited for Robert to do the same and the men clasped wrists in a show of unity before exchanging swords and getting back up on their feet. Sheathing the sword that had killed his brother at Harlaw, Robert felt a chill run up his spine and closed his eyes, remembering the horror of that day, the sight of his brother's blood spilling from his body and staining the green fields red. It would never leave his mind. But life moved forward and, as laird, it was Robert's duty to make certain it did.

"As long as ye hold my father's sword, ye can be certain that the Macleans are allies of the Irvines," Lachlan said slowly as he sheathed Robert's sword. "I dinnae wish to be run through by my father's own sword and I ken ye dinnae wish to be run through by yers, so we shall forever ken there is peace."

"Aye," Robert replied and breathed deeply, hearing Reginald and William stepping forward to flank him in solidarity, knowing he had made the right decision for his people. Reginald smacked him on the back and Robert looked at his brother, nodding in understanding. Alexander died in a battle that should never have happened, led by greedy men with selfish desires. Hopefully, with Robert leading the way, such events would be avoided in the future. Nay, war was always inevitable, but should it occur, Robert prayed there was solidarity amongst his fellow Scots, never against them in vain.

"Ye have traveled far to be here," Robert said to Lachlan, looking at his score of men behind him, all wrapped in plaids and covered in filth.

"Nay journey is too far if it is in the name of peace," Lachlan added. "The Donald is a madman. He will continue to cause trouble in the Highlands, mark my words. My father was little better, I am saddened to admit. The Macleans wish to prove our honor, to show that we will only fight the battles worth fighting. We are mighty warriors and wish to use that might for right."

Grunting, Robert grinned. "Och, I ken ye are a mighty lot. I have heard tales and seen the proof."

"Tales of yer brother have spread, as well. He was a fine man and an able warrior. The bards have been singing his praises with ballads across the land. Have ye heard them?"

"Nay. I have heard rumor of such ballads, yet havenae heard any, myself," Robert said, feeling pride consume him for his brother who may be gone, but whose legend lived on.

"I would be honored to share a ballad or two with ye sometime, should our people break bread."

"Why not break bread now? As I said, ye have traveled far to be here. My wedding is due to occur in two days' time. I shall marry Elizabeth Keith, sister to William Keith, Marischal of Scotland," Robert said, signaling to William who tilted his head in greeting to Lachlan. "She is also Alexander's widow."

"And my wife for a day," Reginald said with a chuckle and a wink.

"Och, are ye wanting me to kill ye now or later, Reg?" William growled and scowled in his direction.

Lachlan looked between the three men and raised a curious brow but must have decided against asking any questions. "Many thanks for the offer. My men and I would be honored to attend."

"Elizabeth and I will be honored to have ye. Follow us back to the castle and we will have the Lady of Drum make ye all most comfortable." Giving the signal to his men in the distance that all was well, Robert walked back toward Drum with the Macleans of Duart following in his wake, the sword that killed his brother sheathed at his side, a bride awaiting him within the tower, and wondering if Alex was watching him now, laughing his arse off at all the unexpected turns in Robert's life.

"WHAT IS HAPPENING?" Elizabeth asked, watching Robert kneel in the grass with his sword in front of him from the slit windows in the tower.

Marta Gordon bumped Elizabeth aside slightly so she could reach up on her tiptoes and view the scene. She had been at the castle for a couple of days and would likely remain for Elizabeth's marriage to Robert, yet the lass seemed jovial and kind – not at all affected by being brushed aside and left without a marriage proposal, though she did talk faster than Elizabeth could understand much of the time. "Och! They are exchanging swords! I have seen this but only once before. It isnae so common, ye ken. Feuds can be quite nasty. Ye ken, we Gordons have rivalries with both the Lindsays and the Douglas' we do."

Tilda looked at Marta and rolled her eyes, making Elizabeth bite her lower lip to prevent from giggling. But fortunately, Marta did not notice and, truthfully, Elizabeth found the lass quite daft, yet harmless.

Throat burning from screaming Robert's name only a moment ago, Elizabeth rubbed her neck and watched as the men stood up and clasped hands before sheathing swords. The pounding in her heart would not cease. For a moment, she had been certain a battle was going to break out with Robert and her brother caught unprepared. The fear had gripped at her, making her feel faint and shaky.

Taking a deep breath, Elizabeth gasped and turned to look at the other women and children huddled around inside the tower, silently awaiting news.

"What it is, my lady?" an elderly woman said with a shaky voice and all eyes stared at her with fear and curiosity. In that moment, she looked around the tower and realized for the first time that she truly was the lady of this castle, of these people. She may be a Keith, but the Irvines were her people. All of the women and children were looking at her for answers, for protection. And more than anything, she wanted to be there for them every day and make certain they knew that she was strong enough to protect the castle and its people when danger arose.

"They are talking! And..." Elizabeth turned once more to look out the window. "And, walking toward the castle!" A loud whistle resounded and Elizabeth gripped her chest. "'Tis his signal that all is well!"

Marta and Tilda ran to the window and gasped in unison. "They are coming here?" Tilda asked?

Mary stood up and slowly walked toward the window. "Aye. They are. Yer brother appears... happy!" Mary said to Elizabeth and grunted. "I havenae seen the man smile since he arrived at Drum. Mayhap I didnae ken he even had teeth!"

"Och! What shall we do, my lady?" Cook asked, wringing her hands in her apron. "I cannae stand to feed an army!"

"'Tis but a score of men. We shall make do, Cook," Elizabeth said calmly. "But we cannae make plans until we ken what is happening. I want ye all to stay here. Dinnae leave this room until I come back. Mary, when I leave, I need ye to bar the door and dinnae let anyone in until I say so."

Mary nodded and the room went silent once more. Opening the door, Elizabeth took a few slow steps down the stairs until she was out of view and heard the tower door slam shut behind her. Picking up her pace and lifting her skirts, Elizabeth sped down the stairs, heart pounding and breath quickening. For one horrible moment, she thought she was going to lose Robert. The sight of a sword being drawn before him would never leave her memory. She had to see him and Will, had to find out what was happening and make certain everything was all right. Robert would be upset that she put herself in danger, but she could not simply sit idly by while the potential enemy walked toward the keep.

Reaching the bottom of the stairs, Elizabeth bolted to the entrance and heard the ancient hinges of the door creak as she yanked it open and ran into the inner bailey and past the stables. Dusk had set and a chill crept up her legs with every swift stride toward the outer bailey and the gates leading out of the grounds, but she was determined to reach the men with haste. Her nerves could no longer stand the unknown.

Just as she reached the outer bailey, voices floated toward her on the breeze and Robert, William, and Reginald rounded a corner, a strange large man by Robert's side.

"Robert!" Elizabeth yelled, nearly out of breath as she ran even faster toward him, knowing in that moment that everything was going to be all right. She had no idea what had happened and knew she would get answers, but Robert was safe, as was her brother and Reginald and that was all that mattered. The women and children were safe in the tower and no blood would spill.

Reaching his side, she jumped just as his arms reached out to her and she embraced him, burrowing her head into the crook of his neck and inhaling his familiar scent. "Lizzie, what are ye doing out of the tower, love?"

"I was so scared," she whispered, forcing back tears. "For all of ye," she added, running to William next and kissing him on the cheek. "We could see everything from above and I thought I would lose ye for a wee moment. I have never been so scared."

"All is well, lass," Reginald said and she smiled at him warmly, clutching her rosary in her palm.

Clearing her throat and regaining her composure when she saw the other men staring at her curiously, she ran her hands over her skirts and looked at Robert. "What is happening here? Who are these men?"

Taking her hand, Robert turned her toward the large man she had seen draw his sword from the tower. "Elizabeth, this is Lachlan Maclean."

"Maclean?" she gasped and pulled back. "But... a Maclean killed Alex!"

"Aye, that man was my father," Lachlan said slowly, sadness in his eyes. "We want no more battles between clans. We have both lost enough and only wish for peace. Ye must be the Lady of Drum."

"Aye. I am Alexander's widow," she said hesitantly, unsure how much these men could be trusted and gripped Robert's hand tighter. She trusted his judgment yet allowing the son of the man who killed Alexander into their home was unexpected.

A forlorn expression washed over Lachlan's face and he dropped to his knees, bowing his head and taking her hand. "My lady, I cannae say how sorry I am that ye lost yer husband in battle to my father. If I could make it up to ye, I would. The best I can offer is peace and the promise that we shall never stand across the battlefield from yer people ever again."

Emotion choked at Elizabeth. She felt his grief and regret keenly and knew all too well that a man went where commanded to go. Pulling her gaze away from the stricken man still kneeling before her, Elizabeth looked behind him and saw the tired, bedraggled men all wearing the Maclean plaids and realized they all truly looked like they needed hot meals, baths, rest, and a warm welcome. They were not men who had come to start a fight.

Elizabeth trusted Robert's judgment on the situation. Looking at these men and hearing Lachlan's plea, Elizabeth sighed, relying on her instincts and making her first major decision as the Lady of Drum. Taking Robert's hand to show a united front, Elizabeth straightened her shoulders and looked down at Lachlan. "Ye are verra welcome to Drum Castle. The Irvines and Keiths will be celebrating our marriage and peace between our people. We wish to have peace with ye, as well. Our clans have had enough of wars with fellow Scotsmen."

"Thank ye, my lady." Relief washed over Lachlan's features as he kissed her hand and got back onto his feet. Nodding, Elizabeth turned toward Drum with Robert by her side as William, Reginald, and a score of men who had once been their enemies now followed them into their home.

Night had set in and stars shimmered in the sky above as a haze of clouds blocked them out intermittently while the wind blew Elizabeth's dress around her ankles. Feeling Robert wrap his plaid around her shoulders, Elizabeth looked up and felt her stomach tighten and her heart lighten as pure love shone back at her in his blue eyes. "Now ye have an Irvine plaid of yer own," he said with a wink, his dimple making her wish to kiss him as soon as they were in private. How she loved this man. Never had she wanted nor expected to find love in this lifetime but now that she had found it, she would be certain to never take it for granted again.

CHAPTER SEVENTEEN

L AUGHTER REVERBERATED OFF the walls of the keep as the hearth fire raged and the minstrels began to play. Serving women took away the empty trenchers and Elizabeth sat back in her wooden chair, feeling fuller than she had in a long time. Looking around the room, she saw Irvines, Keiths, and Macleans dancing and chatting together, all there to celebrate her marriage to Robert and the beginning of peace.

Her light blue silk dress was threaded with silver that sparkled in the light of the fire, as did the adoring blue eyes she felt watching her to her right. Looking up, she caught Robert's gaze and felt gooseflesh climb up her arms. He looked so handsome in his white tunic with a black leather surcoat and Irvine plaid draped over his shoulder, almost like one of the heroes from the love stories she had heard growing up. She never believed in such tales, and yet she could easily write one now about her own journey in love. A maiden passed untouched from father, to son, to son, finally finding happiness.

A smirk spread across her face and Robert wrapped an arm around her, pulling her close as the laughter from a large Maclean warrior boomed across the hall, speaking with an Irvine in the corner. "What are ye smiling about, Wife? Ye seem far away, yet amused." Placing his

MIA PRIDE

lips on the long column of her throat, he gave her neck a gentle nip that sent shocks of pleasure through her body and caused her to shift in her seat.

"I was only thinking about my intense desire to avoid the verra situation I now find myself in," she laughed, then sighed when he flicked his tongue across her sensitive flesh.

"Ye mean, this?" he asked, nipping her neck once more.

"Well, aye. That is quite nice, but I meant falling in love, wanting to marry a man for more than duty. 'Tis nothing I ever expected and, yet, all I have ever needed. I love ye, Robert."

"I love ye, Lizzie. And everyone else loves ye, as well. Look around. Three rival clans are all here together and 'tis because of ye."

"It most certainly isnae," she scoffed. "I made a mess of everything. And the arrival of the Macleans had naught to do with me."

"Mayhap not, but they stayed because of ye, because of our love, because we have united two clans and the Macleans wished to attend and ye graciously accepted them as the Lady of Drum."

"The Macleans wanted food, ale, and baths," Elizabeth added wryly, raising a brow at Robert who shrugged and nodded.

"Aye, mayhap that, too. Do ye ken what I want?" he whispered softly, leaning close to her ear and making her shiver with delight. How did he do that to her? The barest of touches and the softest of whispers made her feel as if she were floating away to the heavens.

"Nay. I dinnae ken," she whispered in return, her stomach fluttering with excitement.

"I wish to take my wife upstairs and finish what we started on the battlements." Robert placed his hand on her thigh under the table and Elizabeth felt flushed as if the hearth fire had taken over the keep entirely. The mischief in his eyes and the dimple on his cheek as a sly grin spread across his face made her squirm in her seat, remembering how he had made her feel and desperate to feel it once more.

"Oh, aye?" Her voice sounded breathless even to herself and she

192

knew he noticed, as well. She wished very much for the same, but the hall was filled with people who would notice if they left for their chamber and embarrass her with bawdy remarks.

"I ken what ye are thinking, love. There is no way around it. They will be awaiting our departure and they will make remarks to embarrass ye. 'Tis simply the way of it. I say we make a run for it," he suggested, lightly tugging on her arm to prompt her to stand. "If we move fast enough, we will make it to the stairs before we can hear most of their jests."

Tapping her fingers on the table, Elizabeth chewed on her bottom lip and shuffled her feet, gathering the courage to bolt from the table. She knew she should stay a wee bit longer, but the feast was over and the crowd was entertaining itself, telling stories and dancing. If she had any chance of getting away, it was now. "Aye. Let's go!" she said in a rush, feeling excitement run through her. Grabbing her hand with a wide smile and a wink, Robert swiftly stood from his chair, pulling her up with him.

"Och! I forgot to share the Ballad of Gude Sir Alexander Irvine!" Lachlan shouted above the music, making the minstrels stop playing their instruments immediately and all eyes land on Robert, who stood frozen in the position to flee.

"This didnae work," Elizabeth said through the side of her lips, feeling like a wee lass caught with her finger stuck in an apple pie.

"Where do ye think ye are sneaking off to, aye?" Reginald hollered from a bench down below where he sat beside Mary and Tilda with a grin across his face.

"I believe I ken where they were going," Mary responded with a chuckle. "It willnae be long until we have an heir."

"Och, do leave them alone," Tilda said, standing up and putting her hands on her hips defiantly. Just as Elizabeth vowed to do any favor Tilda ever asked, her companion smirked and wagged her finger. "After all, 'tis clear they meant to sneak out unnoticed and abandon us all to finally disrobe one another."

"Tilda!" Elizabeth squeaked, knowing she was turning bright red but having no control over the blood rushing to her cheeks. The crowd laughed and started making crude gestures. Scanning the crowd, Elizabeth spotted William who stood beside Lachlan looking uncomfortable yet resigned to the inevitable. Locking a pleading gaze on him, Elizabeth gripped her pearl rosary and hoped he saved her from the attention.

"I wish to hear the ballad honoring my fallen brother by marriage and I am most certain all in attendance wish to hear it as well, aye?" William said just as there was a lull in the shouting and gestures. Relief washed over Elizabeth as the crowd quieted down and nodded their agreement, urging Lachlan to share the ballad that had not yet reached their lands.

Walking across the room, Lachlan approached the head table and stepped up onto a bench, clearing his throat. "The Macleans of Duart are honored to be here with the Irvines and Keiths, and to celebrate peace, love, and unity. We regret our role in Harlaw, as I believe many Highland clans do, and I especially regret my father's ambitions and the pain his greed has caused. We vow to keep the peace and never again be lured by power and greed. In honor of yer fallen laird, Alexander, I wish to share with ye all a ballad a bard has been sharing throughout the land, commending his character and skills."

The crowd had grown silent with anticipation and a sadness hung over the room. Elizabeth choked back a tear and sat back in her chair slowly, daring to make eye contact with Mary, who dabbed at her eyes with a square of linen while she rubbed her belly. Closing her eyes, Elizabeth gripped her rosary and prepared to hear a story about a man she had briefly called husband. A man she hardly knew yet would never forget.

Clearing his throat once more, Lachlan took a deep breath and began to lament, with a voice that brought gooseflesh to Elizabeth's spine. He was a large, rough looking man with the voice of an angel, and more tears welled up in her eyes.

> "Gude Sir Alexander Irvine,
> The much renownit Laird of Drum,
> Nane in his days was better sene,
> Whan they war semblit all and some.
> To praise him we sould nocht be dumb
> For valour, wit, and worthiness.
> To end his days he there did come,
> Whose ransom is remedyless."

Robert gripped her hand and she squeezed tightly, looking at her husband as a tear ran down his cheek and his head hung low. When Lachlan finished, the entire room was silent for an eerie moment before they ruptured into a resounding cheer, men on their feet and saluting both Lachlan for his ballad and their lost laird who would be remembered as a hero and for his courage and devotion.

Standing up in her seat, Elizabeth grabbed a goblet of wine from the table that she had yet to taste and raised her glass high. "To Sir Alexander Irvine, third laird of Drum and my husband of too few days. He was kind, honorable, and loyal to his people. He married for peace and he died for peace. May he always be remembered as his ballad describes him: full of valor, wit and worthiness. To Alexander," she chimed, raising her goblet higher before taking a sip.

"To Alexander!" the room shouted and drank along with their lady.

Robert stood up beside her and raised his glass before taking a drink, giving her a grateful smile, and she was glad to see the tears on his cheeks were drying up. Though her wedding was meant to be a joyous event, it felt right to honor Alexander today and having Lachlan, the son of the man who killed him, be the one to share the ballad meant more to her than she could express.

Soon, the crowd was back to celebrating and drinking, and the minstrels had begun to sing once more. Scanning the room, Elizabeth shook her head and nudged Robert when she noticed her brother and Mary arguing once more in the corner. It seemed the two of them would never get along but, strangely, Tilda and Reginald were missing from the room and Elizabeth crinkled her brow, wondering where they had disappeared to.

"Have I told ye how beautiful ye look tonight, my lady?" Turning toward Robert, she shrugged playfully and took another sip of her wine.

"I dinnae ken. Mayhap ye should tell me once more, my laird."

Taking her hand in his, he placed his other hand on her cheek and looked deep into her eyes, making her breath catch in her chest. "Ye truly are the bonniest woman in all the world, my sweet Lizzie. I vow to love and cherish ye always and to remain a faithful husband until my last breath." Leaning in, he placed a slow, lingering kiss on her lips and she sighed, loving the feel of his soft mouth on hers, knowing she would never tire of the feel of him.

"I love ye, Robert. I cannae believe I almost made the greatest mistake of my life by letting ye go, but I shall never let ye go ever again, I vow," she whispered against his lips, closing her eyes and breathing him in, committing this moment to her memory forever. Looking behind her, she stared at the screens separating the keep from the kitchens and had an idea.

"We may not be able to make it all the way to the stairs unseen, but we can make it behind the screen. I ken how to move through the kitchens without being seen."

Raising a brow, Robert grinned and shook his head. "My mischievous lady. Ye are full of surprises. Lead the way."

Gripping his hand and looking around, Elizabeth knew nobody was truly paying them any attention any longer, which suited her just fine. She would brave the crowds and their taunts if needed, but a private escape was all she wanted. Time alone with Robert in a place nobody would find them. "Now!" she whispered and giggled softly, dragging him behind her as she ducked low and snuck around the screens. She knew the kitchen would be busy with women cleaning up after the meal but, as she suspected, they were far too engrossed in their work to notice them at all. Seeing the door leading out to the garden, Elizabeth silently pointed and Robert nodded, this time taking her hand and leading the way.

The door's hinges creaked and Elizabeth winced but, thankfully, the chatter from the hall drowned out the sound to all other ears.

"Och! Where did the laird and his lady get off to?" he heard a man say loud enough for the entire hall to hear.

"They must have snuck up the tower stairs!" another voice shouted and everyone started chattering all at once.

"If they think they can avoid the bedding ceremony, they had better think again!" a woman said and the crowd laughed and cheered.

"Up the stairs! Let's find them!"

Squealing, Elizabeth pulled Robert through the door and shut it before anyone from the kitchens paid attention. "I think we did it!" she said, panting as she felt the cool night air wrap around them, cooling her heated face with its welcoming chill.

The handle on the door rattled and she froze, looking at Robert, wondering if they would be disturbed after all. When it flew open, her heart sank until she saw Tilda's wide eyes staring back at her. "Shoo! Go! I will keep everyone away! They have made a game of finding ye!"

"Where have ye been?" Elizabeth asked, knowing she had little time but still curious about her maid's whereabouts.

"Ye really want to ask that now when ye have a mob of clanspeople seeking to taunt ye with bawdy suggestions, aye?" Tilda asked incredulously. "Now, go!" She made a shooing sound and waved her arms just as Robert nodded and pulled her away from the door and deeper into the darkness of the night.

As they ran across the grass of the inner bailey, all the sounds of chaos faded away, replaced only by the rustling of leaves, the howling of the wind, and the sounds of their breathing. Robert steered her to the left toward the forest and Elizabeth stopped and pulled back, wondering where they were actually going to escape to. "We cannae go into the woods, Robert!"

"Aye, we can. Trust me," he said calmly, urging her to follow. She did trust him. She had no idea what he intended, but she found that she did not care, for she felt safe and loved and protected wherever she was with Robert and knew she trusted him to take her anywhere.

Reaching the edge of the woods, Robert pulled her in further and guided her through some low brush where a small almost indistinguishable trail could be seen by the light of the moon filtering through the branches overhead. It was midsummer and though it had not rained in a while, Elizabeth could feel the cool earth beneath her slippers sink in with every step.

"I have a surprise for ye. A place we can always go when we wish to escape prying eyes. Just follow this trail," Robert said, holding her hand and leading the way. She giggled and followed with anticipation, always enjoying a good adventure, even if it was a small one into the woods.

A few moments later, she saw a looming shadow in the distance. Something tall and solid, but too dark to fully identify. "What is that, Robert?" When she had pulled him behind the kitchen screens and out the door to the gardens, she had no idea where they would escape to. She simply wished to avoid the crush and have privacy with the man she loved without all eyes on her. Wherever they were heading, it must be a place Robert decided to take her on a whim, and that made it even more exciting.

Pushing open the door, Robert pulled her inside, and the chill within immediately went to her bones. It was pitch black and Elizabeth could not even see beyond her own nose. "Robert?"

"Stand right here," he instructed, releasing her hand and disappearing into the darkness for what felt an eternity but must have only been a moment. She heard shuffling sounds and saw a spark light up the dark just before a fire began to blaze in a hearth to her right. Blinking her eyes and looking around, Elizabeth adjusted to the light and realized they were in a small cabin. One wooden bed lay in the corner of the room with a small table beside it, and another table with a set of two small chairs was set near the hearth.

"A cabin in the woods?" she asked slowly, spinning in a circle to take in the small details of the rather simple room.

"A hunting cabin, aye. This forest is the king's hunting land, dinnae ye forget. I havenae been here in a long time, but my men keep it ready if ever the regent or his men wish to hunt. Few men ever stay in this. 'Tis mostly for emergency use if a man is injured or weather turns on them. When we left the castle, I kenned I wanted to take ye here."

Smiling, Elizabeth walked over to Robert and placed a soft kiss on his lips. The small room was heating up a bit more already from the fire and the thought of being here in this cozy, secluded place with her new husband made her stomach flutter with excitement.

"I am verra glad ye decided to show me. I wasnae so sure where we would go, only that I needed to be away from the madness."

Robert ran his hands through her hair and rested his forehead on hers. "There is nobody around to disturb us now, Lizzie. I love ye. Ye ken that, aye? I have loved ye longer than I ever wanted to believe. Ye werenae meant to be mine."

"Aye, I was. I was always meant to be yers, Rob. Nobody else's. I love ye and have since I laid eyes on ye. Tilda warned me not to fall in love with the wrong brother on my first night, but it was already too late."

A shiver from the cold ran up her spine, and Elizabeth huddled closer to Robert for warmth. "Will ye lay down with me near the fire?"

he asked softly, kissing her temple. "I will keep ye warm." Nodding, she watched as he removed his plaid from his shoulder and laid it on the floor by the fire. Putting out a hand, he helped her sit down beside him and wrapped his arms around her. For several moments, they held one another and stared at the flames, simply enjoying the silence and their first moments together as husband and wife. Elizabeth sighed and leaned closer to Robert, unsure how she had found a love like this when it was all she had avoided her entire life. Now, she could not imagine a day without Robert by her side.

Turning to face him, she felt herself blush, once again remembering their night together on the battlements. He was hers now. She wanted to be intimate with him, to be fully disrobed and know what it meant to make love with him, to see all of him and be one with him. Leaning in, she kissed him, lingering at his lips and feeling a thrill when he deepened it, slipping his tongue against hers as he slowly laid her onto her back.

The fire popped in the background and her flesh warmed up, both from the fire and anticipation of Robert's touch. She ached for more and when his hand started to slowly wander from her waist up to her breasts, she arched into his touch, urging him to continue.

"Ye are my wife now, Elizabeth Irvine. I am sorry ye had to endure so much, but I hope ye will always be proud to be by my side. I should have married ye before Harlaw. I should have said how I felt about ye and fought to be with ye."

"Ye couldnae have. We both ken that. We are here together now, and I want to be yer wife in all ways, Robert," she said breathlessly, biting her lower lip and looking up at his glazed eyes full of love and lust.

When Robert's hand cupped her breast, she shifted beneath him and felt the evidence of his arousal, knowing in that moment that he wanted her as much as she wanted him.

Reaching behind her back, Robert tugged the string of her bodice and began to loosen her dress down her shoulders, taking her linen under tunic down at the same time. When her breasts were free from the confines of the dress, she breathed deeply and felt the heat from the fire warming her flesh.

"By all that is holy, Elizabeth. Ye are the most beautiful woman I have ever kenned," he said slowly, running his finger across her breast and erect nipple before placing a soft kiss on each. Her breath hitched in her chest at the sensation of his mouth on her flesh. Closing her eyes, she felt him suck one nipple into his mouth, then the other, causing her hips to buck instinctively in reaction to his ministrations.

Reaching out, Elizabeth opened her eyes and gripped his surcoat, urging him to remove it. She wanted to see him. Aye, she had seen his bare chest more than once on the lists during practice, but she wanted to feel him, to run her fingers over the ridges of his muscle and revel in the feel of his warm skin, the coarse hairs of his chest against her fingertips.

Wasting no time, Robert yanked off the surcoat and tunic and stayed on his knees, hovering over her as his gaze bored into hers. His dimple showed in the light of the fire as he gave her a small smirk. "I am going to make ye mine. I am going to show ye what it means to be my wife."

The determination in his eyes and the sureness of his words made her tingle from head to toe. She wanted to finally know what it meant to make love to a man and know that she was loved in return. "If it is anything like the night on the battlements, then I cannae wait to be yers," she softly replied.

Leaning down, Robert grazed his lips down her throat, placing soft nips as he went until he reached her breasts once more, his hands tugging her dress down her hips. "It will be so much better than that, my love." She shivered again, gooseflesh covering her arms and her nipples puckering when he flicked his tongue over them. He was driving her mad with need and he had not even fully removed her dress.

With a swift tug, her dress and under tunic were gone and Elizabeth was fully nude in front of a man for the first time in her life. Looking down, she saw his gaze wander her body, like a man studying a sculpture and finding wonder in its details. "Ye are... breathtaking, Elizabeth," he said softly, swallowing hard.

When his hands began to move down her hips and over her thighs, Elizabeth groaned and widened her eyes, not certain what he meant to do next. But when he urged her to widen her legs and lightly ran a finger through her most private of areas, her entire world turned upside down as her body thrummed with some unknown need. It was that same sensation she had felt before, and her body craved more.

"Remember what I did last time?" he asked, slipping a finger inside her, causing Elizabeth to gasp and lay her head back down with a moan.

"Aye, I remember," she whispered, closing her eyes as he slipped another finger inside her and touched her again in that one spot that drove her mad. Dear God, she was going to explode from pleasure.

"Look at me, love." Opening her eyes, she saw him hovering above her, his manhood pressing against his trews, and she knew he was ready to make her his. "If ye are as ready as I am, untie my trews, lass."

Lifting her hand, she did as he requested, then pushed them down over his hips and down his legs. Seeing him fully nude, she swallowed hard and stared at the evidence of his arousal as it stood proudly before her.

Positioning himself above her, he pressed himself against her entrance and looked her in the eye. "Are ye ready, Lizzie?" She nodded and adjusted herself, anxious yet excited to feel him become one with her. As he pushed in, she felt the pressure and wondered if it would begin to hurt. Too many times she had heard women describe the first time as painful, and she gritted her teeth and tensed up in preparation.

He quickly thrust into her and she felt a sting of pain deep within, causing her to gasp, but he stopped and kissed her lips softly, resting his forehead on hers. Breathing deeply, Robert waited for her to recover. "Are ye all right?"

"Aye, the pain has subsided. Is that the worst of it?" she asked.

"Aye, I vow." He began to move again slowly, taking his time, as she adjusted to him. Soon enough, pleasure erased the pain and she started to breathe heavily, moving in tandem with him as he rocked his hips against hers. The fire cast shadows around the room while providing heat, light, and the calming sounds of wood crackling.

Something built deep within her, a feeling that she was going to explode from the pleasure threatening to release all at once from her body. Robert moved faster and his breathing quickened, both their bodies growing frenzied and tensing up around one another. Grabbing Robert's arms, Elizabeth looked up at him and saw the intensity and emotion in his blue gaze. Lips slightly parted, he watched her as she watched him, becoming one for the first time. "I love ye, Robert Irvine," she whispered.

"I love ye, Elizabeth Irvine," he responded in a hoarse voice and gripped her hips tightly, almost painfully, as he thrust harder, deeper, making her entire body thrum with need and pleasure as instinct guided her every move.

A wave of pure ecstasy washed over her, making her call out and dig her nails into Robert's back as he groaned and tensed before collapsing on top of her, their sweat-slicked skin and bared bodies entangled in one another.

"By the rood, Elizabeth," Robert panted. "Ye are my wife, my love, my everything." He kissed her lips and then her neck before rolling onto his back and nestling her into his side.

"That was unbelievable," she whispered, kissing his chest and listening to his heartbeat slow to a normal rhythm after a few moments.

"Ye are unbelievable, Lizzie. I cannae believe ye are mine. I want everything with ye. Laughter, happiness, wee bairns. Everything."

Running her fingers up and down his chest, Elizabeth closed her eyes and breathed deeply, feeling lulled by the warmth of the fire on her back and a contentment she never hoped to feel in this lifetime. She wanted all those things with Robert as well and, deep in her heart, she knew they would have it all.

Their happiness was hard won and though she missed Alexander and wished he had survived the battle, it was a bittersweet feeling to know she would never have been here with Robert as his wife, in his arms, had life not unfolded as it had. Life was unpredictable. The world was always in a state of discontent and battles would continue to rage across their land.

As Elizabeth's eyes fluttered shut and she lay in the arms of a man who loved her in a way she never knew existed, she was reminded of the words of her mother and clutched at her rosary once more. The wheel of fortune was always turning and a man could rise, and then he could fall. For Elizabeth, she knew the truth of it all too well. And though she could not know the fate of her spinning wheel, she did know that as long as she had Robert Irvine by her side, she would always be on the side of good fortune.

Author Note

Thank you, lovely reader, for taking the time to read "For Love of a Laird"! I cannot even begin to tell you how much this story and these characters mean to me, or how much research and love went into telling their tales.

My maiden name is Irvin, a form of Irvine, which has many spellings. While researching Irvine history, I came across the story of "Gude Sir Alexander Irvine" and instantly fell in love with the story of Robert and Elizabeth, who truly did live in 1411 at Drum Castle. Most of the events I wrote about are historically accurate, with some details filled in as needed. Though there are many records, they do seem to vary.

Alexander Irvine was married to Elizabeth Keith for a time before Harlaw, though records do vary on how long the marriage lasted and she is recorded as being his "virgin bride" which means to me that it did not last long or that it was not a love match. What is certain is that Alexander went off to battle with his brother, Robert, to fight at Harlaw in July 1411 and never returned. Robert changed his named to Alexander, which became the tradition for many Irvine lairds, and married his widow, Elizabeth Keith from Dunnottar whose brother was, in fact, the Marischal of Scotland. They had a few children and I am proud to say that, even after I had already plotted out this story, I had not known yet that I am a direct descendant of theirs!

It wasn't until I purchased several Irvine history books and began looking into my lineage in depth that I discovered they are my grandparents 14x removed which just shocked me to no end! As a romance writer, I knew I had to get past the fact that I am related to them to write love scenes, but I admit it was a bit awkward for me to write about my ancestors getting down! However, I would not be here today were it not for them, so I thank them for their love.

It is true that on their journey to Harlaw, Alexander stopped and sat on a stone, still known to this day as the Drum Stone, to ask Robert to marry Elizabeth should he fall in battle. That is well documented. Alexander and Red Hector of the Battles Maclean really did fight until the death and the "Ballad of Gude Sir Alexander Irvine" truly exists to this day to honor the warrior and man he was. He is buried at St Nicholas Church in Aberdeen, just about five miles from Harlaw.

Interestingly enough, the Macleans and Irvines really did exchange swords after the battle to call peace between the clans and it is a tradition to this day that still stands. Every year, the Irvines meet up with the Macleans to honor the original exchange and recreate the ceremony, which I find a wonderful act of good will and true Scottish spirit!

Drum Castle was gifted to the Irvines by Robert the Bruce for their loyalty and it was Alexander and Robert's grandfather, William, who became the first laird. It remained the seat of the Irvine Clan until the 1970s and still stands in Aberdeen and can be visited today. I want to thank the wonderfully kind and knowledgeable people of Drum Castle for taking the time to answer my questions and send me research materials that helped me greatly. In my research, I looked at excavation notes of the castle and original maps to better and more accurately describe the castle, so the reader is truly experiencing 15th century Drum.

Reginald is not necessarily a figment of my imagination. One record I found did mention a brother named Reginald, yet he is nowhere to be found in any other records, but I decided to include him in my story and I am excited to say that he will play a big role in the following books, as will William Keith, who was actually named Robert but obviously that would have been a bit confusing in the story, so I gave him his father's name, William. Tilda and Mary will be present as well, and I hope you continue to follow the history and story of the Irvines of Drum with my upcoming additions to the series: "Like a Laird to a Flame" and "Made for the Knight".

I realize you have many thousands of books to choose from and I am so grateful that you chose mine. To find more of my works, please feel free to check my website and follow me on social media! I love talking with my readers!

Connect with Mia!

FB: miaprideauthor

Twitter: @mia_pride

Newsletter: bit.ly/2vSChr1

Instagram: mia_pride_author

BookBub: bookbub.com/profile/mia-pride

Amazon: amazon.com/Mia-Pride/e/B01M6VEWGX

Pinterest: miapride

Website: www.miapride.com

Blog: miapride.wordpress.com

Email: miapride.author@gmail.com

About the Author

Mia is a full-time writer and mother of two rowdy boys, residing in the SF Bay Area. As a child, she often wrote stories about fantastic places or magical things, always preferring to live in a world where the line between reality and fantasy didn't exist.

In high school, she entered writing contests and had some stories published in small newspapers or school magazines. As life continued, so did her love of writing. So one day, she decided to end her cake decorating business, pull out her laptop and fulfill her dream of writing and publishing novels. And she did.

When Mia isn't writing books or chasing her sweaty children around a park, she loves to drink coffee by the gallon, get lost in a good book, hike with her family and drink really big margaritas with her friends! Her happy place is the Renaissance Faire, where you can find her at the joust, rooting for the shirtless Highlander in a kilt.

Connect with Mia!
FB: miaprideauthor
Twitter: @mia_pride
Newsletter: bit.ly/2vSChr1
Instagram: mia_pride_author
BookBub: bookbub.com/profile/mia-pride
Amazon: amazon.com/Mia-Pride/e/B01M6VEWGX
Pinterest: miapride
Website: www.miapride.com
Blog: miapride.wordpress.com

Made in the USA
Middletown, DE
29 May 2020